A **KILLER** ON CHRISTMAS CAY

A SMILEY AND MCBLYTHE MYSTERY

A Killer On Christmas Cay
Text copyright © 2024 Bruce Hammack
All rights reserved.

Published by Jubilee Publishing, LLC
Ebook ISBN: 978-1-958252-22-2
Paperback ISBN: 978-1-958252-23-9

Cover design: Streetlight Graphics
Editor: Teresa Lynn, Tranquility Press

A **KILLER** ON CHRISTMAS CAY

A Smiley and McBlythe Mystery

BRUCE HAMMACK

BOOKS BY BRUCE HAMMACK

The Smiley and McBlythe Mystery Series
Exercise Is Murder, prequel
Jingle Bells, Rifle Shells
Pistols And Poinsettias
Five Card Murder
Murder In The Dunes
The Name Game Murder
Murder Down The Line
Vision Of Murder
Mistletoe, Malice And Murder
A Beach To Die For
Dig Deep For Murder
A Killer On Christmas Cay

The Fen Maguire Mystery Series
Murder On The Brazos
Murder On The Angelina
Murder On The Guadalupe
Murder On The Wichita
Murder On The San Gabriel

The Star of Justice Series
Long Road To Justice
A Murder Redeemed
A Grave Secret
Justice On A Midnight Clear

See my latest catalog of books at brucehammack.com/books.

1

The door from the garage slammed shut with enough force to rattle the pictures hanging on the wall. Heather didn't care. If Steve was napping, that would be his problem. He'd had plenty of time to sleep.

Steve stepped into the hallway from his suite of rooms without his white cane. "Did someone have a bad day?"

Heather spewed out something unintelligible, then said, "Where's Max?"

"On the couch in my apartment, but I doubt your cat will come to you until you calm down."

Heather marched toward the kitchen, complaining as she walked. "To answer your question, Father called me with a problem. He wants us to fix it."

"Hmm. That doesn't sound like him."

She spoke over her shoulder. "It's going to take two glasses of wine and a hot bath before I'll want to discuss it."

Instead of bombarding her with questions, he turned to walk away. "I'll finish listening to the documentary on television and meet you in the kitchen. Forty minutes should be enough time for you to calm down. I hear lighting candles can help you relax."

She didn't reply, but agreed with Steve's prescription. Four candles should be enough to calm her frazzled nerves. It wasn't long before she was up to her neck in a cauldron of hot, sudsy water. Her shoulders relaxed, as did the tension in her neck. The water, wine, and Alpha waves over Bose speakers worked their magic.

It amazed Heather how thirty minutes of switching her brain off could bring such peace. No need for a second glass of wine. As usual, Steve was right. She didn't always appreciate having a roommate, but today she did.

She and her business partner had not always lived under the same roof. Up until a short time ago, their condos had shared a wall, with a kitty door for Max to come and go between them. That arrangement ended when Steve's former fiction editor retaliated against him by setting fire to Steve's condo. In one afternoon, they had both lost their homes. She solved that problem by leasing a home with a mother-in-law suite for Steve. Living completely separate, but close, proved helpful when they had a murder to solve.

As she dried off, her shoulders sagged as she mumbled, "Why can't Father solve his own problem?"

She dressed in loose-fitting shorts and a T-shirt, then left her room without worrying about what her makeup or hair looked like. It was one advantage of sharing a home with a blind widower.

Heather's thoughts turned to the explanation she'd give Steve as she made her way to the kitchen. As usual, he was waiting on her. "The only reason I'm not a week behind is because I've stayed on top of things. If I were gone for a week, who knows what would happen to my businesses?"

Steve scratched his ear. "Most likely the sun would rise in the east and set in the west like it always does."

"And people would put off what they should be doing," she said with a hard edge to her words.

Steve raised his hands in pretend surrender. "I'm not the one having to drink wine and take a hot bubble bath, as soon as I get home." He placed his palms on the table. His words sounded like he'd chipped them from granite. "Let's skip the fact that you're a perfectionist-workaholic and move on to something I don't know. How long before you have a complete meltdown?"

Heather leaned back in her chair. "Wow. I'm not the only one who had a bad day. You usually save criticism like that for when I really need it."

"Sorry. I'm suffering from a severe case of boredom. It's been three months since our last case. Twiddling my thumbs and listening to Max snore was fine for the first month and a half. Since then, it's gotten a little monotonous."

It was a prick to Heather's heart. She complained about being too busy when she was the only one to blame. No one told her she had to build a high-end lakeside housing development. Her company's other investments were doing all she hoped they'd do and more. She blamed it on a dominant gene she'd received from her father and several prior generations of McBlythe overachievers.

She was on the verge of an apology when Steve put any repentant thoughts to flight. "Forgive me for saying this, but I'd rather not hear about the housing development tonight. Tell me why your father called."

Heather took a breath in, then let it out. "He believes someone is stealing sensitive information and selling it."

Steve ran his palm across his cheek. "That type of theft is a nightmare to prove. It's likely the thief is being paid in cryptocurrency."

"Since when did you become an expert on cybercrime?"

"I listened to a documentary on industrial crime a couple of days ago. It's amazing what you can find on YouTube."

Heather dipped her head. "There's something else. Someone assaulted an employee at Father's corporate headquarters."

Steve sat up straight. "Now you have my full attention. Do you have details?"

"It happened two days ago in the adjoining parking garage. The victim's name is Reggie Scott."

"Did he have access to sensitive information?"

"He wasn't that high in the chain of command. He was described as a perceptive young man who wanted to advance."

"What are the police saying?"

"Father had to make a phone call to Boston's police commissioner to get the cops moving. You know how mugging investigations go. Even after a good shove, the detectives are moving slowly."

Steve tapped a finger on the table. "Back to the problem at hand. What does your father want us to do?"

Sarcasm dripped from her reply. "Drop everything, come to Boston, find out who assaulted Reggie, and uncover the spy."

Steve shook his head. "That would be tricky, especially for you with all you have going on."

Heather stood and paced the floor. "Any ideas on what I'm to say to Father?"

"Not yet. Let's reheat leftovers, have supper, and sleep on it until tomorrow. I might have a tiny grain of an idea rolling around in my mind by then."

What looked like a Scandinavian goddess came into view. Any time their young friend Bella was in the area working, she stayed with them. She entered the kitchen and said, "Unless I'm mistaken, you two are talking about another case to solve. I'll be busy with photo shoots in Houston for the rest of this week, but I can juggle my schedule for the next two weeks if you need help."

Steve lifted his chin. "That's good to know. Thanks for offering."

His phone came to life and announced, "Call from Allister McBlythe."

"Hello, Mr. McBlythe. There must be a recent development."

"I believe you're clairvoyant, Steve. Is Heather where she can hear?"

"I'm here, Father. Bella is, too. We were discussing your problems."

"Good. I heard from the police a few minutes ago. Reggie's in a coma and hanging on to life by the thinnest of margins."

Steve took over. "Can we call you back in two hours? We're going to have something to eat and kick around some ideas about how we can help."

"Let's make it one hour. Nothing like this has ever happened to the business and I want to be involved in any plan you propose."

Heather jumped into the conversation. "Father, expect a video call at nine thirty eastern time."

The call came to an abrupt end, which didn't surprise her. When her father worried, tact and diplomacy went by the wayside.

Heather stopped pacing and addressed Steve. "You have an hour to come up with one heck of a plan." She started toward the refrigerator to mine it for something fast but relatively healthy. "By the way, I'll give you seven days of my time. After that, you and Bella are on your own."

2

Heather turned from the pile of vegetables she'd assembled and asked, "Do you two want any type of protein on your salads?"

Bella moved closer to her and whispered, "Steve's in one of his trances. I don't think he can hear you."

"Probably not. I'll put chunks of ham and cheese on his."

It was then that Heather noticed the white band on Bella's left ring finger. "Where's your engagement ring and wedding band?"

The conversation continued in whispers. "I can't wear them when I'm doing photo shoots, so I picked up a few of these rubber ones." She examined her long, perfectly formed fingers. "It gets the message out that I'm off the market, and I'm not afraid I'll lose it. Adam doesn't mind. In fact, it was his idea that I save the bling for special occasions."

Heather walked to where Steve sat and asked if he wanted to eat or wait.

Nothing moved except his lips, and only enough to issue a one-word response. "Later."

She arranged the ingredients for their salads on three plates and put Steve's in the refrigerator. Bella was right. Steve had

mentally retreated to a place where words had a hard time pene-
trating. Early in their partnership, she found this maddening.
Later, she realized hyper-concentration was one of his
superpowers.

With a nudge of her head toward the formal dining room,
Heather indicated that they should go there to eat. Once settled,
Heather asked, "How's Adam?"

"He's awesome and busy, as always. Mom and Dad are
enjoying living in Puerto Rico and having him there." She looked
down at her salad. "I'm not sure what Adam will say when I tell
him I'm not coming to see them on my two weeks off."

Heather put her fork down. "You don't have to help us if it's
going to cause a rift."

Bella flicked away the statement like it was a fly on a slice of
watermelon. "You have one week to spare, which means Steve
would be alone if it takes over seven days to solve the case. I
have two weeks, so I can stay with him if it takes longer. Besides,
Adam and I have the rest of our lives to be together."

Heather acknowledged to herself that the time-line would be
challenging. "Let's not borrow trouble before the case starts.
We've yet to hear details. There may not be anything to investigate if the police make a quick arrest in the assault case and
Father discovers who's stealing information. It surprises me he
doesn't already know."

Bella had a bite of raw cauliflower in her mouth when
Heather spoke her last sentence, so she didn't respond with
words. The young woman cast a quick glance Heather's way. The
raised eyebrows asked, "Who do you think you're fooling?"

Heather stabbed lettuce and half a cherry tomato, raised it to
her mouth, but didn't pop it in. "As I said, it really surprises me
that Father hasn't discovered who's stealing secrets."

Bella swallowed. "That tells me they're super sneaky. I'd look
for someone with a very high IQ."

"That applies to so many people around him and his
company. The first thing we'll need to do is narrow down the

number of suspects. I know how Father runs his business. It's very compartmentalized, with each department head responsible for their particular area. There aren't many executives who have access to information concerning multiple departments. It will be interesting to see if the thefts are occurring in only one department."

"You're losing me," said Bella as she took a bite of raw carrot.

"You'll catch on when we talk to Father."

Heather checked her phone for the time. "I need to set up the video meeting and make a few notes. He'll blow a fuse if I'm not prepared."

Although she was a married woman, Bella still had a school-girl giggle that bubbled to the surface. "You're a graduate of Princeton, an attorney, a former police detective, and a successful businesswoman. Yet, you're still trying to please your father."

Heather's reply left her mouth without considering her words. "Look who's talking. You're no slouch with accomplishments, and you want to please the men in your life."

"I'm making up for lost time with my dad."

Heather's fork dangled in the air. "I never realized how similar our childhoods were. A kidnapper stole you away from your parents. Mine didn't know what to do with me, so they hired others to do the job." Heather impaled lettuce, a leaf of raw spinach, and a sliver of sweet pepper in one stab of her fork. "I guess we both turned out all right."

"So far," said Steve. "Let's see how you do with a billion-dollar project and a hard case at the same time."

3

After Heather secured the link for the video call, Allister McBlythe IV's face appeared in a matter of seconds. Her father wasted no time. "Good evening. I see everyone's gathered. Let's hear what you've come up with."

Heather responded first. "Before I turn this over to Steve, give us details about the thefts."

"Of course. I first suspected something was amiss about nine months ago when I noticed a particular businessman made unusually high profits on a highly speculative investment. This came at a time when I was poised to buy stock in a copper mine. The geologist's report from samples came back showing the potential greater than anyone ever imagined. I'd paid for the report and was preparing to become the majority stockholder. Before I could purchase additional shares, the price shot through the ceiling."

Heather asked, "Who else knew you were going to purchase more stock?"

"The head of my acquisitions department and my CFO."

Steve asked, "Who had access to the report?"

"Only the head of acquisitions and myself."

Steve broke in. "Something tells me this isn't the only thing that's happened."

"Correct. Four months ago, I was preparing to sell all my stock in a pharmaceutical company that had shown promise in a treatment for dementia. The clinical trials revealed significant adverse effects of the drug. Before I could sell, another large shareholder dumped their stock. The company's stock price tanked, and I was left with near worthless stock shares."

Heather countered with, "The leak could have come from someplace other than your company. Were there any other significant events that led you to believe someone within your organization sold information?"

"I'm not finished. Two months ago, my personal assistant told me she believed someone had been in my office. She intentionally placed a file out of alphabetical order. It was one that I'd been looking at as a potential investment. Someone had placed it back in the correct order."

Heather had to admit that was suspicious. She knew her father's office suite was off limits to all but a few. It was where he kept his most sensitive files. Her mind jumped to who she thought could be an obvious suspect. "Do you think your personal assistant or secretarial staff could be behind these events?"

Her father lifted his chin, which wasn't a good sign. "These aren't events. They're industrial theft." He continued to look down his nose. "As for my PA, I'd trust Dorcas Lindley with my life."

"She's only been with you a few years."

"If she was stealing secrets, why would she set a trap, then tell me someone had been rifling through my files and placed one back in proper alphabetical order?"

He huffed out a full breath. "Besides, I had private investigators look into her finances. There's been no significant monetary inflows to her. She leads a quiet life and has never shown signs of greed or dissatisfaction."

Heather didn't appreciate the condescending tone of her father's words but stayed on track. "Did the investigators consider that someone might have paid her in cryptocurrency?"

"Of course they did. They also investigated her banking records, which included everything they could do legally and a few things that will remain unspoken."

Steve broke into the conversation. "Do you believe the assault on Reggie Scott has something to do with the thefts of information?"

Heather watched as her father rubbed his chin. "I'd describe him as an up-and-coming accountant with marginal executive potential. Our CFO, Habib Patel, had his eye on Mr. Scott for advancement. He had drive, but liked to live large, if you know what I mean."

"Am I right to assume Reggie Scott had access to many of the same documents that the head of accounting did?"

"Some, but not all."

Steve wasn't through. "Is it common in your organization to have multiple people within each department with access to all information?"

"Very few. Janice Peltier is the head of my legal department. She's the only attorney with access to every case. There's no second-in-command. She assigns cases according to the expertise required. There may be water-cooler talk about the individual cases the attorneys are working on, but Janice says it's general gossip, and she's constantly reminding the attorneys to leave all files locked in their desks."

"Does that go for all your department heads?"

"Absolutely."

"I can vouch for that," said Heather.

"What are your major departments?" asked Steve.

"I'm the company president. Answering directly to me are Habib Patel, the chief financial officer, Bob Brown, the head of acquisitions, and Janice Peltier, head of the legal department." He raised a finger. "There's also Louis Crane, our technology wizard. I included him because he has exceptional skills with computers."

"Is he a hacker?"

Heather answered for her father. "Any head of IT knows computers backward and forward. I'd question their veracity if they said they didn't know how to hack into most systems. I know my director of IT can hack into almost anything. She also knows what would happen to her if she did."

Steve allowed a few seconds to pass. "Send me everything you have on everyone you've mentioned tonight. Heather, Bella, and I will start with them and do our own background checks."

"My private investigators have already done reports on those, plus some other employees. Do you want me to send them all to you?"

"As soon as you can," said Heather.

Mr. McBlythe leaned back in his chair and interlaced his fingers. "You haven't said anything about a plan to catch the thief."

Heather and Bella exchanged guilty glances, but said nothing.

Steve cleared his throat. "The silence from your daughter is because she hasn't thought of anything yet."

"That's not true," said Heather. "Bella and I were being polite and waiting for you to go first."

"You never were good at lying," said Allister.

Steve spoke before Heather could dig a deeper hole. "I have something in mind, but right now it's less than half-baked. It's going to be complicated and will depend on what kind of physical condition all the suspects are in."

"Physical condition?" asked Heather.

Steve nodded. "For my plan to work, we need to practice absolute secrecy. Let's do another video call tomorrow night at the same time. We'll spend a day or two completing the plan and the rest of the week making arrangements."

"Don't forget," said Heather. "I can only give you seven days."

"That may be seven more than me," said her father. "I've several overseas trips scheduled in the next few weeks."

"I'll keep that in mind." Steve pushed back from the table a couple of inches. "In fact, it might be best if we didn't include you in anything but the planning."

Heather looked at her father's face on the screen. "What's so important that you won't be available to help plan or implement what we come up with? After all, it's your company."

The corner of one side of his mouth rose a millimeter or two. "You're the one who insisted on doing a billion-dollar housing project on Lake Conroe by yourself. You didn't consult me on any part of it. Why should I feel obligated to discuss my agenda?"

"Because you're asking the three of us to help catch a thief and possibly the person who assaulted your employee."

A wave of a hand preceded her father's excuse. "You'll be even more effective after you get your mind off your project for a while. I've watched you closely since you started solving crimes with Steve. You always come back with renewed vigor after you play detective."

Steve nodded. "He's right. Six months is the longest you can go without taking a vacation to solve a case. You've been working so hard, it's cut the time down to only three months before you need a break from your business."

"That's the silliest thing I've ever heard."

Bella spoke up. "They're right, Heather. Solving a crime energizes you."

Heather had her mouth open to strike back against their logic, but her father interrupted. "I'm looking forward to hearing Steve's plan tomorrow night."

The computer's speakers made a strange metallic sound, and her father's image blinked off.

Mumbled words came from Heather. She pulled down her laptop's screen and announced, "Don't look for me the rest of the evening. I'll be soaking in my tub and drinking that second glass of wine."

"Don't forget the candles," said Steve.

4

The next night, Heather arrived three minutes late for the video call. Steve and Bella were still exchanging small talk with her father, so she didn't think he would scold her. She was wrong.

"Did you lose track of time, daughter?"

She noticed he'd addressed her as if she were a child. "Nice to see you, too, Father. How was your day?"

"Profitable. I find the more punctual I am, the better the results. How was your day?"

"Full and rewarding. Thank you for asking."

"You need to thank Steve and Bella for contacting me to say you'd be late. I took it upon myself to set up the link."

Heather issued a fake smile. "I suggest we not waste any more time and begin." She turned to Steve. "You've had all day to devise a plan to help Father out of the situation he's in. What do you propose?"

Steve sat with Heather on his right and Bella on his left. "It's only a general outline. My inspiration came from a documentary I listened to on what it takes to become a Navy SEAL. Their training breaks down the applicants both physically and mentally before the actual training in warfare begins."

"I don't understand," said Heather. "Are you suggesting we take out-of-shape executives and put them through brutal training?"

Steve smiled. "Not brutal, only unpleasant. It won't take nearly as much to break them down because they won't be expecting it."

"Where would you do this?" asked Allister.

"Before we get to that, let's talk about suspects. I reviewed the reports your private investigators developed. They did very good background research on those they considered the primary suspects. I agree with their conclusion that the person responsible for stealing information from your company is among the top echelon of your employees. It's possible that two or three have worked together to steal from you, but I think it's more likely this is the work of only one person."

Allister asked, "Do you also think this person tried to kill Reggie Scott?"

"I'd say it's likely Reggie discovered something and spooked his assailant. It's possible the thief hired someone to do the assault and they went too far."

Heather asked, "Do you have an update on Reggie's condition?"

"He's still in a coma."

Steve continued. "I propose telling the suspects you're sending them on a team-building vacation. They'll be gone a week to some sort of resort. What I have in mind is a fat-farm where they'll exercise until they can hardly move. They'll eat small portions of salad three times a day."

"Do you have one in mind?" asked Heather's father.

"This is where I need your help. It needs to be a place that's isolated but will appeal to them visually."

"I don't get it," said Bella. "Why do you want to break them down physically and mentally?"

"To reveal character, fears, and secrets. Also, they're more likely not to remember any lies they tell if they're sleep deprived, hungry, and aching."

Heather's father took his turn. "Can you break them down in only a week?"

Steve made a steeple with his index fingers. "If you deprive them of sleep before they travel, I believe it's likely. Give them unreasonable deadlines to complete for a couple of days before they travel."

Heather wasn't convinced. "We're talking about some of the brightest people on the planet. Some of them are bound to see through this plan, especially the person stealing information. They'll know all they have to do is make it through a week and they'll be home free."

Her father challenged her. "How would you improve on the plan?"

Heather held up her hands. "I don't know, but something's missing. My team responds well to challenges. They're all very competitive."

No one said anything, which told Heather everyone was thinking of how they might take the skeleton of Steve's plan and add to it. Bella finally broke the silence. "You're looking for an isolated location. Right?"

"Correct," said Allister.

"The most isolated places I know are islands in the Caribbean."

Steve's head jerked up. "You're on the right track, Bella, but we can't leave the people marooned on a deserted island with no water, food, or shelter."

Allister came to the rescue. "Leave it to me. I know several people who own private islands. They've built homes there. There's one in particular that has a luxury home and independent bungalows for guests. It has a dock large enough to accommodate a yacht and a pad for a helicopter. If it's available, you could come in by boat or air."

"It sounds perfect," said Steve. "You see if it's available, and we'll meet again tomorrow night. There's still a ton of logistics to work out, and Heather's right about someone seeing through our plan. A major part is still missing, but I can't put my finger on it."

Heather's father promised to check on the availability of the island. Steve committed to discovering the missing piece to the plan and to seek help in devising a plan to challenge people mentally and physically. Bella said she'd do whatever was needed once they found the exact location.

This left Heather with nothing to do but wonder what she could contribute to the plan. Oh well, she needed to concentrate on her construction project.

5

It was unusual for Heather to get ideas on her way home from the office. In fact, her body and brain felt like mush after a day of doing battle with crusty contractors and supply chain issues. It seemed everyone had an excuse for not doing what they'd promised. Added to her list of woes was a call from some lower-level bureaucrat in the county planning commission who couldn't locate their copy of a deed of sale to a lot in the middle of the future recreation center. Construction was already under way. The county was threatening to red-tag work if she didn't produce a document that she'd already provided.

Then, everything changed. Someone else, without as impressive of a title, called her back after four hours. She apologized and said her boss had found the document in another file. One more crisis averted, but most of one day wasted.

Heather turned into her driveway and left thoughts about her project behind. That's when the idea struck her. It was the missing piece that Steve hadn't been able to put his finger on. Instead of dreading another video conference with her father, excitement coursed through her. She finally had something constructive to add.

She punched the opener and waited while the garage door

rose. Unlike the previous night, she'd have time to grab a quick bite to eat, unload her laptop, and send her father a text message stating she would take care of the hook-up.

"You're home early," said Steve as he followed Max down the hallway and into the breakfast nook.

Heather reached down and gave her chubby cat a rub under his chin. He rewarded her with purrs of contentment. "I'm not only home early, but I know what's missing in your plan. The answer came to me a few minutes ago."

"That's good," said Steve. "I'm fresh out of ideas."

Bella joined them. "I'm ready to help, but I don't know what to do. I hope your dad scored an island for us."

Heather spoke with confidence. "I don't think Father would have mentioned it if he wasn't sure." She chuckled. "I'm a little surprised he doesn't already own an island."

Steve took his seat. "It's good to see you in a better mood. What brought it on?"

"Perhaps it was having something niggling on my mind besides the housing project. It's even possible you're right about me needing a week off."

Her father logged onto the video call precisely when he said he would. "Good evening. I'm happy to report we have a private island booked and ready. It's not terribly far from Bella's former home and is part of the U.S. Virgin Islands. Only an hour by boat if it has a robust motor."

"How cool!" said Bella. "I might know it. What's it called?"

"Christmas Cay. I'll send the longitude and latitude. You can fly into either St. Thomas or St. Croix. From there, you'll need to charter a boat or a helicopter to get to the island."

Heather broke in. "How many will the accommodations sleep?"

"At least twenty. The island itself is a lush jungle, rises to almost a thousand feet, and has an area of six square miles. There's one white sand beach on the lee side of the island. That's where the pier is located."

Bella was so excited she squirmed in her seat. "What can I do to help?"

Heather broke in. "I need to share my idea before we go on. It will affect the head count."

Steve interrupted. "I count four suspects coming from Mr. McBlythe's company. Add to that three more— Heather, Bella, and me. That's seven."

Excitement rose in the room as Heather took over again. "Here's my addition to Steve's plan. I want to start a rumor in my company and Father's that he and I are planning a merger. This will mean a consolidation of resources and personnel."

"I don't get it," said Bella. "Why would you do that?"

Heather's father understood immediately. "Wonderful idea. There's enough truth in it because someday it will really happen."

"Let's hope no time soon," said Heather. "Anyway, I propose to bring a few of my key employees to give the rumor credence."

Steve nodded in agreement. "I like it so far. Who will you bring?"

"Louise King, the head of IT, Malcolm Swift, the chief financial officer, and Brent Coolidge, my head of acquisitions. I'd bring my PA, but she'll need to hold down the fort."

"What about your lead attorney?" asked her father. "I'm sending Janice Peltier."

"Amy is seven months pregnant. I don't think she'd appreciate a long plane flight followed by a bouncy boat ride."

Heather looked at her father on her computer screen. "What do you think of my idea?"

"It's almost perfect."

Heather bristled. "What's wrong with it? Everyone will be so worried about losing their hard-won positions in their company that they'll not suspect we're trying to find a thief."

Steve leaned in her direction. "It's almost perfect because you failed to consider two things."

"What's that?"

"Food and exercise. We need a chef and someone who'll push them to the limit of their physical endurance."

Her father issued a toothy grin. "Haven't you been around Steve long enough to know he'd not forget about food?"

"How foolish of me," said Heather. "As far as the physical part, I bet my personal trainer would love to spend a week on a private island making people's lives miserable. I'll see if he can get away."

"That reminds me," said her father. "We'll have the island for a maximum of eight days, starting this coming Sunday."

Bella jumped into the conversation. "I know some chefs on St. Croix; I'm sure I can convince one of them to help us. Mom and Dad taught me about ordering food for their resort. We won't starve."

"I'll help you," said Steve.

Heather nudged him. "You're looking out for yourself. I suppose you want to be exempt from the diet and exercise."

"I'll need to keep my mind sharp. It works best if my stomach isn't growling."

Bella took her turn again. "Why don't Steve and I go a day or two early to St. Croix with the chef and personal trainer? We could charter a boat and have everything staged before Heather and the guests arrive."

"Great idea," said Heather. "You can take my airplane. My pilots can come back to get me and my employees a couple of days later. We could meet the ones on Father's plane at either St. Croix or St. Thomas and go to the island from there."

"I'd recommend St. Croix," said Bella. "The airport isn't as busy, and I know the owner of the boat I'd like to charter."

A mischievous grin parted Steve's lips. "Mr. McBlythe, would you mind flying your people down to St. Croix on commercial flights?"

"I was thinking the same thing. I'll put them in economy on a red-eye budget airline from Boston to Miami. They'll arrive very early, then board the first flight to St. Croix. Loss of sleep will jump-start your plan."

Steve gave a nod of approval. "Follow that with a boat ride on open seas, and they'll be tired and grumpy by the time they reach the island." He rubbed his hands together. "This might work."

6

The image of Heather's father sitting in his home's office blinked on, accompanied by audio. He was the first to speak. "Good evening. Where are Steve and Bella?"

Bella was only a short step away, so she eased into her seat. "That's a snappy Hawaiian shirt you're wearing tonight, Mr. McBlythe. I'm used to seeing you in a coat and tie."

"I've spent so much time thinking about the private island and what awaits my executives that I had to pay homage to the Caribbean in some small way."

"The ocean breeze is calling my name," said Bella. "I've worn shorts, sandals, and bright cotton blouses all week."

Steve settled in a chair on the other side of Heather. "A key lime pie got me in the mood for sun, sand, and the sound of waves lapping on the shore."

Heather got down to business. "It's Wednesday night and all arrangements are complete at this end. Steve, Bella, and my personal trainer will leave in my plane from Conroe-North Houston Regional Airport tomorrow morning. Bella arranged for a chef she knows to meet her in St. Croix. She's supervising the loading of provisions and cooking for everyone all week. They should arrive on the island well before dark."

Her father gave her a nod of approval. "Will your pilots fly back the same day?"

"I'm not leaving Conroe until early Sunday morning so they can spend the night in St. Croix. They'll fly back on Saturday and be ready to take me and my three executives to St. Croix."

Her father folded his hands on his desk. "It sounds like your people will arrive well rested."

"Not exactly," said Heather. "My intention is to stay ahead of the construction schedule. I don't mind losing a day or two, but not all seven. That means I'm delegating more to Brent, Malcolm, and Louise before they leave."

"Remind me again. What departments are they over?"

"Brent is acquisitions, Malcolm is the chief financial officer, and Louise is head of information technology."

Her father's head bobbed. "I understand your lead attorney can't come because she's expecting a child soon, but don't you think it would be better if you sent your second-in-command from the legal department?"

"I'd rather he stay here."

"Why?"

Heather gathered her thoughts, took in a deep breath, and launched into an explanation she didn't want to make. "His name is Clyde Pugh, and he's perhaps the most brilliant attorney I've ever met. His knowledge is encyclopedic, and he's an absolute bulldog in the courtroom. He'd be my lead attorney if he'd do something about a personal issue."

Steve's chuckle signaled he had something to say. "What Heather's trying to say is Clyde has hygiene issues."

Heather's father responded with raised eyebrows.

Heather continued where Steve had left off. "Luckily, he's a loner who abhors working with anyone. I gave him the title of Assistant Department Director so he could have his own office at the end of the hall. He comes to work early every day and is almost always the last attorney to leave. He has no supervisory duties, but he's worth every penny I pay him."

It was Steve's turn again. "I think he'd be perfect to throw into the mix, but I can't convince Heather to bring him."

Mr. McBlythe leaned forward. "Do you agree that Clyde Pugh would help uncover the person stealing from me?"

"Yes," said Steve, before she could respond.

"He'd be a constant distraction," said Heather.

"Exactly, and that's what we're trying to do with exercise, lack of sleep, and near-impossible mental tasks." Steve turned his head toward her. "You don't want to take him because you're afraid someone would kill him and we'd have another crime to solve."

Heather spoke under her breath. "If I have to be in close contact with Clyde for a week, you may not have to look any farther than me for your killer."

Bella couldn't contain a laugh. "I was just thinking about how I'd react to being stuck on a private jet for about six hours with an obnoxious, smelly passenger. Yuk!"

"That's my point," said Steve. "Let the misery begin, and keep it up for multiple days."

Heather's father tilted his head, and she braced for the question she knew was coming. "Isn't your judgment being clouded? From what I'm hearing, Clyde Pugh could speed up your plan." He tilted his head a little more. "What's the real reason you don't want him on the island?"

Heather's cheeks pushed out prior to huffing out a full breath. "I can't stand the thought of smelling him for multiple hours in my airplane."

Steve had a quick response. "You don't have to. Pack your bags tonight and come with us tomorrow."

Heather gave her head a vigorous shake. "I can't do that. I've planned out the next three days."

Steve countered with, "That fancy airplane is an office in the sky. There's nothing you do in your office that you can't do on your plane."

"That may be true, but I'm sure the island doesn't have Internet or cell service."

"You're wrong," said her father. "They installed Starlink in the main house last week. You'll have complete Internet access. As for telephone, you have a satellite phone."

Bella interrupted. "If you're so averse to traveling with Clyde and you want privacy, stay in a hotel on St. Croix for a few nights. Then, come to the island by boat on Sunday."

"Excellent idea," said her father. "You can meet your executives at the dock, and there will be plenty of fresh air on the boat ride to the island. All you have to do is sit upwind from Mr. Pugh."

Heather thought about it. "It seems I'm outvoted on including Clyde Pugh. I may live to regret it, but I'll call my PA and tell her I'm leaving for St. Croix in the morning and for her to change all my in-person meetings for the next three days to teleconferences. She'll also need to arrange accommodations."

Steve murmured, "I may have Bella steal your satellite phone once we're on the island. You promised a full week of no distractions."

"If I'm truthful, that's not a bad idea. I want to do my part while I'm there."

A lull in the conversation followed, so Steve took the lead. "We need to hear from you, Mr. McBlythe. Have you completed travel plans for everyone coming from Boston?"

"I implemented the plan we discussed. My people will arrive on the island physically and mentally fatigued. The rumor about my retirement and an imminent merger spread like wildfire. Anxiety is running high. An unexpected benefit has been that the stock price of the company is up significantly. I'm hearing that none of the week's participants believe this will be a series of team-building exercises. They think they're auditioning to save their jobs."

"That's good," said Steve. "I want them to believe their jobs are in jeopardy."

Heather added, "I expect them to believe they'll have to move to Texas in order to keep their jobs. I doubt that's sitting well with some of them."

Mr. McBlythe issued a word of caution. "This plan may have unintended consequences. I'd hate to lose any of my top executives."

"I share your concern, Father, but you taught me a good shake-up every few years can spur growth,"

A warm smile preceded his words. "I didn't think you ever listened to me."

"Speaking of distractions," said Bella. "We could throw out the pirate legend that surrounds Christmas Cay to stir up everyone. It has *cay* in its name, but it's really an island. The cay is offshore on the east side. Legend has it pirates were chasing a ship carrying rum two days before Christmas and it ran aground trying to get to the sheltered bay. The ship's charts showed it was island, but it didn't show the cay. If they'd been approaching from the lee side of the island, they could have found safe harbor and possibly saved their cargo from the pirates. As it was, the crew nor the cargo were seen again. The legend says there are still pirates protecting the island.

Heather scoffed lightly, "We're going to have an island full of very smart people. I don't think pirate legends will cause much anxiety. Besides, we'll be on the island in June, not December."

Bella dismissed her words with a toothy grin. "Everyone knows pirate curses stay in effect all year round."

Heather sighed. "We'll hold it as a backup distraction."

"I like it," said Heather's father. "What else can we do that will occupy their thoughts?"

Silence settled upon the group until Bella spoke again. "Here's a better idea than tales of pirates. Many people are afraid of the sea. The idea of swimming in the same water as sharks might frighten them."

"Good thinking," said Steve. "Did I hear you say you were bringing a speargun along with your snorkeling gear?"

"I thought I'd make myself useful by providing fresh seafood. In fact, it's going to be the primary meat we'll have at our meals."

A sly smile parted Steve's lips. "Why don't we tell everyone they have to catch their own supper?"

"Can everyone swim?" asked Heather.

"If not, I can teach them, or they can fish off the dock," said Bella. "Of course there's no guarantee they'll catch anything from there. I find it's more effective to use a speargun."

Heather held up both hands. "That's enough distractions. Between the physical and mental fatigue, stories of shipwrecks, a threat of shark attacks, and being deprived of all contact with the outside world, everyone's true character should come shining through."

Her father added, "If this doesn't uncover the person who's been stealing and selling company secrets, I don't know what will."

7

Heather's personal assistant met her at the elevator with a cup of coffee. "I thought you might need this."

"You read my mind, but you didn't have to get here so early." Heather took the mug and strode down the hall toward her office.

"I'll catch up on my sleep while you're gone."

"Nice joke. You're taking my place. I promised my father and Steve one full week of my time. Steve reminded me that my plane is an extension of my office. He thinks I should add a few days to the investigation, so we're compromising. I'm working in the air and the hotel for a few days, then I'll focus on the investigation."

They passed through the outer office where the receptionists' desks sat like silent sentinels. Five in the morning was usually too early for the phones to ring, which suited Heather fine. "Any calls or emails I need to know about?"

"Two from Boston. One from Habib Patel and another from Janice Peltier."

"That's Father's chief financial officer and lead attorney. Did they say what they wanted or why they were calling me instead of him?"

"Only that they'd like you to call them back if you weren't too busy."

Heather made it to her desk and placed the valise carrying her laptop on it. "Steve told me to expect this. He described it as sucking up to the prospective new boss. I'd call it jockeying for position over their potential rivals. It tells me those two are more interested in keeping their jobs than remaining in Boston."

"Do you want me to get them on the line for you?"

Heather shook her head. "It's best that I ignore them until we get on the island. They work for my father, not me."

"Did you eat breakfast?"

"Not yet. I'll have a protein drink on the airplane and an energy bar somewhere over the Gulf of Mexico or the Caribbean."

Her personal assistant then gave a rundown on Heather's stay in St. Croix. "I booked you a room for three nights at the Ritz-Carlton. Steve, Bella, and your trainer have rooms for only two nights."

"That's a good hotel choice," said Heather. "As much as I love the resort Bella's parents sold, it still holds bitter-sweet memories. After all, that was the place Jack and I called off our engagement."

Her assistant added, "I wasn't sure how Bella would react to staying at her parents' former resort either, so I played it safe."

Heather let out a sigh. "She said goodbye to that resort after she and Adam were married there. I think you made the right decision to book us someplace else. What about the helicopter on Sunday?"

"You can work all day Saturday at the hotel while the others take a boat to the island. The helicopter will take you from the airport to Christmas Cay at four in the afternoon on Sunday."

Heather nodded her head in approval. "I wanted to make a dramatic entrance." She paused. "What's the weather forecast for that part of the Caribbean?"

"Windy with a possibility of scattered showers."

"That's normal for that part of the world." An additional thought occurred to her. "Winds mean rough seas. We'll find out how many of those on the boat are prone to seasickness. A journey over choppy water will be the perfect way to begin their week."

The early morning passed as Heather checked in with a dozen or more contractors. She extracted personal promises from each that they would stay ahead of construction schedules. About half of them sounded convincing. Falling behind was part and parcel of building anything, let alone a new lakeside housing development.

At eight o'clock, she met with all those scheduled to go to Christmas Cay except Clyde Pugh. It didn't take long before Brent Coolidge, Heather's acquisitions director, worked up the courage to ask, "Is it true that Clyde's coming with us?"

Heather nodded. "Is that a problem?"

"Not if he bathes and puts on deodorant."

Heather wasn't about to back down. Her voice took on the tone she'd used as a police detective. "Mr. Pugh is as much a part of this trip as anyone else. This week is about team building. Do you understand what that means?"

He gave his head a nod.

"Good. Mr. Pugh is going because Amy is too close to having her baby. I chose him to be the number two man in the legal department. Are you having trouble with my decision?"

He swallowed hard. "Not really."

"Not really, or no?"

Eyes cast downward. He mumbled, "No problem."

Heather closed the meeting by saying, "You were each given a list of everything you'll need to bring. Make sure you leave nothing behind. Remember, there's no cell or Internet service on the island. In case of an emergency, I'll have a satellite phone."

Following the quick meeting with her employees, Heather called Clyde Pugh to verify that he knew to be at Conroe's airport and on her plane in the wee hours of Sunday morning. It surprised her that he seemed excited about going and even had everything packed. He then asked, "Can I bring my snorkeling equipment? I can't stand to use other people's things."

"Sure."

"Great. I'll bring my knife and speargun, too."

"I didn't realize you liked the water so much. Are you a certified diver?"

"Of course. I believe everyone should be. Don't you?"

"That's a personal decision."

"You're certified," said Clyde with certainty.

"Yes, but some people have phobias about wearing a mask and breathing through a snorkel or respirator."

"That's because they're weak-minded. A week on the island will toughen them up."

Just when Heather thought there was a modicum of human kindness in Clyde, he proved her wrong. Well, he was still a brilliant attorney.

Heather made it to the airport at ten o'clock sharp. One of her pilots greeted her on the tarmac. "We've stored the luggage, and Bill is going to the terminal to get Steve, Bella, and the personal trainer. That guy looks like a wall of muscles."

"His name is Matt, and he's the reason I stay in fairly good shape."

"The last time I saw him, Matt was doing push-ups and crunches in the terminal."

"Doesn't surprise me," said Heather. "He's intense with workouts."

Her pilot looked her in the eye. "I wanted to thank you for allowing our wives to fly with us to St. Croix. They can't believe they get a full week lounging in the sun."

Heather shrugged. "You and Bill deserve a vacation with your wives. Besides, I may need you nearby if there's some sort of emergency. There's also the chance everyone will leave a day or two early."

Bella led Steve across an expanse of blacktop with Matt

trailing behind. She giggled when she saw Steve wearing a garish, mostly orange, Hawaiian print shirt with white shorts, sandals, and a straw sun hat. Heather looked at Bella. "Did you pick out his wardrobe?"

Steve answered for her. "I told Bella to find me the brightest shirts made. How did she do?"

"Perfect. You could glow in the dark."

"Good. You won't have any trouble picking me out from the crowd."

Bella added, "It was all Steve's idea. He wanted to be different."

"You succeeded."

Steve said, "Let's get going. I was hoping for a couple of hours on the beach this afternoon, but someone insisted on going to her office and wasting half the day."

"It was only three hours, and you'll have time in the sun today."

"Not if we don't get in the air. We're burning daylight."

The two detectives, Bella, and Matt climbed the stairs and took their seats. Twin jet engines came to life, and in a matter of minutes the plane passed over the Texas coast on its way to a sun-kissed island in the Caribbean. Heather sent a text to her father.

In the air. Next stop, St. Croix.

She couldn't tell if Steve was awake or asleep for the next hour of the flight. Her thoughts fixed on a parking garage in Boston, the place Reggie Scott was attacked. The police were still treating the assault on her father's employee as a mugging gone wrong. Was that the truth?

Her thoughts shifted back to Texas. One of the main reasons she was anxious to keep the project on schedule and moving forward was to make sure her and Steve's duplexes were finished in a timely manner. She knew one day the grace would run out on the two of them living under the same roof.

It was time for her afternoon progress report on the construction project. She'd force herself to stay focused on her project while Steve fine-tuned the plan to catch a thief. Hours passed in a flurry of facts, figures, and phone calls.

All went well until her pilot announced they were ten minutes away from landing at St. Croix. A glimpse through her window at the water and the sky in their varying shades of blue, competing with one another for the most beautiful. She wasn't expecting the stab to her heart as the memory of Jack telling her he couldn't marry her shook her world to its foundation. It was on St. Croix that he explained he had a daughter from a previous relationship. He hadn't known the daughter existed, but the death of the girl's mother meant he had to face his parental responsibilities head-on. To his credit, he did, but the decision left Heather with a boyfriend instead of a fiancé.

For all her supposed talents, Heather realized she was woefully inadequate in dealing with a stepdaughter on the verge of becoming a teen. Perhaps someday, after Brianna was in college, or even later, she and Jack might...

Thoughts of lost love came to an abrupt end as the airplane's tires came down harder than usual on the runway. She packed her laptop away and followed the others down the steps into the balmy air of what most people thought was paradise.

Steve made it down the steps without help and came to an abrupt stop on the tarmac. With head tilted back, he took in a full breath of the tropical breeze. "There's nothing like the smell of an island in the Caribbean. I hope there's enough time for me to score a lounge chair and listen to the waves come to shore."

"Aren't you hungry?" asked Heather.

"Always, but that can wait. Let's get to the hotel."

A van from the hotel was waiting outside the hangars. The small size of the islands meant the trip to the hotel didn't take long. Heather turned to Bella. "Steve's intent on listening to the sea before dark. Could you take him to the shore and put him in a lounger while I get us checked in?"

"Sure. This is such an awesome hotel. I know a bunch of people who work here."

Right on cue, the desk clerk let out a squeal. "Bella! Is that you?"

"Hello, Margie. When did you start working here?"

"Not long after your wedding. Where's Adam?"

"In Puerto Rico with my parents."

Bella hooked her arm through Steve's. "This is Steve Smiley, and behind him is Heather McBlythe. Steve's eager to sit by the water. I don't mean to rush off, but—"

Margie raised a hand to blunt her words. "Say no more. We've been expecting Ms. McBlythe and her companions. Take Mr. Smiley to the water's edge. I'll send a server to take his drink order and bring anything he desires from the menu."

Steve held the top of his white cane in one hand. "You wouldn't have conch fritters and an ice-cold bottle of beer, would you?"

"Fritters are one of our specialties, and I'll tell them to bring your beer in a bucket of ice, Mr. Smiley."

"Call me Steve. I'm on island time."

Steve and Bella walked out the door leading to the pool, and beyond it, the beach. Heather was about to turn around and take another look at the hotel when a woman exited through the same door as Steve and Bella. Heather caught only a glimpse, but it was enough to cause her to gasp.

The woman vanished as a noisy hoard of people chose that moment to fill the doorway on their way back from the pool area. The woman Heather thought she saw couldn't be Kate. Or could it?

8

Steve kicked off his sandals before raising his feet on the chaise lounge. Bella had already adjusted the back to the perfect position. The late afternoon sun beamed down, tempered by passing puffy clouds and a steady tropical breeze. Above him, palm fronds rustled. The sea joyfully lapped against the shore, adding to the serenade of peace. He'd imagined the sounds, scents, and texture of the sand ever since they hatched the plan to come to the Caribbean to help Heather's father catch a thief.

The feeling of peaceful aloneness remained with him even when Bella asked, "Do you want me to stay with you?"

"Huh?"

He'd already kicked his mind out of gear and settled into a place where thoughts were in short supply. "I'm fine." He paused. "In fact, I'm more than fine. This is perfect."

"Don't you want me to stay until the server delivers your fritters and beer?"

"You run along and visit with your friend."

"Did you put on sunscreen?"

"No need. I felt the shadow of the hotel on our way to the

shore. It must be a tall building, and I'm facing east. I'd say I have about fifteen more minutes in direct sunlight."

"You always amaze me by how much you know about what's going on around you. How long do you want to stay here?"

"Come for me in an hour. That gives me thirty minutes to finish my snack and another half-hour for a nap."

Bella bid him goodbye. Her footsteps in the sand made little noise as she walked toward the hotel.

He settled deeper into the lounger as the sun warmed him like an electric blanket. Sounds of the sea soothed away any residual cares. It wasn't long before a soft voice eased into his peace. "Good afternoon, Mr. Smiley. I'm Lori and I have your fritters and something cold to drink."

Steve made no move to sit up. "That was quick."

"Special service for a special guest. All the locals read the book about Bella and saw the movie they made of her life. You and Ms. McBlythe are genuine heroes for finding her biological parents after the man kidnapped her and raised her as his daughter. I can't imagine anyone so evil."

"We got lucky, and he paid for his deeds with his life."

"I doubt it was luck." She paused only long enough to take a breath. "I'll leave you alone, but if you need anything, just raise your hand. The staff has instructions to make sure your stay is perfect. The hot fritters and cold beverage are on your right side."

Once again, Steve caught the sound of soft footsteps in the sand fading toward the hotel. His hand found the fritters, and he quickly withdrew it. They'd need to cool before he sampled the tasty treats. His hand then found the bucket of ice and the long neck of an opened beer. The first drink was so cold and pleasing, he followed it with another. He settled it back in the ice and leaned back on the lounger.

He was wondering if this moment could get any better when he caught a scent on the breeze. Strained words followed. "Kate? Is that you?"

"Hello, Steve."

"I'd recognize your perfume anywhere. How's my favorite editor, and what brings you to St. Croix?"

Instead of answering his question, she said. "I saw the three of you checking in. You didn't waste any time getting next to the water. Is your trip business or pleasure?"

"Right now it's pleasure. Starting Sunday, it will be business."

"Another case?"

"Uh-huh."

"Another murder?"

"Not yet, but there's a young man barely hanging on to life. A murder investigation isn't out of the realm of possibility. For now, the case involves stealing corporate secrets."

"How interesting. That has the makings of a fantastic book. Make sure you document everything."

Kate changed the subject. "Are those conch fritters?'

"They were too hot to handle without getting third-degree burns. They should be cool enough by now. Let's try them."

"I shouldn't, but conch fritters are like crack cocaine to me. Let me hand you one."

Talk took a temporary back seat to tasting the crispy fried treats. Moans of satisfaction drifted across the sand.

After polishing off the first fritter, Steve asked, "I thought your Miami condo overlooking the ocean was tropical enough for you."

A pause followed. Kate broke the silence with words that caused his mind and heart to skip like a scratched vinyl record. "Peter and I are here on our honeymoon."

It was as if the wind stopped blowing and the sea pulled away from the shore, afraid to return. Was this a joke? Did Kate say she was married?

He issued a weak, "Congratulations. Do I know Peter?"

"You met him a couple of years ago when you and Heather came to Miami and spoke at the writer's conference. His name is Peter Blake. He's a literary agent." She took a breath. "I'm sorry

I hadn't mentioned him to you, but everything happened suddenly. I had no intention of ever marrying again, but he's a kind man and our careers blend well."

Steve held up a hand. "There's no need to explain. After the disaster of your first marriage, you deserve a man who treats you with kindness."

"I knew you'd understand, and I'll always think of you as the most unique man I ever met."

Steve covered his surprise with a chuckle. "I'll take that as a compliment, but unique is a rather catchall word."

"It's much too weak to express what I really think about you."

Another awkward pause followed until Kate took his hand. "There's something about you that forces me to tell you my true feelings."

"You don't have to say anything else."

"No. I must. I fell hard for you, but I'm damaged goods."

"We both are."

"Right. You'll never get over Maggie and I couldn't compete with her ghost."

Kate was right. Maggie was his one and only true love, even though Kate had made him wonder if another relationship might be possible. Deep down, he knew it wouldn't work. At least he'd convinced himself it wouldn't.

Kate kept talking. "The level of physical and psychological abuse I received in my first marriage took me into the world of writing and editing love stories that have happy-ever-after endings. I invented a world where I'd be safe. Part of that world is Peter."

Steve had a question he wanted to ask but wasn't sure how Kate would receive it. She must have sensed what it was. "You're probably wondering when I decided I needed a safe life partner and not a man who courted danger. Am I right?"

"You read my mind."

"It was after Bucky assaulted you and burned yours and

Heather's condos. From what you told me, you're still in danger from that maniac."

Steve finished her thought. "And you couldn't imagine living every day waiting for a phone call that said he killed me."

"I'm nodding my head in agreement."

Steve knew the conversation was almost over, but he didn't want it, or their relationship, to end on a sour note. "After we both decided I needed to find someone new to help me with my stories, I chose Bucky without doing research. It was my mistake, not yours."

He took in a deep breath. "Considering all we've said today, we both need to move on with no regrets. With that in mind, I need a new writing coach and editor. Could you and Peter make recommendations for someone who won't steal my work or try to kill me?"

Kate had a pleasant laugh that he would miss. She agreed to contact several qualified people who would guide him on his way to become a successful author. He'd make the final choice.

All that needed to be said had been, so Steve patted the hand resting on his shoulder. "Goodbye, Mrs. Blake."

An indeterminate amount of time passed until footsteps approached. They came in a way that made him think the person was trying not to leave footprints. "Are you all right?" asked Heather.

"I'm fine. Your question leads me to believe you watched a private conversation take place."

"I still think you can read my mind."

"Did you talk to her?"

"Very briefly. She told me she's on her honeymoon. I almost swallowed my tongue."

"Don't worry. It surprised me, but it's for the best. She deserves a nice, safe life after all she's been through."

"What about you? You deserve more happiness than anyone I know."

"I had a lifetime of happiness with Maggie crammed into the

years we were together. Now I'm playing with the hand that was dealt me. It's a decent enough hand, and I intend to play it to the best of my ability." He reached to his right. "Who can complain when there's a conch fritter within reach? Grab one. They're excellent hot or cool."

"No thanks. I'm saving my appetite for supper. Are you ready to go back to the hotel?"

"Take me to my room. I'll need to shower and change."

"Bella said she wanted to talk to you when you get to your room. She's really concerned."

"Send her a text and tell her we're on our way."

9

Their walk across the sand was pensive and silent. Heather thought back on Steve's relationship with his editor and coach. He'd always denied that it was, or could be, anything more. But she'd had high hopes that he would have a second chance at love.

Heather watched their reflection in the massive windows of the hotel as she led Steve past the pool. There seemed to be no change in his gait or countenance, but she wondered what kind of turmoil lurked under the calm surface. He was a master at controlling his emotions, but this situation might be different.

The door opened.

"Hi, Bella. We were on the way to Steve's room."

Bella was working up the courage to ask Steve a question when he lifted his chin. "I guess you want all the details about what Kate said to me."

"Not really."

It was a bald-faced lie, which resulted in Steve laughing out loud. He followed the laugh with, "Nice try, but what we said stays between us. What time are we meeting for supper?"

Heather answered before Bella could. "I'll send everyone a

text. We may have to wait on Matt. He's in the gym making up for not getting a proper workout today."

Bella departed with the excuse of needing to call her husband. Perhaps it wasn't an excuse. They were only six months into their marriage, and multiple phone calls and texts a day were still the norm.

Once they were alone, Steve reached out his hand. "Take me to my room and let's get the interrogation over with."

Instead of arguing, Heather took his hand and placed it on her arm. "Our rooms are on the fourth floor. Bella and I were sharing a room, but I changed that plan. You and Matt have your own rooms also."

"I told you I didn't need a private room. Matt is so tickled to have what amounts to a paid vacation that he's willing to sleep on the floor." Steve paused. "Why did you change your mind about Bella getting her own room?"

"I sent my plane to pick up Adam. Puerto Rico isn't that far from St. Croix. I didn't think the newlyweds would want to share a room with me tonight."

Steve's lips parted in a wide smile and he said, "There's a hopeless romantic living inside your tough businesswoman exterior."

They came to a stop in front of the elevators. Even though no one else was around, she kept her voice low. "I'm considering going with the rest of you on the boat."

Steve leaned into her. "Stick with your plan and don't worry about me. I'm fine."

She wanted to confront him on his last two statements, but the elevator door opened and a family of four poured out. The ride up to the fourth floor proved noisy as three giggling teens joined them.

By the time they arrived in Steve's room, Heather had put her thoughts together. He spoke before the door clicked shut. "Have you heard from your father since we landed?"

"I'll answer your question after we talk about you and Kate."

"No."

The abruptness of Steve's word made her take a step back. "What do you mean, no?"

"It's a simple enough word. There is no me and Kate. She's a married woman, and I'm a happy widower. End of story."

Heather considered his statements. "You didn't say she was a happily married woman, and I don't believe you're pleased with how things turned out."

"Happiness is relative. Am I happy that I have to find a new writing coach and editor? Not yet. Am I happy that Kate doesn't have to worry about me being a victim to someone with a score to settle? Yes."

"There's anger in your voice."

Steve shot back, "It's probably because you haven't told me if you've spoken to your father since we landed."

Heather's patience came to an abrupt end. "Yes. Father called. Reggie Scott died. He never regained consciousness."

Steve remained silent. Heather hated herself for being so insensitive. Before her stood a man who'd lost his wife and his sight at the same time in a brutal mugging.

Instead of continuing the verbal sparring, Steve spoke in a clear, businesslike tone. "Reggie's death changes everything. You and I need to go to Boston tomorrow morning."

"Why?"

"To find out if the homicide was premeditated or not."

Revelation hit Heather like a boulder crashing down on her. "You're right. We need to go to the parking garage. I'll call my pilots and tell them we need a quick roundtrip to Boston and back."

Steve had already moved on mentally. "Did you arrange the clothes in the closet so the first shirt will go with my first pair of shorts?"

"You're set for tonight. I'll need to select something more appropriate for you to wear tomorrow."

After a quick tour of his room, Heather wanted to make sure

there were no hard feelings. "Let's agree that we'll give each other space to deal with personal problems."

Steve rubbed his chin. "Not too much space. If I'm still acting like a snapping turtle when we come back to the island, we'll talk about Kate." He held out a hand so a handshake would seal the agreement.

"It's a deal," said Heather.

She then threw both hands in the air. "Who are we kidding? There's no way I can stay in this hotel and work when my mind has already shifted to solving Father's problems. I'm calling my PA to tell her I'm starting my time off as of right now."

"Excellent decision," said Steve. "I was wondering how long it would take you to realize we both need to refocus."

10

Heather boarded the twin-engine corporate jet carrying two white coffee cups with plastic lids. One pilot was already in the cockpit, while the other helped with her travel bag. Streams of early morning light shot through the windows facing east as Heather settled Steve in the seat opposite hers. One at a time, the engines came to life. After a long taxi, the plane turned into the wind. Thrust pushed her back into the leather seat. "Next stop, Boston."

About an hour into the flight, the plane hit turbulence and Steve stirred. After he asked her what time it was, she asked a question she hoped wouldn't offend him. "Didn't you sleep well last night?"

"Not really."

"Thinking about Kate?"

"Some."

For Steve to make this much of an admission was a major achievement. She tested him. "Only a little?"

"Yeah. That accounted for an hour of lost sleep."

"What else kept you awake?"

"The possibility of seeing red at the crime scene."

The simple answer wouldn't make sense to anyone but her,

Steve's former partner at Houston homicide, his late wife, and the psychologist who helped him put a name to his unique gift. He had an ability that bore the rather pretentious name of associative chromesthesia, the ability to see red, or a variation of it, at the scene of a homicide. If he perceived bright red, it was a premeditated murder. Lighter shades indicated lesser crimes resulting in a person's death.

Heather's curiosity got the better of her. "Have you ever worked on a capital murder case? One that resulted in the death penalty?"

He nodded. "Once, and it was the brightest red you can imagine."

"What about one the British would call Death by Misadventure?"

"Pale pink," he said. "Most of those never went to court, but some should have."

She then asked, "Why did you stay up all night thinking about it?"

"The last few cases we worked were obvious murders."

"That's right," said Heather as her head bobbed. "Do you think the gift could fade over time?"

"If it has, this is a wasted trip." Steve didn't cover a yawn. "Either way, I'm going back to sleep. If one of the pilots checks on us, tell him to find a less bumpy road to drive on."

The next words Steve spoke came when the plane touched down in Boston. He asked, "Is there a cab waiting for us?"

"I thought an Uber would be less conspicuous."

He spoke through a yawn. "How long will it take us to get to the parking garage?"

"Thirty to forty minutes, but that depends on traffic."

Steve found his cane but didn't unfurl it. "Coming and going, that's an hour and a half in traffic for less than a minute to find out what we came for."

"That will give the pilots time to get fuel and grab something to eat."

"Speaking of," said Steve. "Have them pick up something for us to eat on the trip back to St. Croix. Any kind of sandwich for me."

Thick traffic didn't surprise Heather, and it took every bit of forty-five minutes to arrive at the parking garage. Steve immediately complained. "These places are echo chambers. I can't tell if I'm about to be run over or which direction is safe to step."

Heather led him to the spot her father had sent a picture of. "Another few steps and we're there." She slowed to a stop and said, "Reggie Scott."

The shudder seemed to start at Steve's head, travel down his torso, and into his legs. "Bright red," he whispered. "Let's get out of here."

Heather had to admit the garage had a spooky vibe. Low concrete ceilings, squealing tires, and shadows cast by dim lights were bad enough without Steve's declaration that they were standing on the spot of a murder.

The flight back to St. Croix was a multi-hour planning session. Heather determined she wouldn't go back to Texas until they'd completed a good-faith effort to uncover the truth of what was going on at her father's business headquarters. A lively discussion took place concerning whether they were looking for one criminal or two. It remained to be seen if an executive from her father's business was also the killer.

They returned to the hotel in time to enjoy a late dinner with Bella and Adam. Heather kept looking for Kate, but the newlywed was nowhere to be found. Good. Both she and Steve needed clear minds for what lay ahead. Steve prescribed a full night's sleep which suited everyone. Tomorrow would be a busy day.

STEVE HAD PREVIOUSLY TOLD HER THAT THE SUN WOULD COME up the next day, no matter what. What he didn't tell her was that her day would start before dawn. Heather received a call from him at four twenty-seven. It wasn't too much earlier than her normal five o'clock, but the jangling phone interrupted her dream of swimming in azure waters. Her first attempt at words fell short, so she tried again. "What's wrong?"

"I can't make it to breakfast."

"Are you sick?"

"I stayed awake all night." He blew out a breath. "Not all night. I went to sleep about ten thirty, but woke up a few minutes after midnight. I've been tossing and turning since then. If I don't sleep, I'll be worthless the rest of the day."

"Why didn't you take something to relax you?"

"I did... fifteen minutes ago, and it's kicking in. That's why I called. Don't count on me meeting you, Bella, and Adam for breakfast. Let's meet for lunch."

Heather wondered if Kate's marriage was the reason for Steve's insomnia but thought it best not to ask. Instead, she said, "The people from my father's company are landing in Miami about now. Bella and I can go after breakfast and help load the boat. There's no reason for you to come with us. We're not leaving the dock until two o'clock this afternoon."

A deep yawn came from Steve. "Wasn't your original plan to have the people from Boston help load the boat and you take a helicopter to the island the next day?"

"That was before my mind stopped working on business."

A few seconds of silence followed. "Let's stick to the original plan as much as possible. The reason you wanted to take a heli-copter to the island was to show the Boston executives you'd be their boss when your father retired. If they see you all hot and sweaty from loading provisions, that's not the look you're after. Let them help load everything."

Steve had a point. It would be best if they believed she held their future in her hands. He kept talking. "Keep your normal schedule. Your pilots are flying Adam back to Puerto Rico later this morning. Bella and Matt are to meet the folks from Boston at the airport and take them to the boat at noon. She can tell them to help the chef load provisions. From what you've told me about Matt, he's an imposing man."

"That, he is."

Another yawn came from Steve, this one louder than the one before. "Let's compromise. You and I will show up after all the work is done. I'm not sure I can pull it off, but you can look fresh and in charge. Is there a place on the boat where you and I can have privacy?"

"There's the flying bridge. It's covered from the sun but is otherwise open to the elements. The captain can operate the boat from the flying bridge or from the main deck, which is more enclosed."

"Perfect," said Steve. "You, me, and the captain will be up top. Bella can stay with the folks from Boston and get to know them. It won't be as dramatic as flying in on a helicopter, but the effect will be similar."

Steve's words proved to her that he hadn't spent all night thinking about Kate. Heather was on the verge of confirming when to meet for lunch, but soft, regular breathing sounds came to her. Whatever he'd taken to relax had done its job. She pushed the red icon on her phone. He needed sleep, and it wouldn't hurt a thing if the employees from Boston had to wait for her and Steve to arrive before they traveled to Christmas Cay.

Heather sipped coffee for the next hour as she checked emails and read the *Wall Street Journal*. She put on form-fitting exercise apparel and headed for the hotel's gym. It didn't surprise her that Matt had already worked up a sweat. She approached him and asked, "Have you been here long?"

"Only about an hour." He slowed the treadmill to a quick walk from a flat-out run. Labored breathing caused him to thrust out words with each exhale. "Couldn't... sleep... well... last... night."

Heather climbed on the treadmill next to him. "Why not?"

"Scared... of boats." He took a deep breath. "Watched *Jaws*... last night. Big mistake."

She couldn't help but smile. The irony was obvious. Next to her stood a man who could bend metal bars with his hands and crush bones with his grip. He was a mountain of muscles who'd been a boxer of some repute before devoting himself to becoming a fitness instructor. She'd seen him do fifty push-ups on his fingertips with one hand behind his back. Yet, he was afraid of riding in a boat.

Heather wanted to allay some of his fears. "I'll make sure the boat has an extra-large life jacket for you to wear."

"That won't stop sharks if I go overboard."

Heather started her treadmill and took steps to get herself ready for a more thorough workout. "I checked the weather. It will be a perfect day for a boat ride."

"I checked it, too." He could now speak in short sentences without gasping. "Wind gusts up to 10 knots... Seas up to three feet."

"That's nothing," countered Heather.

"Nothing to you. Sounds like certain death to me."

"The boat is over sixty feet long."

"How wide?"

"Wide enough to stay afloat in the open sea during gale-force winds, which are between thirty-four and forty knots."

"How fast is that in miles per hour?"

"Between thirty-nine and fifty-four miles per hour."

The shiver started at Matt's head and worked to his shoes. "God didn't make man to be on the ocean. We sink."

"That's why he created man to be smart enough to build boats that can handle the open ocean." Heather was on the verge of chastising the squeamish man, but realized many people shared his fear. Instead of telling him to buck up and enjoy the ride, another idea came to her. "Why don't you take something to relax you before you get on the boat? There's a cabin on the lower deck you can sleep in. I'll wake you after we arrive."

"Where on the boat is the bed?"

"In the bow."

He shook his head. "I've seen enough movies to know that's the front. It hits the waves first. That tells me the crashing against the hull could cause it to spring leaks. I'd be stuck in the boat's bow with no way to get out. No thanks. I'm putting on the biggest life jacket I can find and staying where I don't get sucked under when we sink."

Heather had heard enough. "You could wear two life jackets. One for your chest and back, and the other for your legs and bottom."

"Can you do that?"

"I don't see why not. You'll be the only person wearing one, so there will be plenty to choose from."

Heather turned up the speed on the treadmill and began a two-mile run.

Matt went about his workout, which she knew would include another hour of weight training. She left him doing squats with enough weight on the bar to sink a rowboat.

She considered going to the dining room but didn't want to run into Kate and her husband. Heather examined her thoughts as she made her way across the gym. Why didn't she want to see the newlyweds? Was it because she felt Kate had somehow betrayed Steve? That made no sense because they'd never actually dated. Still, there was an attraction between those two that she felt down to her core.

As she passed a mirror, she stopped and shook her head. "Who are you to judge? You've always been too afraid to commit to anything but work. You're relieved that Jack chose his daughter." She turned and headed to her room but stopped at the next mirror in a long line. "You're a lucky man, Jack Blackstock. Being married to me would have made you miserable."

It then occurred to her that Steve might have made Kate miserable. She looked at herself once more in the mirror. "It's settled. No more talk about Kate or Jack until after the case is over." She looked closer into the mirror. "Better yet, no talk about Kate unless Steve brings it up."

Instead of going on to her room, Heather pulled out her cell phone and punched in Bella's number. It rang only twice before she picked up.

"I forgot to call you. No meeting in Steve's room this morning."

"That's good. Adam wants us to order room service. Do you mind?"

"Steve had a sleepless night and is catching up this morning. Don't call him. I need to shower. Enjoy your time with Adam."

She thought the call to Bella had ended, but Bella kept talking. "Adam said your pilots are taking him back to San Juan. We only have another hour together. Have you called your father to see if the group from Boston left on time last night for Miami?"

"I have their flight information. I'll check with the airline and make sure they're still on schedule."

"This is exciting," said Bella with anticipation in her words. "Sometimes I think I'd like to be a private investigator full time."

"It's better doing it part time."

"I guess you're right, but it sure is fun working with you and Steve. Am I still going to the airport and picking up your father's people?"

"That hasn't changed."

"I bet they'll be tired and grumpy."

"We hope so."

11

A hotel shuttle delivered Heather and Steve to the dock. Matt scurried to the back of the van and grabbed the two largest suitcases as if they were small bags of groceries. Bella and a woman with a dazzling white smile passed Matt on the dock.

Bella took care of introductions. "Heather and Steve, this is Pearl Tee. She's one of the best chefs on St. Croix. She can do things with fresh seafood that will have you purring like a box of kittens."

Steve held out a hand. "You and I are going to be close friends by the time we return."

"I hope so, Mr. Smiley." Her voice blended the accents of the Caribbean and Great Britain.

Heather took a guess. "You must come from the British Virgin Islands."

"The accent gives me away. I was born and raised in Road Town, the capital city of BVI. It's on the island of Tortola."

"It's a lovely island with wonderful people," said Heather.

"Culinary school lured me away, and I never moved back. It's only a short flight from St. Croix. I sometimes catch a ride on a boat going there."

Steve asked, "Is everything and everyone already on board?"

Matt returned in time to answer the question. "All are on board, but not happy. They complained about their flights and loading the provisions. Pearl had the perishables already loaded into huge ice chests. Luggage is in the bedroom at the bow of the boat." He took a breath and looked at Heather. "There's one extra person who wasn't on the list. Did you know your father was sending his personal assistant with the rest of them?"

"Dorcas Lindley is here?"

"You can't miss her. Dressed from head to toe in a loose-fitting outfit that makes her look like an Arab trader. She's wearing a sun hat and is sitting in the shade with zinc oxide covering her nose."

Heather cast her gaze to the yacht. "Thanks, Matt. It shouldn't surprise me, but it does. Father can't stand it if he doesn't know what's going on."

This earned a chuckle from Steve.

Matt grabbed two more suitcases and took off to deliver another load. Heather carried a valise that held her laptop and another leather bag containing her essentials and the satellite phone. Since they were already late leaving, she determined to call her father from the yacht if she could find a place with enough privacy.

Bella placed Steve's hand on her right arm after draping her braid of silver-blond hair over her left shoulder. The sight of a blind, middle-age detective wearing a blazing-red Hawaiian shirt, tan shorts, and sandals being led by a drop-dead gorgeous model pulled Heather's lips apart in a smile. They were a most unlikely sight, but somehow looked perfect together.

They walked down the pier until arriving at a sixty-foot Grand Banks yacht. Heather nodded her approval and mentally switched to her nautical vocabulary. From the top down, it boasted a covered flying bridge, a main deck with a second helm, and ample padded seating. She knew another level existed below with a galley, two small heads, and a salon with even more seating. Finally, a short set of stairs led to the stateroom in the bow.

The aft of the lowest level held twin engines capable of powering the craft at twenty-two knots.

Captain Roger met them at the rail. His skin had the look of a sun-weathered barn, but his eyes were blue as the water. "Welcome aboard," he boomed. His voice would fit a Hollywood pirate. All he needed was a parrot on his shoulder and a peg leg. "Where would you like to perch, Mr. Smiley?"

Heather answered for him. "Steve and I will ride on the flying bridge if that's all right with you, Captain."

"Fine and dandy. I hear you have blue water sailing experience, Ms. McBlythe."

"It's been a while, but I can hold my own under sail, or on a yacht this size."

"Let me get her out of the harbor and set a course for Christmas Cay. You can steer from the flying bridge after I reach open water."

"Thanks, Captain. I'll need to introduce Steve to the guests from Boston. The flying bridge will be the perfect place to talk to them individually." Heather looked at the ropes securing the yacht to the pier.

The captain followed her gaze. "You read my mind. I'll need someone to cast off who won't wind up in the water."

Bella spoke up. "I'll take the bowline."

Heather looked to her right. "That leaves the stern to me."

Heather passed Steve off to the captain, who helped him on board and placed his hand on the ladder. Steve scaled it with no problem. "There's a place to sit on the left when you reach the top. I'll be behind you."

It wasn't long before the yacht shuddered, accompanied by a deep gurgling sound. Mooring ropes came off with no trouble. Bella took long steps onto the craft with sure-footed grace. Heather followed and made quick work of coiling the rope.

"Next stop, Christmas Cay," said Captain Roger. The craft moved forward and away from the pier, barely making a wake. It wasn't long before the boat plowed a path through the water that had changed color from turquoise to deep blue.

Heather looked down at the aft deck. Matt was bent over the rail with a death grip on it. Pearl, the chef, secured a rope around the fitness trainer as he retched. He'd declined taking anything that would allow him to sleep through the trip. It would be a long, miserable voyage for Matt.

"What's that noise?" asked Steve over the throbbing of the motors.

"It's Matt. I told him to take Dramamine, but he played the part of a macho-man."

"How the mighty have fallen," said Steve. "He'll take it before he starts the trip back."

"Pearl's holding on to him to make sure he doesn't go over the side."

Steve didn't respond. This told her he was probably thinking about his first round of questions for the people from Boston.

Captain Roger pushed a button on the control console and turned to Heather. "I'd better check on the lad who's feeding his lunch to the fish. She'll stay on this course for the next thirty minutes. I have her set on eighteen knots. While I'm below, I'll check on the other passengers."

"Aye, Captain," said Heather. She threw in a two-fingered salute and a smile for good measure.

Heather settled into the captain's chair. "Steve, move closer so you can hear me."

She glanced over her shoulder as Steve used his cane to find the seat next to her. "This is nice. I love the smell of the water and the sound of the wind. It's not that bumpy, either."

"Matt might disagree with you."

"You can introduce me to the folks from Boston when Captain Jolly Roger takes over again."

A hearty laugh spilled out from Heather. "I wonder how many people call him that?"

"Admit it," said Steve. "You thought of it, too."

"Aye."

Heather's one-word response preceded a laugh. She controlled herself and asked, "What's the plan?"

"We'll get them up, one at a time. I'll be the good cop with soft questions. You'll be the quiet, sullen cop to start. Be evasive if they press you for details. We have all week to get to know them. Let's go slow and keep them guessing."

"Does it matter who we start with?"

"Not a bit. Grab the first person you come to after the captain finishes making his rounds."

They'd passed several islands before Captain Roger hollered from behind her. "I'll take over from below." This was Heather's signal to retrieve the first suspect. She waited until a light blinked off on the control panel and the craft made a course change before she climbed down the ladder.

Lying on a padded bench was Habib Patel, her father's chief financial officer. She shook him awake and spoke in a firm tone. "Come up to the bridge. I need to introduce you to my partner."

Habib stood, stretched, and yawned. He was a pencil thin man with a slight paunch in his midsection. Dark circles under his eyes told the tale of a sleepless night.

Heather directed him up the ladder and instructed him to stand between her and Steve. The twin captain's chairs had a release on them that allowed both Heather and Steve to swivel so they could face Habib. Heather introduced Steve and allowed him to take over the interview.

"It's a pleasure to meet you, Habib. How was your trip to St. Croix?"

"Not very good, I'm sorry to say." A faint accent seasoned his words.

Steve asked, "India or Pakistan? I can usually tell the difference, but between the wind and the engines, it's hard to hear."

"India, but I'm an American citizen now. I moved my family and my wife's family after I earned enough money."

"That's commendable of you. You must have done very well in college."

"I've been most fortunate."

"I understand you're the chief financial officer."

"Again, I've been fortunate."

"It's my experience that most people make their own luck."

Habib shook his head. "I didn't say I was lucky, only fortunate to have the opportunity to prove my worth to Mr. McBlythe. I'm a firm believer in meritocracy."

"Me too," said Steve. "As a former police officer, I can tell you that not everyone shares that belief. Some people like to take shortcuts. Have you ever known someone who didn't deserve to hold the promotion they received?"

"I try to mind my own business."

Heather made a mental note that Habib had dodged the question.

"That's a wonderful philosophy to live by. Don't you wish more people practiced it?"

"I'm a numbers man. I pay little attention to how others choose to live their lives."

Steve rubbed his chin. "Now I know why Mr. McBlythe trusts you with keeping the company books. Honest workers are hard to find."

Habib didn't respond, so Steve moved on, asking questions he already knew the answers to. "Does your wife work?"

"No."

"Do you have children?"

"Four, and a fifth on the way."

"Congratulations. That's quite the family. Do your parents also live with you?"

"My parents and my wife's parents."

"Holy smoke! It's a good thing you have such a high-paying job."

Habib turned away. "Perhaps we could continue our talk when I'm rested?"

"Sure, Habib. I hope we didn't wake you out of a pleasant dream."

"I don't waste energy on dreams. You'll soon discover I'm a very practical man in all things."

Instead of allowing Habib to go, Steve held up a hand. "One more question, please. What is it you want most from your career?"

"Right now, it's sleep."

"Go back to your bench, Habib," said Heather without a trace of sympathy in her voice. "We have much to do once we get to Christmas Cay. You'll need all the rest you can get."

Habib moved to the ladder and descended it. Once his head was out of sight, she asked, "What do you think of father's CFO?"

"One outright evasion and two half-truths. He doesn't mind his own business all the time."

Heather agreed. "I caught that. What else?"

"He's definitely a numbers man, but he was lying about not paying attention to what others are doing. I'd say he sees and hears things others don't."

"You're right. He wouldn't be Father's CFO if he had his head down in spreadsheets all day."

"Finally," said Steve, "everyone dreams of something. If nothing else, he dreams of coming home to a quieter house. Two sets of grandparents, four kids, and a pregnant wife would make me long for a hammock on a quiet beach."

"Amen to that. He wasn't lying about wanting to go back to sleep."

A few seconds of silence followed before Steve said, "Bring the next one."

12

A woman's voice sounded from the ladder leading to the flying bridge. Heather and Steve spun their chairs until they faced Janice Peltier. Their visitor was the first to speak. "I saw Habib come down, so I thought you might want to meet all of us."

"Yes," said Steve. "I wanted to introduce myself before we arrived on the island."

Janice gave her head a nod, but didn't respond otherwise. Heather had to begin the interview with an instruction. "Steve is blind. You'll need to respond to him with words."

She lifted her chin and her eyebrows narrowed. She opened her mouth to speak, but closed it just as fast. Heather interpreted this to mean Janice didn't like to be corrected, but knew better than to argue with her boss's daughter. Not surprising for an attorney. Standing before a short-tempered judge trained attorneys to choose their words carefully.

"My apologies, Mr. Smiley and Ms. McBlythe."

Steve took over by brushing away the apology with a flip of his hand. "People nodding a greeting happens so often that I've learned to expect it. Heather's overprotective of me." He extended a hand for her to shake. "Let's start over. I'm Steve Smiley and I assume you've met Heather."

"Never in person," said Janice, as she shook Steve's hand. "Of course, I've heard of you both."

"What have you heard? I hope it was something good."

"Only good things."

Heather broke in before Steve could respond. "I want to apologize on my father's behalf. I understand your travel arrangements left much to be desired."

Once again, Janice chose her words with care. "How can one complain about a week on an island in the Caribbean?"

The words didn't match her posture. She stood too erect, and there wasn't a trace of joy in her tone. She was an attractive woman in her early forties with slender fingers and long legs that mid-thigh shorts showed off well.

Steve asked, "Are you ready for a week of sun and fun?"

"Is that what I'm to expect?"

Heather again interrupted. "Spoken like a fellow attorney. Whenever you're unsure what to say, respond to the question with one of your own."

A spark of anger came from Janice's gaze, but died away just as fast.

It was time for Steve to play good cop again. "What I'm expecting is a relaxing week of eating fresh fish and feeling the sun bake away all my troubles."

Heather scoffed, "What troubles?"

"Deciding if I'm going to drink a *pina colada* or a *Cuba libre* is a tough decision to make. My brain may explode from the pressure."

Janice showed no reaction to Steve's attempt at humor. Was she a cold fish or simply worn down from lack of sleep?

"Tell me, Janice," said Steve. "How long have you worked for Mr. McBlythe?"

"He hired me fresh out of Harvard law school."

"And you're now his lead attorney?"

"That's correct."

"You made fast progress."

"I earned his trust and promotions by outworking everyone else."

"What do you like most about your job?"

This question seemed to stump her as she stared straight at Steve. She finally said, "Like and job aren't two words I normally put together. I find my position fulfilling in that I work with some of the best minds in the world. I don't tolerate mediocrity in myself or those I supervise."

"If that's the case, I hope my slovenly habits don't rub off on you."

"You don't expect me to believe that."

Steve allowed a smile to part his lips. "That tells me you've done your homework."

She didn't answer again, nor did she need to.

Steve asked, "How many hours a week do you work?"

Janice took a half-step back. "That's an interesting question. I don't count them, but I'm consistently the first attorney in the office and the last to leave. I like to come in on weekends because it's quiet. That allows me to get work done without interruptions."

"Will you be able to refrain from work while you're on the island?"

"I downloaded all the Supreme Court cases for the last five years onto my computer. I plan on filling my free time with going over them again."

"You can forget that plan," said Heather. "This week is about team building, physical health, and meditation. One of your assignments will be to clear your mind."

Janice's eyes shifted back and forth as she took in the information. Heather was sure she'd challenge the assignments. It surprised her when Janice's lips formed a thin line. Whatever she wanted to say stayed bottled inside the poised attorney.

Steve broke the silence with words of dismissal. "Thanks for coming up to meet us. Could you ask Bob Brown to climb up here?"

"My pleasure, but I'll have to wake him."

Heather ended the conversation with, "He should have slept on the planes or at the Miami airport."

"I agree," said Janice. She turned, grabbed the ladder, and was soon out of sight.

The two chairs turned to face the bow. Heather scanned the horizon and asked, "What did you think of Janice?"

"Chronic overachiever. That was a brilliant touch, telling her she'd have to meditate. Be sure you take up all the phones and laptops. I'm guessing Janice isn't the only one who'll go into withdrawals when they can't look at a screen of some sort."

It took a full five minutes before Bob Brown's thatch of gray hair poked above the last rung of the ladder. Puffy eyes and one red cheek showed he'd come from deep slumber. Heather greeted him with, "You must have been sleeping hard."

"Uh-huh."

"You don't sound happy to have a week off. Would you rather have stayed in Boston and worked on acquisitions?"

"A week off is fine as long as it includes traveling in first class."

"I agree," said Steve. "We had a great flight on Heather's plane. There's nothing like a corporate jet. No waiting in ticket or security lines, a comfortable leather seat, no crying babies sitting close to you—"

"Hey. That's exactly what happened to me last night and this morning. Not the leather seat. I might as well have been sitting on a metal bucket, and the kids.... Jeez Louise."

Heather noted the thick Boston accent. Bob didn't always sound this way. Fatigue must have caused him to lapse into a thick brogue. He'd worked his way up the ladder in her father's company and now headed an important department. He'd trained his voice to mimic various dialects of the country and had a talent for languages.

"You must be uncomfortable in slacks and a dress shirt," said Heather.

"I stepped off one airplane and onto another last night. My wife met me at the airport and we traded suitcases. Barely made it through security in time. I hope she packed everything on the list Mr. McBlythe gave us."

Steve took his turn. "You must travel a lot. Doesn't it get old?"

"It's all part of the game of looking for companies to buy or invest in. I'm usually in business or first class. I don't know what happened with this trip, but it was lousy with a capital L."

Steve asked, "What do you expect to get out of this week?"

"I hope to leave the island with my job. I'm not a young pup."

"Are you willing to change with the times?"

Heather knew Steve was baiting Bob with the question. Also, he wanted to keep the rumor going that a merger of companies was imminent and competition for jobs would be fierce.

Bob drew a hand down his face. "Corinne and I are on the downhill side of raising our girls. One's already out of college, and the other graduates next year. Her wedding is in September. I was hoping for five more years, but things might not work out that way. I love Boston, but that doesn't mean a change wouldn't do me good."

Steve took the conversation a step further. "Would you be willing to take a pay cut and move?"

"It depends on how much of a pay cut you're talking about. There's no state income tax in Texas and I'd get more house for the money. Our eldest daughter lives in Florida and it's doubtful Julie will stay in Boston. Although, I'd miss the Red Sox and all the things that make Boston such a special place."

"It sounds like you're willing to take whatever life hands you. Is that a fair assessment?"

"I'm not under any illusions about my age and that change is coming. It's all a matter of timing. Either change will beat me to the finish line of my career, or I'll break the tape first."

"One more question. Why do you think someone attacked Reggie Scott?"

A wave picked that moment to jolt the boat, causing Bob to resettle his feet to keep from falling. He took his time responding. "I don't know Reggie very well, but from what I picked up around the office, he lives beyond his means and made himself into a target for muggers."

Heather perked up. "Do you blame him for the assault?"

"Wearing a Rolex into Boston's bars isn't a wise thing to do. He's a junior accountant. Those people sit in cubicles behind closed doors. The only time I remember meeting him was at the last Christmas party. He did magic and card tricks after a few drinks loosened him up."

Steve thanked Bob for his time and told him they'd talk again about the Red Sox's chances to make it to the World Series in October.

Heather asked him to send Dorcas to them.

"Your thoughts?" asked Steve after he was sure Bob was down the ladder.

"I like him, but there's something he's hiding," said Heather. "Father says he has a great intuition for evaluating companies."

"You must have known Bob for quite a while."

"Yes, he's been with the company a while. He still gets the job done, but he used to be ruthless in negotiating deals. He made my father a ton of money."

"Enough for him to feel slighted by the prospect of being put out to pasture?"

Heather hesitated as she tried to push her emotions back into their closet. She'd always liked Bob and his family. "I'm having a hard time imagining Bob as a seller of secrets, but now that I shine a bright light on him, it would make sense if he did."

Dorcas Lindley was the next person from Boston to climb the ladder. Heather let out a chuckle when her father's personal assistant arrived. Her choice of clothing made her look like she stepped off a camel in a desert caravan.

"Hello, Dorcas," said Heather after wiping the smile off her face. "Aren't you hot in that outfit?"

"I didn't know if I'd be in the sunshine all day and didn't want to take the chance of being incapacitated." She lifted her hat. "Most natural redheads have very fair skin, and I'm no exception."

Steve asked, "Did Mr. McBlythe send a satellite phone with you?"

"How did you know?"

"Knowing things is what Heather and I specialize in."

Heather took her turn. "Did Father tell you to call him daily?"

"He's expecting nightly updates."

Steve then asked, "The others will want to use it once they know you have it."

"I'll tell them no."

"It would be best if I kept it," said Heather. "You can come each night and make your call from my room."

Dorcas shook her head. "I'll need instructions from your father to do that."

Steve asked, "Will you need instructions from Mr. McBlythe to comply with the schedule of events we're planning?"

"Mr. McBlythe told me to use my judgment. He's expecting detailed reports, and that's what I'm going to give him."

Steve smiled. "The best way to get to know a group of golfers is to play a few rounds with them and then listen to what they say after they've had a bad day. We designed this week to be mentally and physically challenging. We want you to take part in as many activities as you can. You won't be able to make full reports if you're not around the executives."

"Then that's what I'll do, metaphorically speaking, of course."

"No metaphors. The challenges are real," said Heather.

"We're requiring everyone to exercise, swim, and catch their own fish. You'll also play sand volleyball, take hikes up a steep hill, and participate in problem-solving exercises. Some events will measure individual performance while others involve team efforts. We could excuse you from some things, but to get inside information to report, the more time you can spend with the others, the better."

Dorcas's eyes widened. "What about people who can't swim?"

"Bella will teach them."

"I don't know the first thing about fishing."

"Bella and others are here to help. You can fish off the pier and not have to use a speargun."

"A speargun? Good lord. I oppose guns of any type. The idea of me causing harm to a fish is abhorrent."

"Do you eat them?" asked Steve.

"Of course I do, but..."

"No one will force you to catch fish, but you'd better like rice and vegetables if you don't."

Dorcas shook her head. "I foresee non-compliance and rebellion among the participants."

Steve widened his smile. "You underestimate how competitive these people are. They each earned their position and now change is threatening their jobs. We can't require them to take part, but if they don't, there will be consequences."

"What about me? I'm not an executive."

Heather stared into Dorcas's eyes. "My father and I haven't always been on the best of terms, but all that changed a few years ago. As you know, he and I communicate regularly. Is it your intention to report only to him about what goes on at Christmas Cay?"

Dorcas didn't hesitate. "Yes."

"Even though you know he'll tell me everything you say?"

"He's my employer."

Steve concluded. "Your loyalty is commendable. Be sure to

wear sunblock, drink plenty of water, and pace yourself physically if you choose to take part in physical activities. Most importantly, listen and look for the person who's stealing and selling information from Allister's company."

"That's why I'm here."

Heather dismissed Dorcas with a wish of good luck. She and Steve were now alone on the flying bridge. It was out of character for Steve to use her father's first name with one of his employees, but she dismissed it as being part of the informal vibe of the Caribbean.

Her thoughts about Dorcas took flight when the satellite phone rang. Her father's name appeared on the screen.

"Hello, Father."

"Are you on the island yet?"

"Another forty minutes of open sea and we'll arrive."

"Can anyone else hear us?"

"Only Steve. The others are on the decks below. If they're awake, the noise from the engines insures privacy."

"Good. The Boston police aren't happy that you're transporting a group of potential murder suspects to a far-flung island."

Steve responded with silence to the news.

"Be careful," said her father. "You now may be looking for a killer and a thief."

The call ended and Steve said, "Only one more department head to interview."

13

Heather's mind churned away at the revelation that the police were looking at the people on the boat as suspects. It shouldn't surprise her; she'd been rolling the possibility around in her mind since she heard Reggie died. Steve brought her back on task by saying, "Let's see what we can get out of Louis Crane."

"I forgot all about him."

"By the way," said Steve. "Is Matt still at the rail?"

Heather looked down. "He's on the deck in the fetal position. Pearl has a wet towel over his head."

"You'll need to take his place leading exercises until he recovers."

"I don't know about the others, but the physical challenges will do me good."

"I'll be cheering you on from a distance."

"Thanks. If nothing else, join us for sunrise yoga and a morning swim."

Heather had her sea legs firmly under her and soon returned with her father's technology wizard. Louis Crane had pleasant features and a ready smile, even after two cramped flights and a long boat ride. His black hair spiked outward in every direction imaginable. She knew from his bio that he was thirty-four, but his baby face took off ten years.

Steve met him with an outstretched hand. "Hello, Louis. Steve Smiley. Your coworkers didn't fare well on the flights to the islands. How are you?"

"Great," said Louis with energy powering his words. "I use technology and good habits to improve my physical and spiritual well-being."

"Technology and habits?" asked Steve. "That sounds interesting. Tell us more."

"I trained myself in middle school to use biofeedback to go to sleep at the same time every night. My body and mind relax when I tell them to. It doesn't matter if I'm sitting or lying down. The idea came to me from studying soldiers. Did you know it's possible to sleep while riding a horse or bouncing in a tank?"

"I've heard of it, but never gave it much thought."

Louis became more animated. "While everyone else was drinking coffee as we waited to board our plane in Boston, I was already asleep. Listening to Alpha brainwaves on earbuds triggers a sleep response. It takes less than a minute for me to go to sleep. I was out all the way to Miami and slept again in the terminal until my normal wake-up time."

"What happens if you don't have your music to cue you?"

The question resulted in hesitation and pinched eyebrows. "I'm not sure. Fully formed habits are hard to break, but they all start with a trigger, or as you said, a cue. Change-induced anxiety may be stronger than the habit. That's why I keep an adequate supply of battery backups to power everything I depend on. All my habits begin with something auditory."

Heather looked up at him from her chair. "Let's try an experiment for the next week. My father and I want to challenge everyone from both our companies to perform tasks while feeling a level of physical and mental discomfort. You may have an unfair advantage over everyone else. Then again, you may not.

The only way to tell is for everyone to go cold-turkey from all electronics."

To her surprise, Louis beamed a smile. "What a fascinating experiment." The smile left him. "I assume it will only last three days, at the most. That will be plenty of time to measure the results, and I don't want to lose all my good habits."

Heather shook her head. "A neuroscientist recommended seven days for an accurate reading." This was a complete fabrication, but one that sounded good enough to fool him.

Louis thrust his hands deep into the front pockets of his baggy shorts. "That's not long enough to fully form a good habit, but I may start developing bad ones."

Heather tilted her head. "Don't you trust yourself and the science behind your good habits?"

"I guess so. What I'm having difficulty understanding is the purpose of the experiment. If I can use technology to increase efficiency, why not use it?"

Steve responded with, "What you're really saying is, why not use it all the time? Is that right?"

"I believe it would maximize efficiency."

"What about creativity and problem solving?"

"Significant advances are being made in those areas through technology, too."

Heather asked, "What percentage of jobs will technology replace in the next ten years?"

He didn't hesitate. "At least fifty percent of human work could be replaced, but it remains to be seen if management will move that quickly. Early adopters will reap untold benefits."

"What about the displaced workers?"

"I don't understand?"

Heather was on the verge of explaining how sudden mass reductions in personnel can change the reputation of a company, but Steve broke in. "Have you done studies of Mr. McBlythe's companies to see which ones could benefit the most?"

"That's much too big of a project for my small department.

I've focused my studies on the departments at corporate head-quarters. In fact, every person chosen to come on this trip represents a department that I've studied, or soon will."

Heather took over. "Which department will be the most affected?"

"Your father has already streamlined human resources. We replaced twelve percent of the workers with existing technology. It could have been three times that number, but your father decided natural attrition was more palatable to him. Next on the list is accounting. I'm hoping to increase the percentage."

A smile came to Louis. "My recommendation is for a fifty-five percent reduction in force, and that's just the beginning. Machine learning is advancing so fast. There's no telling where it will take us."

Steve thanked Louis for his time and slowly spun his chair around. Heather guided the young man to the ladder and echoed her appreciation. Once they were alone and both faced the sea, she asked, "What did you make of Louis?"

"He's hyper-pragmatic, cold, and calculating. Machines will disrupt traditional jobs, but perhaps not as much as he'd like to believe."

Steve took off his sunglasses and rubbed his eyes before putting them back on. "I believe we might have stumbled onto the motive for someone stealing secrets from your father's company. A systematic reduction in employees doesn't sit well with department heads."

Heather nodded in agreement. "Some people measure success by the amount of money they make. Others, by the number of people they supervise."

"If that's the case, which department head has the most to lose?"

Heather considered the question before saying, "It depends on how they measure success. Habib Patel may eventually lose the most employees. That results in a loss of prestige."

"What will happen to his salary?"

"Knowing my father, it will probably go up. Efficiency reaps rewards."

Steve kept his face to the wind. "We need to find out what motivates Habib. Is it money or perceived status through staff? In fact, we need to discover that about everyone who works for your father."

"How do you recommend we do that?"

Steve rubbed his chin for several seconds. "Let's create a survey and ask their peers in other departments to rate each department head. These people know each other well."

Heather joined in. "I'll weave some questions into a long, boring questionnaire." She chuckled and said, "A few more questions won't add much time to a three-hour survey." A dark dot appeared in the distance. "There it is, dead ahead, Christmas Cay."

"How much longer?" asked Steve.

"It's just a speck on the horizon, so I'm guessing thirty more minutes."

Captain Roger spoke from behind them. He'd made it up the ladder with stealth enough not to be noticed. "That's a fair estimate, Ms. McBlythe. It shouldn't take long to unload if everyone pitches in. I'll be long gone by the time you carry everything up the hill to the main house and cabanas."

Heather swiveled the captain's chair around. "The bridge is all yours, Captain. She's a fine ship."

In a matter of seconds, Heather was on the main deck and announced, "Everyone below. I have instructions to give you."

Those enjoying the wind in their hair moved to the ladder that took them to the deck below. Her first task was to awaken those who were taking advantage of the time to catch up on lost sleep. "Good afternoon," she shouted above the noise of the engines. "Christmas Cay is in sight. We'll dock in about thirty minutes. The first thing you'll do is unload provisions and luggage onto the dock. Decide among yourselves the most efficient way of staging. Provisions go to the main house first. Pearl, our chef, will tell you how she wants things arranged in the kitchen. After completing that task, you can retrieve your luggage. Everyone carries their own to their assigned cabana. Bella has a map of the island that shows locations of places you'll need to know."

"Like what?" asked Bob Brown.

"The main house, the trailhead of the path to the tallest hill on the island, the cabanas, the beach volleyball area, and several other places you'll be required to go to." She took a breath and continued. "Your first challenge will be to memorize the map before we reach the dock. Bella will show it to you one at a time."

"When do we eat?" asked Janice Peltier.

Heather took in a deep breath. "I don't think you understand how this week will go. You'll receive instructions to perform certain tasks. These will follow a strict schedule. You will focus on one task at a time and do it to the best of your ability. My father and I are looking for high levels of competency and cooperation."

Heather replaced her drill sergeant voice with her normal tone. "Since this is your first day, I'll answer your question about eating. There's still several hours of daylight left. That gives us enough time to hike Christmas Mountain and play sand volleyball until dark. I'll be leading both events. If you're still worried about eating, that's Bella and Pearl's assignment."

Heather's nod meant Bella was to explain. She stood. "While you're taking a hike and playing volleyball, I'll be in the water spearing enough fish for Pearl to prepare us a banquet." She paused. "At least that's the plan. You never can tell about fishing."

Statements of appreciation sounded. Heather ended the meeting by looking at her watch. "You now have approximately twenty-five minutes to memorize the map, determine how you'll unload all provisions and luggage, and arrange everything on the dock. I'll be observing and taking notes. You're on your own and

I'll not answer any more questions until we gather at the trail-head. You can ask me anything you want on the trail, providing you can catch me."

"Is that a challenge?" asked Louis Crane.

"Get used to it. Everything about this week is a challenge, and you wasted twenty seconds asking that question. All decisions result in consequences. Some good, and others you won't like."

She gave Louis a hard stare. "Your consequence for wasting time is you'll be the last to look at the map." Her gaze swept over those assembled. "The other participants from my company will be here in a day or two. Consider carefully how you'll conduct yourself with increased competition."

14

With clipboard in hand, Heather looked on as her father's lead attorney, Janice, and Louis Crane, the IT guru, argued about the most efficient way to unload. The result was predictable. Those who abstained from the leadership role quietly left and returned to the room one at a time as Bella called their name. By the time Louis and Janice realized the boat had docked, it was too late for them to memorize the details on the map. Others would have to show them where to go. The infighting continued, with others joining the fray.

Heather said nothing, but made a show of frowning and scribbling notes. Her father's team had failed before stepping on dry land.

She made sure Steve was safely off the boat and on his way with Bella to the house that overlooked one of the most spectacular beaches Heather had ever seen. The bay faced west and looked like a horseshoe, with the curve of an expanse of white sand. A three-hundred-foot pier pierced the bay to the south, and a coral reef guarded the north side. Also on the north side of the bay, a jagged hill looked over the reef that extended out into the sea. Fish abounded in the pristine water. Bella would have no problem providing a bountiful selection of fresh fish for the evening meal.

A clearing of her throat was all it took for the passengers to realize they needed to unload the boat. The executives were too busy schlepping provisions off the yacht and complaining to each other to comment on the beauty of the bay.

Heather broke her silence. "Don't forget your luggage. Captain Roger needs to be back at St. Croix before dark."

What she didn't tell them was St. Croix was only an hour away. They'd zig-zagged across the Caribbean to give her and Steve time to get a read on the people her father thought might steal and sell information. It turned out only her fitness trainer, Matt, suffered from severe seasickness. Dorcas Lindley had placed patches of scopolamine behind both ears after her interview. One would have sufficed. She'd slept after returning below and now wobbled her way off the boat.

Pearl hooked Matt's arm over her shoulder and led him to the safety of terra firma. He fell to his knees and stayed in the sand as the cook took over her area of responsibility. Pearl barked orders and soon had the provisions off the dock and on the way to a futuristic looking home made of steel and glass.

Heather followed the last person, Dorcas, who struggled to carry two cloth bags stuffed with onions, cucumbers, bell peppers, and containers of spices. It took the five-person crew from Boston three trips to transport everything needed to sustain the gathering for a week. Dorcas made it as far as the living room, collapsed on the couch, and fell fast asleep.

Between the June sun, the humidity, and the physical exertion, most participants were wet with sweat, and they hadn't yet retrieved their luggage.

Heather gathered them in the home's massive living room where floor-to-ceiling glass offered a panoramic view of the bay below. "Don't get comfortable. You have fifteen minutes to remove your luggage from the pier, find your cabana, change into the hiking clothes you were told to bring, and meet me at the trail-head." She gave them what she hoped was a wicked smile. "Let's hurry down the hill to get our luggage. We're on a tight schedule."

"What about Dorcas's luggage?" asked Janice, as a drop of sweat fell from her nose.

"How you treat each other is up to each of you. Do you believe it's worth it to help Dorcas, or will it cost you if you don't make it to the hike on time? You'll find this week is all about decisions and consequences."

Steve sat in a recliner facing the group, who stood with their backs to the windows. "I'm sure you've noticed by now that the heat and humidity are more than you're used to in Boston. There will be a water bottle for each of you with your name written on it. Bella's filling them now. You can either wait here for her to finish, or pick it up after you change."

Heather moved to the door. "Little choices can have big consequences." She opened the door and ran toward the dock.

Habib Patel tried sprinting down the hill but misjudged his speed. Feet and head traded places as he tumbled several yards before coming to an inglorious stop.

Louis Crane was the only person who made it to the trail-head within the allotted time, but he came without a water bottle. She spoke to him while watching her footing. "How often do you work out?"

"My workouts are on a high-tech stationary bicycle. I can ride any course in the world."

"It's not the same as being outside. I work out in a gym that's not climate controlled. There's plenty of heat and humidity in our part of Texas."

"It's too cold in Boston most of the year to do that," said Louis.

"You'll soon see what a difference it makes."

Louis caught up with her again. His words came between breaths. "How long is... this trail?"

"It's not long, but it's steep. It also has several switchbacks. I should reach the summit in about fifteen minutes." She broke into a jog.

Louis matched her stride, but with labored breathing. "Narrow... path... cut out... of the jungle. Very steep."

"That's why it's so humid. The jungle traps the heat." She increased the pace. The aggressive tread on her hiking shoes bit into the damp dirt and threw it behind her. It didn't take long for sweat to form tiny streams on her face. Once out of sight, she slowed enough to take a few large gulps of water.

The view from the craggy summit took her breath away. She could see the entire island and even a couple of dots of green and brown, tiny islands on an otherwise royal blue and azure seascape. She could also see the curved strip of sand that lay off the east shore of the island. This was the true Christmas Cay from which the island borrowed its name.

Billows of fluffy clouds played far overhead as the trade winds from the southwest cooled and refreshed her. This was indeed an island paradise. Too bad she, Steve, and Bella had to find a thief and possibly a killer.

Water and wind worked their magic on Heather, and she soon recovered from her run. She hustled from the summit and encountered Habib and Louis. They sounded like trains huffing their way up the trail elbowing each other as they approached the top. The last thing she heard was Habib's response to Louis's plea for water.

"You should... have considered... the heat... and humidity."

Heather passed the others on her way down the hill. Everyone but Louis carried a water bottle. She noted Dorcas wasn't among the participants, which came as no surprise after her overdose of motion-sickness medication. There was little doubt that Steve would pump her for information when she woke.

15

Steve closed the lid to his laptop, took off his headset, and left his bedroom. He'd familiarized himself with the layout of the home enough that he could navigate the living and dining rooms with the aid of his cane. The sound of a woman yawning greeted him as he located the chair that suited him best. "You slept through the hike, and you're missing the volleyball game."

"How long have I been asleep?"

"Almost two hours. I've been in my room dictating notes."

"I should follow your example. Mr. McBlythe expects a full report every evening at nine o'clock." Concern filled her voice. "Are we still on Boston time?"

"The U.S. Virgin Islands are on Atlantic standard time and don't recognize daylight savings time. If this was winter, we'd be one hour later than Boston. Since it's summer, we're on the same time."

"Thank goodness. I'd die if my first report wasn't on time."

Steve allowed the hyperbolic comment to pass, but wanted to find out more of what Heather's father expected of Dorcas. "What will you report of your first hours on the island since you slept through them?"

She hesitated before answering his question with one of her

own. "How would you gather information for a report when you missed an event? They have to be accurate and complete."

Steve considered her question for several seconds before responding. "The only thing you can do is become like a newspaper reporter and ask a lot of questions."

He quickly changed the subject. "Are you physically unable to do strenuous activity?"

"To be frank, I could stand to lose weight."

Steve raised his chin and took in a bouquet of odors coming from the kitchen. "There's nothing like the smell of authentic Caribbean cooking. While you were sleeping, Bella speared enough fish for supper and breakfast."

"She's such a beautiful young woman."

"That's what everyone says. All I know is she's one of the finest people I've ever had the privilege of knowing." Steve smiled. "Where were we? The smell of food cooking has a way of clouding my mind."

"You were answering my question about the best way to glean information for today's report to Mr. McBlythe."

"Uh-huh. I remember. Am I correct to assume you're not in good physical shape?"

"I loathe exercise, and it shows."

Steve drew a hand down his face. "If you get too tired from exercise, it will impair your ability to observe. If you don't take part in some activities, the others will view you as an outsider and you risk being shut out. My advice is to join Heather and Bella early tomorrow for yoga. If you're up to it, do the morning hike up the hill. Don't try to keep up with those trying to prove themselves. After that, avoid most physical activity in the sun."

Something else occurred to him. "The participants don't know it yet, but everyone will be required to catch their own fish. You could trade fish for information."

"I don't understand."

"The way we've arranged the schedule, it will be impossible for everyone to take part in every activity. They'll have to choose what they're willing to cut out of their schedule. If you catch an abundance of fish, you could trade it for information."

A hint of hope entered Dorcas's voice. "You and Heather have planned this well. Do you believe all the executives from Boston will relocate when the merger takes place?"

"That's one thing we hope to discover this week."

Steve shifted in his chair. "That reminds me. What are your plans when Mr. McBlythe retires?"

Absolute confidence filled Dorcas's voice. "He'll never completely retire, and he'll never leave Boston."

"Don't you think the merger is imminent?"

"It doesn't matter. I've been his personal assistant for years. I know Allister McBlythe better than he knows himself. Trying to live without another deal to close isn't in his nature."

"What if you're wrong?"

"I'm not. He'll always need to work."

Her certainty took him aback. He semi-agreed with her as he said, "Heather says her girl-Friday is a complete god-send. I guess Mr. McBlythe will continue to need a limited staff."

"Like father, like daughter." Dorcas followed this with, "In case you're wondering, I have no intention of competing with Heather's PA. My only goal this week is to provide accurate and complete reports to Mr. McBlythe. If that means daybreak yoga, a morning hike up a steep hill, and learning how to fish, then so be it."

The door opened. He could tell by the footfalls that Heather, Bella, and Matt entered. Matt's footsteps didn't fade until he reached the hallway leading to one wing of the bedrooms. Steve asked, "Is it sundown already?"

The sound of Heather falling into a chair close to him preceded her response. "Not yet. Bella, Matt, and I are the undisputed champions of beach volleyball."

"How are you three physically?"

"Not too bad. Matt overcame his sea-sickness by drinking

water with added electrolytes. I'll need to slack off exercising tomorrow."

"Me, too," said Bella. "Between spearing fish and two hours of volleyball, I'm going to hurt in the morning."

Steve had one more question. "How long until we eat?"

Heather rose from her chair. "I gave them twenty minutes to shower, dress, and be sitting at the table. The glorious smells coming from the kitchen tell me Pearl is grilling the fish Bella caught."

"Only twenty minutes?" said Dorcas. "I'd better get to the women's bungalow and get ready."

Steve rubbed his hands together as the door closed behind Dorcas. "Let's fill their bellies until everyone's miserable and see how well their brains work when faced with trick questions and impossible situations."

Heather must have found a sudden burst of energy. "I'll race you, Bella. Last one to finish showering and sit at the table has to take the yoga mats to the front yard in the morning."

Steve chuckled as bare feet slapped against the tile floor. So far, the plan was on track. He wondered how the group from Boston would react after Heather's executives arrived, and the competition began in earnest.

Following the evening feast, Steve led a three-hour session of value clarification exercises that required people to decide between equally distasteful options. They then had to defend their choices to the group. What started out as lively discussions morphed into shouting matches. Habib Patel and Louis Crane continued their competition for alpha male. Janice Peltier proved herself to be excellent at cross examinations, with snarky comments thrown in for good measure.

The verbal jousting was precisely what Steve had predicted would happen, and this was only the warm-up to the arrival of Heather's staff.

16

Steve lowered his coffee cup when Heather entered the living room the next morning. "You're up earlier than I thought you'd be. Sore muscles?"

"I thought I was in decent shape. Sand volleyball killed my calves. I can only imagine how the five people from Boston feel this morning."

"Only four. Dorcas stayed out of the sun."

Heather retrieved a cup of coffee and returned. "Speaking of Dorcas, did you speak with her yesterday afternoon?"

"Uh-huh. I asked her to call your father and get his permission to hand over personnel files on the crew from Boston."

"How did you do that? I thought no one from Boston was to know we have internet access."

Steve placed a finger over his mouth in a sign of secrecy. "He wanted to make sure everyone from both offices believes all outside contact is impossible, but he told Dorcas so she can follow up phone conversations with emails."

"We confiscated everything electronic. What difference does it make if they know there's Internet capability?"

"Do you really think a tech guy like Louis Crane didn't bring an extra device of some sort? You told them to turn in everything, but you didn't search them or their suitcases."

"I thought about it, but decided not to." Heather let out a scoffing huff of air. "He probably has something with a screen." She took a sip of coffee and placed her cup on a side table. "There's more to this story than you're telling me. I know how you think. What aren't you telling me?"

Steve shrugged. "The best way to keep a secret is don't tell anyone."

"If I wasn't so sore and tired, you'd get a piece of my mind."

"Save it for your father." Steve changed the subject. "Is it still dark?"

"First light. It won't be long before I'll need to take the yoga mats out to the yard."

"You're too late. Bella beat you to the punch."

Heather went to the window. "Why'd she do that? I lost the bet."

Steve didn't answer because he didn't need to. Bella was hardwired to help people, and not only her and Steve. Instead, he asked, "What time do you expect the people from your office to arrive?"

"Noon-ish. If the plane catches a strong tailwind, they might be here as early as eleven-thirty. Things could get interesting this afternoon."

The door opened and Bella walked in wearing her body-hugging yoga outfit. "Everything's ready. Do you think they'll show up on time?"

"I doubt it," said Steve. "I'm expecting a mini-rebellion this morning."

Heather bristled. "They'd better come."

Matt walked in wearing a sleeveless shirt and tight shorts. "Only Dorcas is moving this morning, and she's in slow motion."

"Told you," said Steve.

Bella puffed out her cheeks. "What do we do now?"

Steve had the answer. "Follow your schedule of yoga and a

hike up the hill. Take your time this morning. They'll come here looking for breakfast, but won't find any. I'll break the bad news and have a heart-to-heart talk with them."

As predicted, the only person to show up for sunrise yoga was Dorcas. She wore a loose-fitting, lightweight jogging suit. This was her first experience with early morning stretching. Audible moaning accompanied every change of position.

Heather wanted to use the time on the trail to get to know Dorcas, while Matt attacked the hill like he was competing in a race with a cash prize. Bella set a brisk walking pace, so it wasn't long before they lost sight of her also.

Dorcas opened the conversation. "I'm so disappointed in everyone from Mr. McBlythe's office. I feel like it's a personal affront to the best man I've ever known."

"We told them making choices and living with the consequences was one of our goals."

Sweat formed on Dorcas's forehead. "It's an unorthodox plan, but I think it's brilliant. Your father must have come up with it."

Heather overlooked the slight and kept a lookout for straight sticks, about four and a half feet long. She found one, and then another.

"Why are you carrying those?" asked Dorcas.

"They're hiking sticks. They help you keep your balance on uneven or steep terrain. I picked up the habit of using them one summer in the foothills of the Alps. Here. Try them and see if it helps."

It seemed to take all of Dorcas's mental energy to get into the rhythm of swinging the sticks forward as her foot took a step. The trek proved to be a mostly silent journey, punctuated by greetings to Matt and Bella as they descended.

Upon reaching the summit, Dorcas took a seat on the least jagged rock and surveyed the panoramic view. "This has to be the most beautiful place I've ever seen."

"It's certainly a strong contender," said Heather.

Dorcas's appreciation of the scenery didn't last long. "What's the schedule for the rest of the day?"

Heather grinned. "Steve reminded me this morning that the best way to keep secrets is to not tell anyone."

"That's what your father says."

Heather fixed her gaze on a distant island. "They're both wise men." She brought her gaze back to Dorcas. "What do you like most about being my father's personal assistant?"

Dorcas's eyes shifted to something in the distance as she took her time responding. "That's hard to say since he has such a dynamic personality. I've definitely found my dream job."

"That's nice of you to say, but every job has its highs and lows. What do you like least about yours?"

The response rolled off her tongue like she'd practiced what to say. "I detest people who speak ill of the company because they don't see the entire picture of how the departments work together to form a single team."

"Does anyone come to mind?"

"All the department heads to some degree."

"Who's the worst?"

"There's two. The CFO, Habib Patel, and Louis Crane. They're both consumed with ideas concerning company profits. They don't understand your father's generosity. Both call him a fool for supporting philanthropic causes."

The candor came as a surprise, but Heather pressed on without comment. "Anyone else?"

"Janice Peltier is frank in the extreme, but she's brilliant and so far has proved herself loyal. She's not an easy woman to like, but your father trusts her implicitly. I still have reservations."

"You said she's been loyal so far. What did you mean?"

"Please don't take this wrong, but I don't trust attorneys. It's a bias I picked up a long time ago and has to do with the entire legal profession. I don't see how two lawyers can stretch the truth until it screams, employ every legal maneuver available to them, tear each other apart in court, and then have drinks and laugh together after work."

Heather chuckled. "There are many ironies in life and you've identified a big one." She didn't want to explain more, so she said, "It seems we're down to Bob Brown for the people from the Boston office."

"I'll let your father discuss Mr. Brown with you."

Heather tilted her head. "An evasion. Are you sure there's not more attorney in you than you're willing to admit?"

Dorcas rose from the rock she was sitting on. "I need to get down the hill before something happens and I'm not there to report it."

The trip down the hill was quiet. She assumed Dorcas had spent her morning supply of words and needed to focus on using the walking sticks to steady her descent. With only the sound of their footfalls and birds in the trees above them, Heather's thoughts drifted to how detailed she'd be with Steve about her talk with Dorcas. His mantra was, the more information the better, so this would be her first contribution. Although scant, the information Dorcas gave was an insider's perspective on Habib, Louis, and Janice. That she refused to discuss Bob was also significant.

Heather walked behind Dorcas to allow her father's personal assistant total concentration on the trail. This left her mind free to ruminate on who was stealing secrets. She'd need to call her father and find out why Dorcas refrained from talking about the acquisitions director.

As the home came into view, she spied the four remaining Bostonians in the front yard.

The strident voice of Janice Peltier greeted them. "Why are we being kept out of the main house?"

Steve shot back. "You overslept and failed to take part in today's first two activities."

"That's not fair," said Habib. "We're sleep deprived and can hardly move."

"Yeah," echoed Bob Brown. "They almost killed us yesterday."

Heather joined the fray. "Bella and I did more physical activity than any of you. She spent two hours in the water providing your supper, and neither of us took a break from volleyball. You took breaks."

Louis Crane had his own complaint. "How do you expect me to wake up without my phone?"

Steve swept his cane in front of him until it touched the railing. "You sound like a flock of bleating sheep. Heather, didn't we make the purpose of this week clear last night?"

"I thought we did. Perhaps you need to explain again."

"Both Heather and Mr. McBlythe are firm believers in meritocracy."

"We know that," said Bob. "We all had to prove ourselves as the best in our field."

Steve nodded. "To quote the sentiment of an old song, *that was yesterday, and yesterday's gone.*"

Janice fixed her hands on her hips and cast her gaze to each of her coworkers. "Don't you see what they're doing? We're fighting for our jobs and they're looking for weak links."

Steve held his ground. "Janice is correct, and right now I'm seeing very little competition to Heather's employees."

"I'm not sure it's worth it," said Bob.

Steve replied, "That's a decision each of you will need to make."

Habib asked, "Are you planning on closing the Boston office?"

"My father and I haven't decided." It wasn't a complete lie. Someday it would happen, but there were no immediate plans.

"Of course they are," said Janice. She set her jaw. "I don't care what the rest of you do, but I didn't make it to lead attorney by quitting when things got tough. I've done my homework and my counterpart in Heather's company will be out on maternity leave in two months. There's no guarantee she'll come back. While I have the advantage, this is my opportunity to prove my worth, and I'm taking it."

Steve placed both hands on the top of his cane. "As a demonstration of goodwill, missing yoga this morning will not count against you. However, if you want breakfast, the hill awaits you."

"Are you saying if we don't go up the hill, you'll withhold food from us?" asked Bob.

Steve spoke in a flat tone. "You've done nothing to earn it."

"Neither have you," snapped Bob.

Heather took in a deep breath to propel the words of chastisement. Steve's roaring laugh overpowered her prelude of, "Now, listen to me, Bob Brown."

While Heather reloaded with another breath, Dorcas played peacekeeper. "It's still nice and cool. I want to go again."

Matt, who was standing off to the side, spoke up. "Everyone who's going, follow me. Run if you want to, but I'm walking."

Bob grumbled under his breath, but he followed the group. Heather caught up with Steve inside. "That was close."

"They're all competitive. Let's eat and tell Pearl she has about forty minutes before they return."

Bella asked, "What do you want me to do after breakfast?"

"Teach them to catch fish. For the time being, that will be the only meat on the menu. They have until the people from Heather's office arrive to catch enough for lunch, supper, and breakfast."

"What about me?" asked Heather.

"You and I will teach Matt to swim. It's ridiculous he doesn't know how."

"How many more days until we start individual interviews?"

Steve rubbed his chin. "At least two, possibly three. In the meantime, we'll wear them down until the only things they can think about are rest and keeping their jobs."

17

The morning sun was well up in the sky by the time the Bostonians finished breakfast. Everyone gathered in the living room as Steve stood with his back to a view he couldn't enjoy. "I have good news and bad news," he said.

"Bad news first," said Habib.

"No. Let's start with something positive," said Louis.

Steve pretended to flip a coin and announced, "Heads. Good news first." He kept talking over Habib's groan. "No beach volleyball this morning."

"Wonderful," said Janice. "After climbing that mountain again, I can barely take a step. What's the bad news?"

"From now on, everybody catches and cleans their own fish. Bella will teach you this morning."

Bella spoke up. "You'll have your choice of a rod and reel or snorkel gear and a speargun. After today, you need to fit fishing into the day's schedule of activities, which will be non-stop."

"How do you expect us to do that?" asked Janice.

"Exactly," said Steve. "There are no free times. You'll have to decide if you want to eat fish or earn points. By the way, the boat carrying Heather's crew from Texas will be here around noon. Instead of more sand volleyball this morning, you'll need to catch your supper and tomorrow's breakfast. There won't be any lunch today since you had such a late breakfast."

Bob Brown raised his hand even though Steve couldn't see it. "What if we catch more than we need?"

Steve drew his hand down his face. "I like it. You sound confident, Bob."

"If there's a fish in the bay, I'll catch it."

"Then you'll have more decisions to make than the others. You can catch and release to give others a better chance, give some of your catch to those with less skill, barter with them, or you can even go to your bungalow and take a nap until the next event starts."

"Are you saying we don't have to fish if we don't want to?" asked Habib.

Heather took her turn. "It's your choice, but you'll eat what the chef prepares for you. It will keep you alive, but food is fuel and you've already experienced how many calories you can expect to burn."

Janice gave a scoffing laugh. "What's the matter, Habib? Afraid of the sharp teeth, or can't you swim?"

He didn't reply.

"Ah," said Janice. "You're afraid of both."

"I'll fish," announced Habib with as much vigor as he could muster. "But you won't catch me in the water."

Steve broke into the conversation before it devolved further. "There's one more thing we need to cover before you change and we all go to the beach. You have three minutes to pick a leader who will establish a schedule of dishwashers. Heather arranged for a cook, not a galley slave. Mouths to feed will increase by four this evening, and for the rest of the week."

Janice didn't hesitate. "I say we elect Dorcas to make the schedule. It will give her something to brag about to Mr. McBlythe."

Dorcas's head snapped upward, but she refrained from saying anything.

"I second the nomination," said Bob. A series of 'ayes' followed.

The group didn't pay attention to Dorcas's weak complaint.

Steve added, "More good news. The other group will alternate washing dishes and cleaning the kitchen."

Dorcas pushed her lips over to one side. "All five of us will need to work every other meal."

Complaints filtered in, but Steve put a quick end to them by saying, "You each gave Dorcas the authority. Now, you'll live with your decision. You have thirty minutes to finish cleaning the kitchen, change, and collect your gear for fishing. Meet Bella on the dock and don't be late."

Heather stood to signal the end of the meeting. "You'll clean the kitchen to Pearl's standards."

The room cleared and Heather drew near to Steve. "Do you think they'll be able to complete the challenge without a riot?"

"I doubt it. Dorcas doesn't impress me as someone they'll listen to. I told Pearl to tell them what to do only once, then go to her room."

Matt asked, "What if they don't make it?"

Steve grinned. "I hear the view from the top of the hill is spectacular."

Bella giggled. "Come with me, Matt. Let's move the fishing gear to the patio. They'll need it, eventually."

Steve turned to face the windows but spoke to Heather. "Let's take a walk."

Heather took his hand and placed it on her arm. She led him onto the patio and down a short flight of steps to the yard where the yoga mats lay on a flat area with thick grass.

"Can anyone hear us?" asked Steve.

Heather scanned the area. "All clear. Is something wrong?"

"We need details on Reggie Scott's attack."

"Be patient. I called my old partner at Boston P.D. last night. She's not assigned to the case, but she's working back-channels to get information. She's supposed to call me tonight. Also, my father is sending everything Human Resources has on Mr. Scott and all the executives here. All we brought with us was summary reports."

Steve nodded his approval.

She then asked, "How do you think things are going so far?"

Steve turned his head toward the bay below. "They're focused on aching muscles right now. The arrival of your people will keep them distracted for a few more days. They're all exceptionally smart, which means it's only a matter of time before one of them sees through our plan to find out who's stealing secrets. Dorcas told me Habib figured it out by examining the unusual fluctuations in lost revenue. If he knows, others may, too."

"What about the murder of Reggie Scott? Do you think the thief could be the same person who killed him?"

The shrug of Steve's shoulders told her he'd considered the possibility, but didn't have enough information to reach a conclusion. Instead, he said, "You and I need to keep in mind that the people from your office in Texas are here as distractions. The more eyes and ears we have on the Boston execs, the more we'll learn about who might have a motive for both crimes. Let's meet with Bella, Matt, and Pearl throughout the day. They might pick up on something important."

Heather joined Steve in facing the bay. "The seas aren't as calm today. Captain Roger probably won't arrive until after noon."

"Choppy seas are a good way of describing what will happen when the two groups meet." Steve lifted his head. "Did you hear that?"

"I can't hear anything but the wind."

"It's coming from inside. I left the patio door open on purpose. Janice has a shrill voice when she's excited."

"Who's she arguing with?"

Steve stood perfectly still for several seconds before saying, "That's a surprise. I thought it would be Louis or Habib, but it's Bob Brown."

Heather led Steve to the steps leading to the patio and whispered. "Can you hear what they're saying now?"

Multiple shouts sounded from inside, followed by a loud crash. Steve said, "I was wondering how long it would take."

Heather bounded up the stairs and sprinted into the living room. Louis and Habib rolled on the floor, both trying to free their hands. Bob shouted at them to stop while Janice laughed. Dorcas wrung her hands. Louis freed a hand and delivered a solid blow to Habib's eye.

Bob caught Louis's next blow on its way to do more damage and pulled him off the chief financial officer. Both regained their footing as Bob pinned Louis's hands to his sides. Habib took full advantage of the opportunity to even the score. The right hook caught Louis square on the nose. Blood flowed onto Bob's arms and he released his grip.

"Enough!" shouted Heather.

The unlikely pugilists dropped their hands as Dorcas looked on with horror.

Matt and Bella arrived and stared with expressions of unbelief. Heather turned to Matt. "It seems my father's executives have extra energy this morning. They're still dressed to hike up the hill. Once the bleeding stops, would you mind escorting all five of them two times up and down?"

"My pleasure."

"I did nothing," said Janice. "This isn't right that I'm about to suffer for their buffoonery."

Steve responded. "Cleaning the kitchen is a team event. That means you all pass or fail together. We've told you repeatedly that there'll be consequences for failure."

Dorcas swallowed. "Does that apply to me? I'm here as an observer."

"Not anymore," said Heather. "My father gave me authority to implement any decisions I think are necessary. You're in charge of cleaning the kitchen, and you failed miserably."

Dorcas's eyes widened. "You can't report this to Mr. McBlythe."

"Why not?"

"You just can't. I'll run up and down the hill if you promise not to tell him."

Steve spoke in a calm voice. "You don't have to run, but a brisk walk seems in order. While you're at it, keep track of anyone who doesn't go all the way to the top."

Louis expressed his opinion about Dorca's new task with one word. "Snitch."

Steve kept his voice to a loud whisper. "As a show of mercy, we're willing to wipe all demerits off your record and start fresh when the people from Texas arrive." He paused a moment. "What about the rest of you? Do you want to restart the day with a clean slate after you complete two quick trips up and down the hill?"

"This is extortion," said Janice.

"Shut up," said Louis as he pinched the bridge of his nose. "I don't want to go into the competition with a deficit of points."

"Me either," said Habib.

Janice stood in front of the two fighters. "If either of you two idiots cost me another trip up that hill, I'll make you regret being born."

Dorcas found her voice. "Bob, you have the dining room. Wipe off the table and sweep the floor." She turned to Habib. "Finish rinsing the dishes and silverware and put them in the dishwasher."

"What about me?" Louis asked sullenly.

"Scrub the pans and skillets. Janice will dry and put them away." She scanned all four. "I'll sweep and mop the kitchen. We have ten minutes to finish."

Heather nodded her approval. "That's more like it. With cooperation like that, you stand a slim chance of beating one or two of my executives."

Matt set the pace up and down the hill. The time was

approaching late morning when the crew finished their two treks to the summit and back down. Dark splotches marked sweat dampened shirts. Bella met them at the base of the hill. "Change into bathing suits. Bring a towel, hat, sunblock, and the long-sleeve shirt and pants you'll find on your beds. If you're snorkeling and spear fishing, you don't have to wear the pants. Otherwise, wear both. You'll burn to a crisp in this sun. Matt, Heather, and I will distribute the fishing equipment to you on the deck."

Heather added, "You have twelve minutes to be on the deck. None of you remembered to take water with you on the hike, so I'll give you an extra five minutes to hydrate."

She looked at her watch. "We're running an hour behind schedule, so you won't have as long to catch your supper and breakfast." Her gaze took in each of the sweaty faces. "Steve and Pearl were kind enough to fill each of your water bottles. I suggest you pick them up on your way to change. You look wilted."

Everyone took Heather's advice and swigged water as they quick-walked to their bungalows. Steve waited for her in the living room. "Are their tongues hanging out?"

"Pretty much. I'm not sure they'd make it up the hill again."

"They'll feel better about life when they watch your crew from Texas hike up the hill in the heat of the day."

Heather took a long look at Steve. "You're enjoying this, aren't you?"

He grinned. "Almost as much as you are."

"Does that mean we're both a little twisted?"

"We wouldn't be looking for a thief and a killer if we were normal."

Heather took a long pull from her water bottle. "Here comes Janice. She's leading the pack."

A sly smile came across Steve's face. "I wonder how she'll get along with Clyde Pugh and his body odor."

Heather looked out to sea. "We'll find out tomorrow when

we put people into two-person teams. Until then, I hope he didn't smell up my plane too much."

"Did you warn your pilots?"

"They told their wives to put cologne or perfume on paper face masks. They'll warn my department heads to sit close to the cockpit. Clyde's seat is at the rear of the plane."

"That may not be enough."

"Everyone knew what to expect. They'll have to cope as best they can."

Steve shook his head. "You're enjoying this more than I thought you would. Let's keep in mind what we're trying to accomplish."

18

Steve retreated to his room while Heather watched Bella and Matt pass out equipment that would allow the crew from Boston to catch their food. Habib and Dorcas each chose a rod and reel. Louis, Janice and Bob grabbed masks, snorkels, flippers, and spearguns. Bob also grabbed a rod and reel. The trio made for the reef on the north side of the bay. Everyone remembered to refill their water bottles and carry them down the hill.

Bella led Dorcas and Habib onto the dock and stopped about halfway down. Heather followed and looked on as Bella began her tutorial of baiting the hooks and operating the reels.. "Put the bait on so the fish can't see the hook. They're smarter than you think. I'll bait Dorcas's hook. Habib, you'll watch and bait your own."

With bait on each hook, Bella took Dorcas's rod and reel in hand. "Watch carefully to see how the reel works. Push this button and the line releases." She demonstrated, and the baited hook and weight plunked into the water and unwound line from the reel. "When the weight hits the bottom, turn the handle on the reel. This engages the drag, which puts pressure on the fishing line. Reel in some line to adjust the depth of the bait."

"How much?" asked Habib.

"Fish swim at different depths. You'll need to experiment."

"This seems very arbitrary."

Heather broke into Bella's lesson. "It's called fishing, not catching. There's a lot of skill and some luck involved."

Bella spoke with more hope. "Look down into the water. There's plenty of fish. Watch as I try to catch that yellowtail."

Habib lay on his stomach and peered over the side of the dock. Dorcas, dressed from head to toe in loose fitting, sun-blocking apparel, placed hands on knees and stared into the clear water. Bella lifted the bait and twitched the rod to entice the fish to strike. With a sudden burst of speed, the yellowtail closed on the bait and seemed to inhale it. Bella set the hook with a firm jerk of the rod upward. Dorcas took a step back. "My goodness. I wasn't expecting it to be so violent."

The fish soon broke the surface. Bella's pole jerked and bent as she kept constant pressure on the line until the fish ran out of fight. With smooth turns of the handle, the thin line fed back onto the reel, and the fish rose out of the water. She allowed it to rest on the dock, where it thrashed a few more times.

"What now?" asked Habib. "It has teeth."

"Most saltwater species do," said Bella. "You'll need to kill it and put it on ice. I brought everything you'll need."

Heather spoke before the novices could ask for details. "If you strike the fish hard in the head with the priest Bella brought, you'll kill it."

"Priest?" asked Habib.

Bella answered. "That's what anglers call the wooden club. After you kill the fish, remove the hook with needle-nose pliers and put it in the ice chest."

"This is barbaric," said Dorcas.

Heather shot back with, "I didn't hear you complain last night when you raved about the meal."

It came as a surprise when Habib grabbed the priest and made quick work of dispatching the fish. Her first thought was of Reggie Scott, whom someone had beaten the life out of. Could Habib have done to Reggie what he did to the yellowtail?

The fishing lesson came to an abrupt halt. Heather cast her gaze to the north side of the bay. "You two are on your own. Bella and I need to check on the others."

Bella said, "I'll be back. Enjoy catching your supper."

Heather added, "You'll need to move when the boat arrives. Don't get in their way as they're unloading."

Habib looked down the long dock. "That means we'll need to go all the way to the end."

Heather couldn't help but smile. "Don't fall in."

Once out of earshot, Bella leaned into Heather as their toes dug into the firm sand where the turquoise water foamed onto the beach. "Habib surprised me when he took the bat and killed the fish."

"I noticed that, too. I'll have to tell Steve about it."

They approached three piles of clothes. Matt looked on from the shore and pointed at two snorkels poking up from the surface of the bay. Both were a considerable distance from the shore, but close together. "Louis and Janice couldn't wait. They challenged each other for the most fish and the biggest."

"Good for them," said Heather. She turned to Bella. "Would you make sure there's plenty of distance between them? I'd hate to have them shoot each other with spearguns."

Matt wore a baseball cap backward, so he shaded his eyes with his hand. "I told them they'd forfeit their right to fish with spearguns if they didn't maintain forty yards of separation."

Heather tried to judge the distance. What looked like two periscopes broke the surface only ten yards apart. "Bella, tell them I want to see them immediately."

Bella pulled off her pants, but left her long-sleeve shirt on to cover her swimsuit. She donned a mask, snorkel, and flippers and cut through the water with powerful kicks.

Following suit, Heather pulled off her pants but kept her water shoes on. She waded until the warm water lapped against the tail of her long sleeve shirt. Bob spoke as she approached. "Did you see the fish on my stringer?"

"They look like mahi-mahi. You know your way around a rod and reel."

"That's what I thought they were. They're both decent size."

"I thought you'd be spearfishing instead of using a rod and reel."

He shook his head. "Too crowded."

"You won't have long to wait if you want to fish with a speargun on your own."

Bob gave his head a firm nod as he kept his eye on a cone-shaped cork with an orange top and a white torso. "I knew they'd compete for the same fish, so I stayed closer to shore. Are you going to make good on your threat to make them use a rod and reel?"

Heather was now alongside her father's head of acquisitions. "Rules lose their effectiveness if they're not enforced. They forfeited their fishing privilege for the day."

"Good. That means I'll be the only one fishing on this side of the bay."

"Only for today. Enjoy the solitude while you can. Four more anglers will be in the water tomorrow."

Heather watched as the orange top of the cork dove under the surface. Bob jerked his rod. "There's number three, and it's pulling harder than the others. I told you fishing was my strong suit." He walked backward to the shore while reeling in the fish. He soon landed the third mahi-mahi and secured it to the stringer he had attached to a belt loop on his pants.

"Are you going to continue fishing?"

He nodded an affirmative answer. "I know the value of building goodwill. People are going to owe me favors if I have fish to trade."

"You're a very strategic thinker."

"That's why your father promoted me to lead what I believe is his most important department."

The comments struck a nerve with Heather. Bob believed he was of extreme value to her father. Yet, he was on the downhill side of his career. She watched as he walked out into the bay and cast again. He was a shrewd man, capable of waiting for other people to make mistakes. She wondered if the thought of being put out to pasture could turn a loyal employee into someone who'd take a shortcut to retirement by stealing company secrets.

She didn't have long to think about it as Bella led Janice and Louis toward the shore. They swam a wide arc around Bob while Heather waded back to shore.

The rule violators arrived at the shore and jerked off their masks. Janice had one fish on her stringer while Louis had two, but they were much smaller.

Heather didn't waste time explaining. "You were told to keep a safe distance between you. You broke the rules."

The attorney in Janice made itself known. "That's not exactly true. I informed Louis where I intended to fish. My boundary is a coral outcropping that extends well out into the bay. He was to stay this side of it."

"Says you," said Louis. "I never agreed to a rule you created out of thin air."

A hand went up to block any additional comments. "You both know it takes an agreement from both parties to form an enforceable contract. Did you two agree to the boundaries?"

"No," said Louis.

"It's unnecessary if the first party states their position clearly and the second party doesn't object," countered Janice. "He didn't, so there was a reasonable expectation on my part that the contract was in effect."

Heather shook her head. "Good try, Janice, but the purpose of my instruction was to keep you safe from harm." She pointed to the bay before them. "Look at how much water you two had to choose from." She let the words sink in. "It's my ruling that you've forfeited your fishing privileges for the rest of the day."

"I'd like to appeal the decision."

"To whom?"

Janice's gaze shot from side to side. "To Steve."

"Very well," said Heather. "Your appeal is scheduled for one week from today."

"That's ridiculous. We'll be off the island by then."

"Apply for an emergency review in writing. You can file it first thing in the morning. Until then, my ruling stands."

Heather pointed to where Bob was focused on his cork. "He's not having any trouble catching his supper."

Louis turned and walked away. Janice spun and shouted at his retreating back. "Wait. I'm not through with you. Where are you going?"

He threw up his hands. "You fool. This isn't a courtroom, it's a private island in the middle of the ocean. We didn't follow the rules they established, and now we'll pay the price. I'm taking my gear back to the porch."

Matt let out a shout. "There's the yacht."

Those gathered on the shore cast their gaze toward the sea that spread before them. Sure enough, the boat was heading for them.

Bob let out a whoop as he walked backward toward the shore and pulled in another thrashing fish. He drew alongside Heather and Janice. "This one's big enough for two meals."

Bella announced, "It's a wahoo and very good to eat."

Janice took a quick glance at the size of the fish, turned, and ran to her pile of clothes. She then shouted at Louis. "Don't get anywhere near where I'm fishing tomorrow or you'll have to pull out a fishhook."

"Same to you."

Matt approached Heather and Bella as they watched Bob string his latest fish on a braided line, re-bait his hook, and walk back into the water. The reel zinged as he made another cast to a spot where the reef met the sandy-bottomed bay. Heather turned to Bella. "Take Matt down the beach and teach him to swim."

Matt took a step back. "Wait. That wasn't part of the deal."

Heather took a step toward him. "We're playing by island rules. Besides, it's ridiculous that a fitness trainer doesn't know how to swim. By the time you leave the island, I'll expect you and Habib to swim like dolphins."

Bella led the way. "Come on Matt. We'll start in water that's not over waist deep. Any time you feel afraid, tuck your knees to your chest and find the bottom with your feet. We'll also practice putting your face in the water."

Matt groaned but followed Bella like an obedient dog... a very large, muscular dog.

Heather spoke to Bella's back. "I may send Habib to you after Matt learns to float." She picked up her pants and carried them while allowing her shirt and bathing suit to dry.

The corners of her mouth pulled up as she walked along the shoreline toward the pier. Everything with the group was going as Steve predicted. Fatigue, aching muscles, and the sweltering heat and humidity had all conspired to bring the group to the point of mental and physical misery. They were verbally striking out against her and each other.

Heather shaded her eyes against the sun as she gazed out to sea. The yacht bearing down on them carried four perceived threats to their livelihood. How would they respond? She'd soon find out.

19

Clouds temporarily blocked the sun as they scuttled across the sky, leaving dark, moving shadows on the bottom of the bay. Heather walked onto the wooden planks of the long pier and took only a few sure steps until she stood in front of Habib. "Any luck?"

"Not yet." His mouth formed a thin line of disappointment.

"It's because you moved too close to shore. Why don't you try in deeper water?"

"It would be over my head if I fell in, and you and Bella weren't here to save me."

"That reminds me. You'll go with Bella after the new group clears the dock of their luggage."

"With Bella?"

"You're going to learn to swim." Heather pointed. "She's teaching Matt now."

"That's not acceptable. I refuse to get in the water."

Heather wondered what Steve would do. As if on cue, he came down the hill with his cane as his only guide. He wore a purple shirt with yellow flowers so bright they looked like the sun overhead. His baggy bathing suit almost matched the colors of his shirt, but not quite. A tan straw hat had the circumference of a small umbrella, with a chinstrap that kept it anchored to his head.

She rushed to meet him and made her presence known. "Keep coming to the sound of my voice. There's nothing to run into."

They met about thirty yards from the dock's steps. "I'm glad you came. I'm having a problem with a reluctant non-swimmer. He refuses to get near the water."

"Habib or Matt?" asked Steve.

"Bella's with Matt. Habib has an unreasonable fear of water."

"Take me to the water's edge near the pier. Bring him to me and we'll both work with him."

It wasn't long before Habib stood in front of Steve, who'd discarded his cane on the white sand. He began the conversation while standing in water that barely covered his toes. Habib stood in the wet sand.

"Come stand by me, Habib, and tell me everything you know about Reggie Scott."

Water lapped over Habib's feet. "Not much to tell. He's a junior accountant."

"I can tell that you're watching the water. Focus on my face. Pretend we're in a business meeting."

"All right. I'm looking at you now."

"Good. Don't look down. True business leaders focus on the person they're talking to. I'm testing you to see if you have what it takes to be a leader, and Heather's watching."

Heather stood beside Steve and matched his almost imperceptible step into ankle deep water. "Is Reggie a CPA?"

"He's a young man who does light bookkeeping and runs errands."

"How long have you known him?"

Habib seemed to search for the answer in a puffy cloud passing overhead. "About a year."

Steve kept on the subject as he inched into the water up to his calves. "What do you think of him?"

"To tell the truth, I have sparse interaction with him."

Steve held out his hand toward Habib. "Put my hand on your arm. Let's walk and talk instead of standing here."

Habib did as instructed and the two took slow steps as Heather walked on the shore side of Habib. She realized what Steve was doing and followed suit by asking questions. "Tell me, Habib, what made you want to work for my father?"

"It was the best offer I received out of graduate school."

Steve fired the next question at him as he slowly drifted into knee-deep water. "You must put a lot of stock in education."

"I'm pursuing a Ph.D."

Heather kept his head turned her way by asking him another question. "How long until we can call you Dr. Patel?"

His chin rose with apparent pride. "I'm defending my dissertation this coming fall. I'll go through ceremonies in December. My family will be very proud of me."

"As they should be."

Steve took his turn. "What would you do if you discovered someone embezzling funds from the company?"

Heather paid particular attention to the reaction. She didn't have to wait long. "I'd recommend his termination and turning him over to the authorities for prosecution."

"How much time do you believe he should serve?"

"Whatever the maximum penalty is."

Steve stopped. "Habib, close your eyes as tight as you can. Have you ever wondered what it's like to be blind?"

"Uh... I guess everyone has, but I've never dwelt on it."

"I want you to experience my world. Heather's going to lead you, and you'll lead me. She'll put her hand on your arm as the three of us keep walking."

They took slow steps through the warm water as she and Steve peppered him with questions. Ever so slowly, they drifted into deeper water.

Heather was almost thigh deep. That meant Habib was in

slightly deeper, and Steve had water lapping at the bottom of his bathing suit.

Steve stopped. "Keep your eyes closed as tight as you can. Heather and I are going to squat down, and I want you to do the same." He waited only a second and said, "Now."

All three bent their knees as warm water covered their chests. Steve asked. "Are your eyes still closed?"

"Yes."

"This is all I see every day, and I'm in water that's up to my chin."

"I'm afraid."

"That's understandable, but a good leader has to face fears and overcome them. In a few seconds, I'm going to ask you to open your eyes. This is as deep as you're going today. Tomorrow you'll go with Bella. She won't take you into water that's above your waist, and you'll practice floating and swimming. The way the water feels on your chest right now is how it would feel if you were in water up to your chin."

Steve waited for a tick of the clock and said, "Open your eyes."

Heather watched as Habib blinked and laughed. "I'm practically on the shore."

"Now," said Steve, "tell us more about Reggie Scott."

"He could rub people the wrong way."

"How so?" asked Heather.

Habib ran his hands through the water. "As previously stated, I had minimal contact with him, so my opinions are based on secondhand comments. The rumors were that Mr. Scott was the type of man who'd insult you and immediately follow it by saying he was only kidding."

"Does anyone come to mind when you think of someone he offended?"

Habib continued pulling his hands through the water. "Janice Peltier came to a meeting a month ago complaining about something Mr. Scott said to her. It didn't concern me, so I don't know what sparked her anger. I can think of no one else."

Heather cast her gaze toward the dock and rose. "Habib, you're responsible for Steve. I've a yacht to greet."

Habib asked, "What's the name of your CFO?"

"Malcolm Swift. You'll like him." She paused. "He earned his doctorate several years before I lured him away from his prior employer."

Habib's pained expression didn't match his words. "I look forward to meeting him."

Heather twisted the proverbial knife. "Don't worry. He's a very modest man who prefers we not call him Dr. Swift." She stood and made for the pier.

Dorcas stood at the same spot where Bella had caught the first fish of the day. Heather's water shoes squeaked as she padded her way down the dock. "How's the fishing?"

"Not good. Bella made it look so easy."

Heather looked over the side. "Reel in your line and I'll check your bait."

Dorcas did as instructed. Her eyelids widened. "How did that happen?"

"Look down. Do you see those little fish?"

"I've been watching them. There's loads of them."

"They're bait thieves. Too small to catch, but big enough to nibble until you have nothing to attract a larger fish. You need to check your bait every few minutes to make sure you're still fishing and not wasting time."

"There's more to this fishing thing than I thought."

Heather pointed to the end of the dock. "Reposition yourself near the end and keep trying. The yacht will soon be here. It won't be long before you run out of time to catch your supper."

Dorcas picked up her gear and began walking. Heather followed behind until she reached the spot where Captain Jack had delivered his first load of cargo and passengers. The yacht seemed to grow in size as it throttled down, made a half circle in the bay, and approached the dock. Heather noticed Clyde Pugh was riding on the front of the boat and had the bowline in hand. He was wet from hat to deck shoes.

The boat faced out to sea as Clyde threw her the rope and she secured it to a metal cleat. "You're soaked. Did you swim part of the way?"

"I rode on the bow of the main deck," replied Clyde, over the gurgle of the boat's motors. "The swells were enough to drench me with spray. It was a glorious trip."

Heather didn't believe that was the full story when she caught a whiff of the man who smelled like a gym bag filled with sweaty clothes left too long in the sun.

She tied off the bow and moved to the stern. Once secured, a backpack landed with a thud near her.

"Sorry." The voice came from Brent Coolidge, Heather's head of acquisitions. "That belongs to Clyde."

The rest of her executive staff came from below deck and gathered in the shade of the flying bridge. Heather took charge. "Unload everything. Put the provisions in the main house first then come back for your luggage. We'll meet up the hill on the deck, and I'll assign you to your bungalows."

Brent was the first one off the boat. He was close to her age of mid-thirties, trim, and casually dressed in khaki shorts, an untucked cotton shirt, sandals, and a straw hat. "Heather, we need to talk."

They walked toward the shore but stopped after twenty paces. He wasn't smiling. "Something has to be done about Clyde. The flight was like riding in the back of a garbage truck. If I'm assigned to the same bungalow as him, I'd rather sleep on the dock."

Heather was at a loss. She delayed the inevitable by saying, "Try to stay away from him. If that's not possible, get upwind."

"That's not good enough."

Heather realized this was a challenge to her leadership, so she came back at Brent with force. "Replace your emotion with motion. There's cargo and luggage to unload, and we're on a tight schedule. Did you eat on the way here as instructed?"

"Not everyone did. They were still recovering from the stench of the flight and the ride in the van from the airport to the pier."

Heather pointed to the growing stack of provisions and luggage. "Pass the word. The crew from Boston has already learned that this is a no-complaint island. I expect the same from my department heads. Steve and I will treat everyone the same."

The shriek from the end of the pier pierced the midday calm. Heather took off at a run, closing the distance between her and Dorcas. When she arrived, the woman was looking into deep water with a look of horror. "It jerked the rod out of my hand. I couldn't hold on to it."

Heather looked into the water that she estimated to be twenty-five feet deep. "Oh, for heaven's sake. Go get me a mask and flippers."

"I'm so sorry. It must have been an enormous fish."

"Forget the problem. Focus on the solution."

Hurried footsteps approached. Clyde spoke as he approached. "What's wrong?"

Heather pointed toward the crystal-clear water. "Dorcas is a first-time angler. She allowed a fish to pull the rod and reel from her hands. I've sent her to the house to get me a mask and flippers."

"No need for that," said Clyde. "I brought my own."

Clyde retrieved his backpack and jogged back to the end of the dock. Heather hadn't noticed it before, but his backpack had black flippers dangling on the outside. He pulled off quick-dry pants and a matching hooded shirt. Wearing only a black bathing suit, he displayed a broad chest completely covered with hair so thick it looked like a rug. His back was also a mat of hair, so thick that if painted green, it would look like a lawn that needed mowing.

It was then that Heather realized Clyde's thick black hair grew from his forehead to his heels. The front was no different. A neatly trimmed black beard almost connected to the hair on his chest. She'd never seen him in anything but a coat and tie suitable for court, so his bearlike appearance took her aback.

She stood with mouth agape as he pitched his mask, with snorkel attached, into the water and followed it in with fearless abandon. He rose to the surface with the mask in hand and gracefully treaded water. After emptying the water, he spat on the inside of the glass and rubbed it in with his fingers.

Clyde was no novice to diving and knew how to keep his mask from fogging. Once he secured it, he looked at the bottom before resurfacing and giving a report. "I'll get it and swim back to shore. It looks like she hooked a nice grouper. With any luck, I'll get the fish along with the rod and reel."

He took in several deep breaths before diving. Mask and snorkel went down while flippers shot him to the bottom. Heather thought about how at home he was in the water. With the almost full covering of hair the color of coal, he resembled a seal effortlessly propelling itself. He soon surfaced with fishing gear and the catch of the day.

Steve, Matt, and Clyde were waiting for her after Heather bid farewell to Captain Roger. Clyde held up his trophy for her to admire. "That was a blast. Amazing water." He cast his gaze down the pier. "It looks like my suitcase and backpack are the only things left on the dock."

Steve put words to what Heather was thinking. "The others should have seen you were busy and carried your suitcase and backpack."

Heather let out a huff. "Matt, take the rod, reel, and fish to the house. When you've done that, change into your hill climbing clothes. It's time my people had a lesson in teamwork." She shifted her gaze to Clyde. "Get your luggage and go to the deck in front of the main house. I have a special assignment for you today."

20

Matt ran ahead while Heather led Steve up the hill. Clyde went to retrieve his suitcase and backpack, which meant she and Steve could talk without fear of anyone hearing them. He broke the silence. "The tone of your voice tells me you're not pleased with your troops."

"I'm not. They're ostracizing Clyde."

"Can you blame them?"

They took several steps before Heather tried to answer his question with one of her own. "What am I supposed to do? This situation has me stumped. I've reviewed everything I know about leadership. None of the experts addressed what to do if you have an exceedingly competent employee with atrocious hygiene."

"I have to admit, it's a unique situation. As I see it, you have two problems to solve. The most immediate is what to do with your department heads and how they're treating Clyde."

"I know how to handle them. A couple of trips up the hill in the heat of the day will give them a fresh perspective. With all the sweating they'll do, they may not smell much better than Clyde."

"That won't fix the underlying cause of Clyde's problem. Have you ever wondered what causes body odor?"

Frustration settled into Heather. "I must have missed that lecture in law school. It's going to take a miracle. Do you have an extra one in your pocket?"

"Sorry. I'm fresh out of miracles."

"That's what I was afraid of." She walked on. "The best I can do is keep Clyde separated from the group like I do at the office." She gave Steve a sideways glance. "You're the one with the vivid imagination. Surely you can come up with a solution."

"Me?" said Steve. "When did this become my problem?"

"You're the lead detective, and you have time to think." She couldn't help but smile. "Look on the bright side. You wanted to keep all the suspects from thinking we were trying to find a thief and possibly a killer. Clyde's custom made for distracting them."

They arrived at the ultra-modern home and climbed the steps to the deck. Heather placed Steve to one side and wasted no time in addressing her employees. "This week is about team building. We're expecting you to take part in all scheduled events without complaining. You'll soon learn that controlling your tongues may be the hardest thing you'll do all week."

Heather stared into the eyes of the employees before continuing. "The first words spoken to me when you arrived were complaints about Clyde."

Brent took a half-step forward. "You'd complain, too, if you had to spend hours with him on an airplane."

Heather straightened her spine. "Did you wear the masks I provided?"

"What masks?"

"The paper masks. They were available if you'd taken the time to look for a solution instead of stewing in the problem."

Louise King, Heather's head of IT raised her hand. "They were on each seat. Mine smelled like perfume. It was a pleasant flight as long as I kept the mask on."

"I can't stand to wear a mask," said Brent in a loud whisper.

"Let's move on," said Heather. "Clyde told me he rode on the bow of the yacht all the way to the island. He did that to make the trip more pleasant for you. He showered with salt water the entire way."

Brent wasn't through complaining. "That was after we had to endure the stench in the van from the airport."

"You survived," said Heather. "How long was the trip in the van?"

"About ten minutes," said Malcolm Swift, Heather's CFO. "The open windows helped."

"Easy for you to say," said Brent. "I had to sit next to him."

Heather ignored the last complaint. "I want to address your actions on the dock. None of you but Clyde responded to the scream from Dorcas. She was trying to catch your supper. Unlike the rest of you, Clyde made a quick assessment, took action, and solved the problem. You didn't even lift a hand to help carry his luggage while he swam to shore."

"By the way," said Steve. "You'll be expected to catch your own fish after today."

Heather nodded. "It will be the only meat on the menu." Heather cast another searching gaze. "You're off to a poor start. You'll have ten minutes to study a map of the island, change into hiking clothes, and be back here. As a way of helping you remember the purpose of coming to Christmas Cay, Matt, my personal trainer, will lead you up a jungle trail to the top of the hill behind me."

Steve added, "A water bottle with your name on it will be waiting for you. Don't forget it."

"What about Clyde?" asked Brent.

Heather tilted her head. "That's progress. At least you're not ignoring him." She gulped a breath. "Don't worry about Clyde. He'll be catching your supper."

She stepped to a table and moved a rock that anchored a map. "Ten minutes to memorize the map, deliver your luggage, change, and be back here. The time starts now."

Clyde arrived as everyone was leaving. He'd put on his long-sleeve shirt to cover what looked like a blanket of fur. His gaze shifted to the scattering of people. "Do I follow them?"

"Heather has something better for you," said Steve. "How would you like to spend the afternoon fishing?"

Heather affirmed Steve's question with a nod. "We need enough fish to feed everyone from Texas and our chef."

"I'm all in."

"Speargun or rod and reel?" asked Heather.

"Speargun. I doubt it will take all afternoon."

"Take your time and enjoy the water. The kitchen has a walk-in freezer and two commercial refrigerators. If you catch more than we can eat in a single day, they won't go to waste."

Heather watched as Clyde left his luggage on the deck, grabbed his snorkeling gear, and selected a speargun. He skipped down the steps and whistled an upbeat tune as he descended the hill.

Heather noticed Steve's pinched eyebrows. "What's on your mind?" she asked.

"What causes body odor?"

"I assume it's from not bathing."

He paused. "Did you notice a strong odor coming from him?"

"Not much, if any."

Steve rubbed his chin. "Was he wearing the same shirt he wore on the boat?"

"No. It looks like a quick-dry fishing shirt like Bella wears."

"We were both downwind from him, and it wasn't bad at all. I wonder... He hasn't been out of the water long. Perhaps bathing in salt water is the solution we're looking for."

"Perhaps," said Heather, even though she had her doubts.

Steve seemed to put the problem aside and said, "I think we've created enough distractions. Let's focus on your father's department heads."

"Who do you want to talk to this afternoon?"

"Let's start with Bob Brown. He seems a little too easygoing." Steve jerked his head up. "I just thought of something. We haven't been able to extract much information from Dorcas. You have her in a vulnerable spot because she lost the rod and reel."

"Not that vulnerable. Clyde came to her rescue."

"More than you think. She's a perfectionist. Let's speak to her first and see if she'll tell us some inside information about Bob."

Heather looked at her watch. "The group from Boston will be here in a few minutes for lunch. We can speak to Dorcas while the rest of Father's staff are eating."

It wasn't long before Janice led the pack up the hill. She arrived with a question. "Who's the winner of the hairy-man contest?"

Heather gave her a straight answer. "That's Clyde Pugh, attorney at law. He's the acting department head while my lead attorney is having her baby."

"He looks like a cross between a black bear and a Chia pet."

"Don't let that fool you. He has the best legal mind of anyone I've ever met."

Janice looked toward the bay where Clyde was preparing to enter the water. "He reminds me of a rugby player I dated in college. I thought the pelt was sexy, but I couldn't stand the way he smelled." Her head wagged from side to side. "Poor guy. He showered twice a day, but it wasn't enough. When the summer heat arrived, I had to let him go."

"That's interesting," said Steve.

All but one of the Bostonians arrived with meager offerings of fish. Bob Brown was the exception. He proudly displayed six keepers. Habib asked him, "What are your plans for the excess fish?"

Heather broke into the conversation. "He can do whatever he wants. Catching more than he needs gives him options."

"Like what?" asked Bob.

"If he doesn't want to miss any of the required sessions and accumulate more points, he can keep them for himself. Or, he can trade them for favors."

Janice cast a piercing stare at Louis. "It's your fault we had our spearguns taken from us. Now, I'll have to give up points in order to eat."

Louis placed hands on hips, looking as if he was winding up for a comeback when Bob broke in. "I might make a deal on an extra fish or two."

"What kind of scam are you trying to run?" asked Janice.

"No scam, and I prefer to conduct negotiations in private." He then looked at Heather. "Do we have to clean our own fish?"

"Unless you surrender ownership."

Habib groaned.

A conniving smile parted Bob's lips. "It seems I'm the only person from Boston who knows how to clean fish."

"I can," said Habib. "I had to do it once a long time ago."

Bob issued a scoffing laugh. "But first you have to catch the fish. How do you expect to catch anything if you won't walk out on the pier and look over? That hairy lawyer might or might not catch anything. I'm a proven producer."

Habib's next words showed he was ready to trade. "I may not catch any fish this week, but I'm willing to clean them. I want to hear what you want for two of the fish you caught."

Bob rubbed his chin. "Let's talk."

Habib turned to face the group. "Bob's not the only one who can make a deal. I'll clean anyone's fish for a portion of the catch."

Bob's clenched fist signaled he wasn't pleased to have competition.

Heather broke into the multiple voices that rose. "Negotiate on your own time. Take your fish to Pearl and sit at the table. Your lunch is waiting for you."

"What are we doing after lunch?" asked Janice.

Steve answered with a single word. "Brainwork."

Heather followed his obtuse response with, "You have forty

minutes to eat, clean your fish if you caught any, wash dishes, and leave the kitchen and dining room spotless. If you work together, it's plenty of time."

The group didn't need to be told twice. Heather and Steve stood some distance away and whispered. "They're inhaling their meal," said Heather. "Next time, we may have to reduce the time we give them to eat."

"You're assuming they'll work together. I'm betting fatigue and petty grudges will rear their ugly heads."

Empty dishes were being carried to the kitchen when the team from Texas arrived on the patio, two minutes late. Water bottles and a look of disappointment awaited them.

Heather cast her gaze to Matt. "Three trips to the top at a quick pace. The first is to get them used to the jungle and to give them a view they'll never forget. The second is to help them remember this is a no-complaint island." She took a breath. "Have them refill their water bottles before they make the third up the hill. That one is to remind them this is a team building trip. When they return, I'll help you confiscate all electronic devices."

Heather's head of technology, Louise King, gasped. "Everything?"

Steve answered with, "Heather says we made quite a haul from the Boston group. It wouldn't be fair if she treated you differently."

Brent Coolidge raised his hand. "If this is supposed to be team building, why isn't Clyde going up the hill with us?"

Louise let fly with a quick response. "Would you please stuff a sock in your mouth?"

Heather had to bite the inside of her mouth to stifle the laugh that almost escaped. Louise had figured out that the jungle path in the heat of the day would be like hiking in the boiler room of a steamship. Clyde's problem would raise the misery level to unbearable if he went with them.

Matt's voice boomed. "Follow me! The view from the top is

worth the effort." The porch cleared and Heather checked on the progress being made in the kitchen. Steve's prediction of disharmony proved correct as Janice's shrill voice blasted into the living room. "How are we supposed to clean the kitchen when you're smearing fish guts and scales all over the counter?"

The door swung open so fast it rebounded off the wall and flew back into Dorcas. She stopped it with outstretched hands before it did any physical damage. Tears poured from red, puffy eyes. Her fight for words resulted in short bursts of frustration. "I... can't take... any more... from these people."

Janice followed Dorcas into the dining room. "Dorcas, get a grip on your emotions."

"Leave me alone."

The attorney's voice held not a drop of sympathy. "I can't imagine why, but you are in charge of cleaning after meals. That idiot, Bob Brown, is trying to sell fish instead of helping us clean. If we don't up our game, all of us can say goodbye to our jobs. That includes you."

Panic came across Dorcas's face. Louis appeared in the doorway. "Janice is right. We all know you're here to spy on us and give reports to Mr. McBlythe. You're not the only one who'll be submitting a report. Mine won't be flattering if you don't buck up and do your job."

"You wouldn't dare say anything bad about me."

Janice laughed. "Dorcas, how can you be so naïve? Everyone knows Louis climbed over the backs of more qualified people to get his job."

Louis didn't deny it.

Steve leaned into Heather and whispered. "Now we're getting somewhere. Send everyone up the hill but Dorcas."

21

Dorcas pushed on the door leading into the kitchen with both hands. She'd dropped the timid persona and replaced it with pinched lips and a firm voice. "Bob, you'll cease selling or trading fish while you're in the kitchen. Is that clear?"

"Who elected you queen of the kitchen?"

The rebellion didn't last long when Heather entered and said, "You did, along with the others." Heather glanced at her watch. "In five minutes, you'll cost your team another trip up the hill to go along with the one you're already responsible for."

"There's no way I'll finish with these fish and have my area of the kitchen clean in five minutes."

Janice Peltier moved into Bob's personal space and let loose with a verbal broadside. "You idiot. Are you so far in debt that you have to supplement your income with part time work as a fishmonger?" Her eyebrows drew closer together. "It wouldn't surprise me if you're the one selling company secrets."

Bob stared back. "That sounds like a guilty dog barking."

The sharp-tongued attorney had to get in the last word. "Putting two girls through Brown University while keeping a mistress must put a strain on the old budget." She sucked in a quick breath. "I never heard how much you paid for the yacht, but it had to be in the millions. And those trips to the Bahamas must set you back a pretty penny for gas alone."

"At least I'm not trying to become the next Mrs. Allister McBlythe."

The words stunned everyone in the room. Bob looked at the wide eyes and open mouths of those gathered. "Don't look so surprised. Haven't you noticed Janice making frequent trips to Mr. McBlythe's office? She's trying to set herself up for when he retires."

Janice found the hole in his argument. "First, Louis accuses me of selling company secrets. Now you say I'm maneuvering to marry my employer. Do you need to have a moment so you can come up with another unsubstantiated accusation?" Sarcasm dripped from her words. "I'll give you credit for trying to deflect guilt. Too bad you're such a poor liar. That twitching left eye gives you away every time."

Bob took a cleaver and whacked off the head of a fish. Heather took it to mean he'd had all of Janice that he could stand and actions could soon replace words. Janice may have spoken the last word, but Bob's display had a more profound effect.

In a firm voice devoid of emotion, Dorcas said, "I can only imagine what Mr. McBlythe would say if he were here. Everyone pitch in and get this mess cleaned!"

Heather cast her gaze at each of the now silent executives. "It's a good thing you still have on your bathing suits. When you're finished here, all you'll need to get from your bungalows is your hiking shoes. Make sure you fill your water bottles. One trip up the hill followed by a swim to help you cool off should help you remember to stay on task."

Steve broke in. "We'll start the afternoon session later than Heather planned. It will be all mental work, nothing physical. Best of all, it will take place in the living room where it's nice and cool."

"I hope you all can complete your cleanup task now. I'd rather not assign you another trip up the hill on such a hot day."

The threat shifted the group into action, even though furtive glances passed between the executives. Heather wondered how many secrets lay underneath the surface of each of them. She moved to the doorway where Steve waited. "Did you hear everything?"

Instead of giving her a simple yes or no, he said, "Make sure you tell Dorcas she doesn't have to climb the hill."

They moved into the living room while the crew finished in the kitchen then jogged to their bungalows to change shoes for their hike. Dorcas had little to say as she watched the Bostonians disappear around the corner of the home and onto the trail.

"They're upward bound," said Heather. It was Steve's cue to extract what he could from Dorcas.

"That was an interesting conversation between Janice and Bob," said Steve in an even voice. "Do you know what I learned from listening to them?"

Dorcas turned from the patio doors and sat on the couch. "That they suspect each other of doing terrible things?"

"That goes without saying. What's of more importance is how much you've disappointed Heather and me."

"Me? What did I do?"

"You already knew about Bob's financial troubles, yet you failed to tell us."

"I don't work for you."

Heather took her turn. "While we appreciate your loyalty to my father, you know that Steve and I are private investigators. You also know that my father wants us to find out who's been stealing secrets from his company. I spoke with him this morning, and he told me to tell you that he expects full disclosure and that he's not happy about your reluctance to tell us what you know. Also, your reports lack details."

She was not normally a woman who relied on lies to get

someone to reveal what they knew, but in this instance, stretching the truth about having spoken with her father seemed necessary.

Steve piled on. "Would you like for Heather to call Mr. McBlythe and have him instruct you to divulge all you know or suspect?"

It was a bluff. Hopefully it would be enough to crack a tough nut. Near panic filled Dorcas's words. "No! Ask me anything."

Steve put steel in his voice. "You're to give us details about each executive that's here from Boston. We're going to give you names one at a time, and you're going to tell us what you know. That includes rumors, gossip, and things you believe are outright lies." He leaned forward in his chair. "Don't think about holding anything back from us. We're both highly skilled in spotting deception and evasion."

Heather softened her tone. "My father depends on you. He wouldn't have you as his personal assistant if he didn't trust you. Now, tell us about Bob Brown."

Dorcas sat up straight with feet flat on the floor, a sign she wasn't trying to deceive. "Everything Janice said about Bob rings true. I don't know all the details of his current romantic interest, but he appears to be going through a serious mid-life crisis. Bob is a likable man who's been a dynamic employee in the past."

Steve asked, "What about his financial situation?"

"Rumors are that he'll be all right when he sells the yacht and rids himself of the woman."

"Ah," said Steve. "Tell us about her."

"She won't last." The words came out with certainty. "His daughters know about her and have given Bob a deadline to end the relationship. Both girls are smart and cunning. They know how to play the game of protecting their parents from permanent harm."

"It may be too late if Bob's selling company secrets," said Heather.

Dorcas shook her head. "He's impulsive and may have sold

secrets, but he's not stupid enough to stay with a gold-digger. The rumor going around is that she already has her sights on an investment banker. It's only a matter of time before she moves on. When that happens, he'll sell the yacht."

Heather took her turn. "Are there any new rumors of secrets being stolen?"

"Not that I'm aware of."

Steve wasn't ready to move on. "Are you saying you're not sure Bob sold company secrets?"

Dorcas took more time than necessary to answer, and when she did, it wasn't a definitive response. "Bob had an exemplary record with the company until he became entangled with that woman."

"So, you believe it's possible he stole from the company."

"I guess anything is possible."

Steve remained quiet, which was Heather's cue to move on. "Tell us about Janice Peltier."

"I don't trust her," said Dorcas as she crossed her arms.

"Why not?"

"She has a serpent's tongue. You saw how she attacked Bob in the kitchen."

Heather saw the verbal attack from a different perspective. "It sounded to me like she was in a pre-trial conference. There's nothing unusual about staking out a position and vehemently defending it."

"She takes it too far. She has a temper that's hard to control."

Steve asked, "Have you ever heard of Janice becoming physically violent?"

"I've seen her provoke others to violence."

"That's not the same," said Heather. "Attorneys sometimes do that on purpose."

"It's not right," said Dorcas. "It disrupts the harmony of the company and upsets your father."

Steve asked, "What about Janice's loyalty to the company?"

Dorcas sniffed. "She's like all the other attorneys. She'll move on if someone offers her more money."

"What makes you so sure?"

"It's their culture. You wouldn't believe how many lawyers I've seen come and go over the years. I'm shocked Janice hasn't set up her own practice. That's what most of them do."

Steve folded his hands in his lap. "That seems to bother you."

Dorcas didn't respond, so Heather asked a direct question. "You don't like Janice, do you?"

"No."

"Do you think she's an asset or a liability to my father's company?"

"That's not my call to make."

Steve attacked the question from a different angle. "Do you believe Heather should seriously consider Janice as lead attorney when Mr. McBlythe retires and the two companies merge?"

Heather didn't see a significant reaction, which came as no surprise. Dorcas uncrossed her arms and her shoulders dropped a quarter of an inch. "I have no opinion on that."

To Heather's amazement, Steve moved on. She would need to quiz him about it later. "What about Habib Patel? Any secrets or skeletons in his closet?"

Dorcas looked up and to the left, as if she was looking for an answer on the spinning ceiling fan. "Habib is a very smart man. What he lacks is awareness of what's going on around him."

Steve asked, "Is he something like an absent-minded academic?"

"Not exactly. More like an uncaring machine. He wants to maximize profits, regardless of the consequences to others. I think it's a cultural thing." Dorcas closed her lips, looking as if she thought her brief explanation was sufficient.

Heather had to probe deeper. "We'd like to hear you expound on what you said. What do you mean by a cultural thing?"

"You know, the entire caste system of his home country influences his every action. He's expected to excel in business, and the pressure on him is tremendous. Both sets of parents arranged his marriage. His parents and his in-laws share the home with him and his wife. To hear him talk, he's expected to keep advancing until he takes over the company and makes it more profitable than it's ever been."

Steve ran a hand down his face. "That's a lot of pressure."

"I'm sure it is. I don't think he cares if he gets a doctorate degree, but he'd never hear the end of it if he didn't. Mr. Patel doesn't sound nearly as impressive as Dr. Patel."

"Is he loyal to the company?"

"So far, but I can tell Heather is an unwelcome intrusion into his plans."

Heather lifted her chin. "And what would those plans be?"

"To continue to work as Mr. McBlythe's CFO and hope to take over if the opportunity presents itself."

Steve cut in. "I wouldn't think Habib has the money it would take to buy his way to the top."

"He doesn't. At least not yet, but don't underestimate him. He's very smart, thrifty, and cunning. He keeps close tabs on your father's investments and mirrors those purchases and sales."

Heather couldn't help but ask, "Do you think he'd take a shortcut and sell inside information?"

Dorcas lifted her shoulders and allowed them to fall. "Like I said, anything's possible, and he knows everything there is to know about the financial side of the business."

Steve resettled in his chair. "That leaves us with Louis Crane, the department head over all things related to technology. What can you tell us about Louis?"

"He's odd," said Dorcas. "But that may be because he spent his formative years in a basement with the computers he built. I hear he can hack into almost any system and not leave a trace."

The implications were clear to Heather. Louis Crane could sell company secrets anytime he wanted to. The IT guru moved up on her list of suspects. It also occurred to her that everyone from Boston had a motive for stealing. She and Steve would need time alone to sort through the newly gained information.

Steve thanked Dorcas for her time and told her to rest in her bungalow. The patio door closed and Steve stood. His penchant for going off-script picked this moment to bubble to the surface. "We've already done this a time or two, and we're seeing results from it. I want us to continue doing it."

Heather's response skipped a beat. "I... I don't have any idea what you're talking about."

"We've been changing the rules as we go. Harsh punishments followed by announcements of mercy is one. Assigning Clyde to provide fish for the team from Texas by himself when the plan was for everyone to catch their own." A conspirator's smile came to his lips. "You made up rules on the fly when Bob was hawking his fish instead of cleaning."

"I still don't understand what you're getting at."

"We're keeping them guessing as to what we'll change next. It's keeping them distracted, and it's producing information." He took a breath. "I'm going to my room to do a little research."

"Research on what?"

"Something that's affecting everyone."

22

Heather moved the lawn chair to a spot on the deck shaded by the fronds of a tall palm tree. If it weren't for nature's umbrella and the constant breeze, she'd be sitting in the walk-in refrigerator to cool off. She realized she'd forgotten about Clyde Pugh and his assignment to provide fish for everyone on the island. Her gaze slid to the dock as his head bobbed to the surface.

Her eyelids came together for a long second. The peace and beauty of the private island overwhelmed her. It was as if the chair had a magnet in it that wouldn't allow her to rise and check on the lone fisherman. Oh well, a few more minutes of solitude wouldn't hurt anything. Her chin bounced off her chest twice before she surrendered to the island.

It surprised her when voices drifted toward her from a gaggle of people coming down the hill.

"It must be nice to take a midday nap," said attorney Janice Peltier.

Heather came back with, "If your team had completed their work in the kitchen on time, you could do the same thing. A nap was on the schedule before you failed your—"

"Don't remind us," said Habib.

Heather inspected the group as they approached the porch in a sloppy single-file line. Sweat dripped from noses and chins.

"Janice, hold up a minute," said Heather. "Go check on Clyde Pugh. Tell him to bring whatever fish he caught to the kitchen."

She looked toward the bay. "I don't see him. Do you know where he is?"

"Look under the dock. That's where I'd be fishing in the midday sun."

The rest of the sweaty group passed by on their way to take a dip. Heather spoke loud enough for all to hear. "Everyone but Janice hold up. I have your next instructions."

A groan rose that Heather ignored. "After you rinse off in the bay, go to your bungalows, shower, and put on clean clothes. Bring all your dirty clothes here to be washed. You'll be in the shade the rest of the afternoon."

"Thank goodness," said Louis Crane.

Janice had separated herself from the group and was most of the way down the hill by the time the rest left the yard. Heather wondered if they would relay her last instructions to the feisty attorney. This would be a test of thinking as a team.

The group barely took the time to take off their hiking shoes before wading into the bay. All but one walked until the water was up to their chins. Habib's introduction to the water had taken away at least some of his fear as he ventured into waist-deep water and squatted.

Janice walked down the pier, looking over the side. She was almost to the end when she launched herself into the water. She and Clyde surfaced together and swam to shore. Both looked at home in the water.

They arrived at the deck with wet hair, struggling under the weight of two stringers of fish. Heather greeted them with, "Well done, Clyde. You exceeded my expectations. That's enough to last most of the week."

"I could have speared a lot more."

Janice said, "We need to get them cleaned. Do you mind if I help Clyde? I'm pretty good with a fillet knife."

Heather nodded her permission. "You're earning extra points. That's the teamwork we're looking for. For the afternoon session, we're dividing everyone into two-person teams. You two are partners."

Clyde scratched his well-trimmed beard. "You must be arranging teams according to areas of specialization."

"Of course," said Janice. "That means the CFOs and the heads of IT will be on the same teams."

"Don't forget the acquisition directors," said Clyde.

Heather ignored their suppositions and looked at her watch. "With all those fish to clean, you may not have time to shower before we start our afternoon session."

Janice threw back her shoulders. "Follow me, Clyde. Let's show her what we can do."

Clyde didn't hesitate. "Lead the way. I'll sharpen the fillet knives while you get out the cutting boards."

They ran up the steps with the bounty from the sea and disappeared inside.

Steve spoke a word of greeting as they passed. "It smells like fresh fish."

"No time to talk," said Janice. "We have work to do."

Heather told him to follow her outside. Once there, he said, "It seems the two lawyers are negotiating a partnership."

"I'm not so sure," said Heather. "Partnerships can be tenuous. Most don't last long and end with bruised feelings."

"True, but those that last are very special."

"Not this one. If Clyde could stay in the water, I'd say the chances would increase. Unfortunately, he's not a merman and Janice isn't a mermaid. His problem will become clear in no time."

"You're probably right," said Steve.

Heather turned her head like a confused kitten. It wasn't like Steve to surrender a position once he'd staked out his ground.

She determined he had something up his sleeve other than his arm.

Matt returned from the trips up and down the hill with Heather's crew from Houston. All were wringing wet with sweat, but the personal trainer looked as if he could go again. The other three, Brent Coolidge, Malcolm Swift, and Louise King, looked like the leftovers from a plate of buttered spaghetti.

Heather spoke to them over the patio rail. "I was going to tell you to take a dip in the bay, but we're running behind schedule. Cool off under a cold shower, put on clean clothes, and return here in twenty minutes."

The group trudged to their bungalows. Steve leaned into her and asked, "Are they all right?"

"They'll survive. I'm interested to see who gets along with their counterparts in this afternoon's session."

"Can you give me Clyde, Janice, and Matt? I've come up with a special assignment for the two attorneys."

Heather tilted her head again. "You're up to something sneaky. What is it?"

"I'm solving a problem that will hopefully buy us some goodwill." He hesitated. "For this to work, I'll need all three of them."

"Take whoever you need except Habib. I'm hoping deducting points from him will be enough to cure his fear of the water and learning to swim."

"What about his partner, Malcolm Swift?"

"Malcolm will work on his own and earn points. I believe that should be enough to motivate Habib to overcome his fears."

Steve spoke in a dead-pan voice. "It seems I'm not the only sneaky person on the island."

Heather shrugged, even though she wasted the gesture on Steve. "Whatever it takes to help us find the person stealing from my father."

Steve settled in a lawn chair and took on a sphinx-like appearance. This was his posture for serious thinking, and she knew not to disturb him unless it was an emergency. She wondered if he heard Clyde and Janice as they rushed past him. Heather caught a whiff of body odor as Clyde passed. It wasn't intense, but she was glad he was heading toward the men's bungalow and a shower.

One by one, the members of both groups arrived back in the main house while Steve remained on the porch, lost in thought. Clouds had rolled in. The wind shifted to a northwesterly breeze, taking a good portion of the humidity with it. Heather checked a thermometer. It had fallen ten degrees in the last hour. What had been a hot, sticky day morphed into pleasurable comfort.

Once everyone was present and accounted for, Heather stood with her back to the patio. "Your attention, please. I'm going to divide you into two-person teams. Each team will receive a problem specific to your area of expertise. The first team is Janice and Clyde, our two attorneys. Steve has your assignment."

Brent Coolidge chuckled as he spoke under his breath, "Be sure to sit downwind."

Clyde ignored the comment. The group from Boston appeared confused by the inside joke.

Heather shot Brent a look that conveyed displeasure, but kept talking. "Clyde and Janice, you may leave now with Steve."

Heather waited until they descended the steps of the patio before she turned her attention back to the group. "The next pair is Louis Crane and Louise King. Your problem to solve will deal with information technology. I'll tell you what it is in a few minutes."

She shifted her gaze. "Bob Brown and Brent Coolidge will be solving a problem dealing with acquisitions."

The team members traded glances with each other, as if they wanted to size up the competition. Heather's gaze drifted over each person as she gave more details. "What I'm about to tell you will apply to every group. You must develop a multi-faceted solution to the problem that addresses all contingencies, variables, and unforeseen circumstances."

"That's impossible," said Bob.

Heather shrugged. "I suggest you start with a positive attitude and do the best you can."

Habib asked, "May I work alone? That will allow me to develop an efficient plan."

Malcolm spoke up. "Hold on there. Who says this will be your plan?"

Heather held up her hand as a stop sign. "Both team members must be in full agreement with every aspect of the plan you submit." She turned her gaze to Habib. "Mr. Patel. Due to your hesitancy in learning to swim, you'll forfeit points earned until you're able to swim twenty yards. Bella will work with you until you pass this simple test."

A combination of fear and anger fueled Habib's accent-heavy response. "This is not right. You should judge me on my skill as the chief financial officer, not by an arbitrary display of physical ability."

Heather expected an objection and had a ready answer. "What good is awarding a top job to someone who poses the risk of a premature death? Every time you drive or fly, you pass near or over water, not to mention the number of times you walk near a lake or a pier. Learning to swim solves needless tragedies. Your reticence to learn makes me wonder about your competence to lead."

The muscles in Habib's jaw flexed as he rose and looked at Bella. "Shall I meet Bella at the shore?"

Bella entered the room from the direction of the kitchen, wearing a quick-dry shirt over her bathing suit. "I'll be in the water waiting for you."

Habib spoke as he followed her to the patio. "It will take me only thirty minutes to learn to swim."

Malcolm showed he wasn't above goading the other CFO. "I'll have my plan finished by the time you learn to float." He smiled a toothy grin. "Whatever you do, don't think about sharks."

Habib stopped in his tracks. "Your attempt at psychology has fallen upon deaf ears. Many have thought they could get the better of me, and all failed. I always succeed... no matter what it takes."

As Heather saw it, both CFOs had scored points, but she received the most benefit from the exchange. Habib had revealed his desire to win at all costs. It remained to be seen if that included theft of secrets or homicide.

She shifted her attention back to Louis Crane and Louise King. "Your assignment is simple. Develop a firewall that will ensure no one can hack into my father's company."

"Is that all?" asked Louis.

"That's a foolish question," said Louise. "With enough super-computers, I can hack anything."

Louis stuck out his chin. "If the assignment is too complex for you, I'll do it."

Louise snorted a breath from her nose. "You look like the type who'd leave a back door open so you could always have access. Hackers like you are in basements all over the world. Real IT experts know how to lock doors that won't open."

The statement must have struck very close to home as Louis's eyes shifted left to right and back again. Heather thought back to what Dorcas had said about Louis's ability to gain access to all her father's data.

The confident voice of Malcolm Swift, the Houston CFO, took her thoughts away from the two computer experts. "What's my challenge?"

Heather refocused. "The problem is for you and Habib to solve together. You may proceed on your own until Habib proves he can swim."

"That could take the rest of the week."

"I don't think so. Habib now has ample motivation to prove himself capable of overcoming a serious fear."

Malcolm shrugged like he didn't care. "Let's hear the problem."

Heather had a seat and leaned forward. "You've examined the books and have found a minor discrepancy."

"How minor?"

"Three hundred dollars is missing from petty cash. When confronted, each person with access denies their involvement, but they all implicate each other. Write a detailed plan of how you'll find the thief, what you recommend as punishment, and how you'd ensure it wouldn't happen again."

Malcolm smiled. "This won't take me long to finish."

"Bob and Brent, let's go into the dining room. I'll explain your assignment."

Heather left the acquisition directors to begin their work and went out on the deck, casting her gaze to the beach. Habib's arms flailed while Bella held him up in waist-deep water.

Thoughts turned to Steve. She wondered what problem he'd given Janice and Clyde to solve.

23

S teve removed his hand from Janice's arm as they stopped outside the men's bungalow. Habib rushed by without a word.

"What's the rush?" asked Janice.

Habib gave no response.

Steve filled her in. "He can't begin working on the problem Heather gave him and the other CFO until he learns to swim."

Janice let out a scoffing laugh. "That's brilliant. He may be the most obsessive-compulsive person I've ever met. The fear of failure will outweigh his fear of the water. I predict he'll be swimming in an hour."

"Thirty minutes," said Steve. It was then he caught the first whiff of Clyde's body odor. It was faint, but losing his sight had heightened his other senses.

The sound of Clyde shifting from foot to foot preceded his question. "Are we going inside?"

Steve asked, "Is there seating for the four of us? I've asked Matt to join us also."

"There's a living area overlooking the bay."

"Lead the way. I have a lot to say, and we might as well make ourselves comfortable."

Janice took his hand and put it on her arm. "This is the same set-up as the women's bungalow. Three bedrooms with two queen beds in each and private bathrooms. There's a dynamite living room with a sectional couch and two chairs, not to mention a killer view of the bay. If you want something cold to drink, there's a kitchenette."

Steve swept his cane in front of him across the tile floor. He tapped something and asked. "Is this a chair or the couch?"

"A rocking recliner," said Matt.

"Perfect."

The sound of people sitting preceded Janice saying, "I'm looking forward to hearing about the problem Clyde and I are supposed to solve."

Habib's footfalls rushed toward the front door that slammed behind him.

Steve cleared his throat. "I hope you'll keep an open mind when you hear what your assignment is."

"That's an intriguing thing to say," said Clyde.

"Let's hope you're still intrigued when you find out what it is." He took a deep breath. "As you already know, I haven't always been blind. I lost my sight and my wife on the same night in Houston."

Clyde spoke up. "The punishment those street thugs received didn't fit the crime. It was a miscarriage of justice."

Steve spoke over Clyde's attempt to expound. "As a result, I had to learn to depend on others to help me. It was a steep learning curve, and change wasn't easy. I resented people helping me until I came to my senses and realized they were doing it for my good."

Janice proved her agile mind by saying, "You're nibbling around the edges. What are you trying to say?"

Steve lifted his chin. "Clyde has a problem that I want to address, and hopefully, find a solution to."

Clyde sprang to his feet. "If this is what I think it is, don't go there, Mr. Smiley."

Janice unleashed a demand. "Sit down and let him talk."

Steve wondered if both Clyde and Janice had reverted to their training as attorneys and imagined themselves in court. If so, he'd start by playing the role of an expert witness.

Steve continued, "Today, we are going to address the elephant in the room. Heather's father put me in contact with a leading dermatologist in Boston. What he told me was most illuminating."

Janice said, "I've always wondered what caused my college boyfriend's body odor."

"I don't want this discussed. It's my problem to bear," said Clyde.

"Overruled," said Janice, who'd switched to play the part of a judge.

Steve spoke as if he were teaching a class. "Did you know there are two types of sweat glands? The first is called eccrine glands. They release sweat directly onto the skin's surface. The second is apocrine glands. They release sweat into hair follicles. This sweat mixes with bacteria, travels upward to the skin, and becomes entangled in more hair and bacteria. It's the leading cause of body odor."

"Fascinating," said Janice.

"Not to me," said Clyde in a softer tone. "You don't know how embarrassing it is to smell like a mule. I live close to the office so I can go home for lunch. I shower and change clothes twice a day. It doesn't last."

A hint of optimism seasoned Janice's words. "What else did the doctor say? Is there an effective treatment?"

"It's a trial-and-error approach, but he recommended shaving."

"How much?" asked Clyde with a squeak in his voice.

"Everything and everywhere. The more the better."

Matt broke into the conversation. "You have a well-shaped beard. Did you bring a trimmer?"

"Yeah, but—"

Janice spoke up. "I always wondered what Miguel looked like under all that hair."

"Who's Miguel?" asked Clyde.

"My old rugby-playing boyfriend. You and Miguel could have been brothers. He smelled like a goat, too."

Clyde released a huff of air that sounded like defeat. "If you're intent on humiliating me, don't let me stop your fun."

"Buck up, counselor," said Janice. "I used to have breath that could stop a charging elephant. Having enough money to afford regular dental care changed my life. Advanced gingivitis took a while to cure, but now people don't mind having a conversation with me."

Steve took over. "Once you remove the hair, doctors recommend regular showers with an antibacterial soap. Bacteria and sweat from hair follicles are like thousands of petri dishes producing odor."

"That makes sense," said Janice. "What else?"

"Use an antiperspirant, or a combination antiperspirant with a deodorant. Then, watch what you eat. Sulfur-rich foods like onions, garlic, cabbage, and broccoli can exacerbate the problem. Also, watch out for certain spices and foods that promote sweating. The general rule is, if it has a strong odor or makes you sweat, leave it alone."

Clyde said, "So much for jalapeños." The lawyer's propensity for arguing was still active. "It's going to be impossible not to sweat while here on the island."

Steve had an answer. "I mentioned that, and the Doc said you could make a paste of baking soda and water. Use it under your arms and down yonder if the antiperspirant doesn't work. He also said to make an appointment with a dermatologist when you get home. They'll do blood work to rule out other potential causes like diabetes, gout, an overactive thyroid, or other diseases."

A clap came from the direction of Janice. "Let's get started.

Who knows, there might be a nice chest and back buried under that thatched cottage."

Clyde surrendered. "I'll grab my beard trimmer. We'd better go outside, away from the bungalow. The wind should disperse the hair."

Janice spoke as if this were some sort of competitive sport. "Don't stop with the clippers. Matt, do you have an extra razor and shaving cream?"

"Sure. I shave everything but my eyebrows. Started doing it when I took up competitive cycling and liked the way it felt."

Clyde must have had second thoughts. "Let's not get carried away."

Janice punched through his hesitance. "Why are men so weak from the neck up? All you have to do is stand there. Isn't it worth taking a chance? You and Matt get to work."

Unexpected silence settled on the room. Steve waited for someone to speak. Clyde came through with flying colors. "Do any of you realize what a big deal this is to me? I haven't seen my chest since I was fourteen. Are you sure the hair on my head and the beard have to go?"

Janice answered with twin cliches. "Nothing ventured, nothing gained. Also, like the British say, 'in for a penny, in for a pound.'" She ended with, "It will grow back, and you're wasting time by standing here."

Steve listened as Matt and Clyde's squeaking footsteps on the tile floor faded. They soon returned and Clyde surrendered to his fate. "Let's find a spot where no one can see us and get to work. The clippers have a full charge on them. The battery should last about an hour."

Steve turned in Janice's direction. "Could you put me some-place where the hair won't blow on me? I don't want to miss this."

"Do you expect me to watch this lamb get sheared?"

"You can supervise."

"Latch on," said Janice. "This is going to be a first for me."

"Me, too," said Clyde with little enthusiasm.

Matt spoke in a matter-of-fact tone. "It's not that big of a deal. I shave from head to toe two to three times a week."

They walked out of the bungalow into a brisk breeze as Clyde asked, "How do you shave your back?"

"That's the best part. My wife helps with the hard-to-reach places."

Janice didn't miss a beat. "That must do wonders for your love life."

A chuckle came from Matt. "She came up with a new saying: 'The couple that shaves together stays together.'"

What sounded like a huff of frustration came from Clyde. "That works for you, but potential wives are in short supply for me."

Steve put in his contribution to the discussion. "If what you're about to do helps as much as I hope it will, you shouldn't have any trouble finding someone special to help you."

The procession stopped when Janice said, "This is a nice spot. Take off your shirt, say goodbye to the old bearskin rug, and hello to the new Clyde."

The sound of clippers and the rustle of palm fronds filled the air for the next twenty minutes. Toward the end, Matt had a slight modification to the plan. "After Clyde and I take care of the bottom half, he'll go in and shave in the shower. Stubble won't clog the drain."

Janice gave her opinion of Clyde's partial transformation. "So far, so good. There's antibacterial dishwashing liquid in the kitchen of the big house. I bet they have the same brand here in the kitchenette. Steve and I will go inside while you and Matt finish out here."

Once inside, Steve settled into the same chair he'd previously occupied. By the sound of her footsteps, Janice had moved to the window overlooking the bay. He asked, "What do you see?"

"Paradise."

"What about Bella and Habib?"

"No one's in sight, just blue water from here to the horizon."

"Ah. That means Habib can swim enough to save himself."

The flat tone of Janice's words told him she was staring, probably mesmerized by the beauty before her. "Water isn't the only thing he's afraid of."

"Oh?"

"He's scared he'll lose his job when Mr. McBlythe retires."

"Scared enough to do something foolish?"

He could tell by the increase in volume that she'd turned to face him. "We're all concerned. Some much more than others."

"Does that include you?"

He heard Janice take in a full breath. "I'm a practical, confident woman with a thick skin. The type of law I practice allows me to rub elbows with people who make and lose fortunes. One lesson I learned from successful people is to expect and plan for low points in any career. My skills are easily transferable, I practice thrift, and I've invested well. The future doesn't frighten me."

"What does?" asked Steve.

"Growing old alone, same as Clyde."

Steve reached into his pocket and pulled out the plastic cap from a bottle of water he drank on the boat ride to the island. "I'd like to hire you, counselor." He handed her the worthless piece of plastic.

"This isn't legal tender."

"Island currency," said Steve. "Whatever you normally charge, this will more than cover it on this island. I have it on good authority that there's not another bottle cap like this one."

"Perhaps you should tell me how I can help you before we discuss fees."

"I need someone from Boston I can confide in."

He imagined her nodding, and somewhat confirmed it when she said, "Please, go on."

"I've eliminated you as a suspect from our inquiry related to stealing company secrets."

"I suspected there was more to this week than weeding out employees." She paused a moment before saying, "I'm glad to hear I've been eliminated."

"It shouldn't come as a surprise. You already knew that Mr. McBlythe recruited Heather and me to find who's been stealing and selling inside information."

"How did you surmise my innocence?"

"That's between me and Heather. What's important is your confidentiality for what I want to tell you."

"Is my silence all you want from me?"

"Not quite. I'd like for you to meet with Heather and me privately to discuss possible suspects that accompanied you from Boston." He took a breath. "Do we have a deal?"

"If there's one thing I'm exceptionally good at, it's maintaining client-attorney confidentiality. I'll accept your payment of the island's special currency as a retainer."

Steve handed over the bottle cap. "Are you aware that an employee named Reggie Scott received serious injuries in a street mugging?"

"He works under Habib Patel's supervision."

"Correct," said Steve. "Mr. Scott died of his injuries."

The sound of Janice taking in a labored breath reached his ears. He waited for her to speak, which she did after several seconds. "Now it all makes sense. This isn't just about theft. You and Heather are conducting a murder investigation, and you suspect Habib."

Steve didn't correct her. Instead, he said, "Murder investigations are our area of specialization."

Matt's voice shouted from the bathroom. "Janice, we're ready for the antibacterial soap."

Steve flipped his hand as a way of dismissing her. "Take care of Clyde. I want your honest opinion on how he looks."

Janice whispered. "If the soap and antiperspirant do the trick, he'll be a much sought-after man."

"You included?" asked Steve.

"I'm years overdue for an island romance." She paused. "By the way, what knotty legal problem did you and Heather have in mind for us to solve?"

"It had to do with personal hygiene and how it relates to workplace discrimination. I believe you and Clyde did an exceptional job in dealing with the problem. You both scored very high. It will be interesting to see how the other teams do with their problems."

24

Heather retreated to the solitude of her bedroom after assigning the almost impossible problems for the teams to solve. She couldn't help but wonder how the two attorneys were dealing with whatever problem Steve had given them.

It came as no surprise that Steve had slipped into his motif of not divulging all his plans to her. He usually kept something from her in every investigation. It was maddening and endearing at the same time. Just one of the many things that made him special.

The sound of angry voices cut through the peace of being on an island so far from civilization. She closed her laptop, uncrossed her legs, and set out to find the people responsible for breaking the tranquility. Bob Brown and Brent Coolidge sat on opposite sides of the living room, scowling but silent. Their gazes fixed on the patio.

"What's happening?" asked Heather, as her gaze also shifted to the patio.

"I had to shut the door," said Brent. "Malcolm and Habib are at each other's throats."

The argument on the patio took a more serious turn when Habib took a swing at Heather's chief financial officer. Malcolm artfully dodged Habib's blow and gave the off-balanced aggressor a push. It wasn't hard, but enough to send Habib sprawling on the deck. Rage overtook Habib. He sprang upward with surprising agility, spread his arms, and charged into Malcolm. Both men went to the planks.

She reached the door and slid it back. "Stop!" Her command floated away on the wind. Habib flailed with his left hand while Malcolm pinned the right arm. The awkward blows from the Bostonian did no apparent harm.

Heather knew the fight was a mismatch from the outset. Malcolm, in his early fifties, had served as an officer in the Marines and was still trim and fit. It didn't take him long to pin both of Habib's arms while sitting on the inept fighter's chest.

Malcolm looked up at Heather. "This guy is nuts. He told me I should have waited on him before starting on a plan to solve the problem you gave us."

"Get off me!" shouted Habib. "This isn't a fair competition. I shouldn't have been required to learn to swim."

Heather drew closer and looked down at Habib. "I gave you the opportunity to learn to swim yesterday. You didn't take advantage of it, and today you paid the price by having to repeat the lesson. You have only yourself to blame for your failure."

His gaze shifted to Heather as he spat out hatred. "I can't believe your father required me to waste an entire week on this island. It makes me question your leadership capabilities, and if I could ever work for a woman like you."

She tented her hands on hips. "You can quit the team building exercises any time you want, but there won't be a job waiting for you back in Boston."

Heather knew it was a lie wrapped in a bluff, but it worked all the same. Emotion choked Habib's words. "You don't under-stand. I can't fail. It's not permitted."

Heather hadn't noticed, but Steve and Matt had arrived and stepped onto the patio. "Do you want to continue fighting?" asked Steve.

"I have no choice," said Habib. "It's now a matter of honor."

"All right, you'll get your wish."

"Wait a minute," said Heather. "We can't have them harming each other this far from medical care."

Steve waved away the protest. "I know a way that will minimize the risk." He took in a full breath. "Malcolm, I have a new task for you and Habib. You're to build pugil sticks."

"Huh?" said Heather.

The former marine explained. "They're heavily padded sticks with an overall length of fifty inches. The only exposed hard surface is where your hands grasp the stick. In the olden days, people fought with wooden staffs. Pugil sticks are the modern version, only you shouldn't be able to inflict damage on each other."

Steve took over. "To make sure, you'll each make the other's stick. Use as many pillows on the ends as you want. Malcolm, since you know what I'm talking about, you're to teach Habib. Spend the rest of the day working together to make each other's weapon. The contest will take place tomorrow morning after you both warm up with two trips up the hill."

Heather placed a hand on Malcolm's shoulder. "You have your assignment. If I were you, I'd make sure there was plenty of padding on the stick I was going to be hit with."

Malcolm stood while making sure Habib didn't get in a cheap shot. She pointed toward the hill. "There's the forest. You'd better get busy finding two stout sticks that are fifty inches long."

"We'd better get started."

Habib's blood-lust cooled enough for him to respond with words instead of blows. "I agree. It may take some time to find two sticks that are exactly alike."

"Let's get a couple of knives from the kitchen."

"Something to chop with would be helpful," said Habib.

Heather flinched when she heard the idea and that both men were in favor of it. She made a quick decision. "I'm sending

Dorcas with you to carry a knife and observe. No violence of any kind until tomorrow. Is that clear?"

"Good idea," said Steve.

Heather noticed that Bob Brown and Brent Coolidge had joined them on the patio. She trained her gaze on the two men. "What progress have you two made on your problem?"

"Not much," said her director of acquisitions. "Bob's not up to date on many of the current opportunities in emerging markets."

"That's not true. I know what's going on, but the opportunities are too uncertain," said Bob, looking at Heather instead of Brent. "Mr. McBlythe is shifting to a more risk-averse portfolio."

Heather shook her head. "That wasn't your assignment. You two are to develop a ten-year plan of your own for maximizing profits while minimizing risk. Don't try to out-think my father."

Bob didn't back down. "It's obvious he takes unnecessary chances."

"I balance my portfolio allocations across a broad spectrum of assets," Brent stated in his rebuttal. "The speed at which things change dictates a minimum of twenty percent investment in developing technologies. I'm putting my money where my mouth is and bumping the allocation to thirty percent."

"Seven percent is all I'm willing to go," said Bob.

Steve interrupted. "It seems you two are at an impasse. Do you want to settle the matter with pugil sticks like Habib and Malcolm? I'm sure they'll let you use theirs when they're finished."

Bob held up his hands. "Not me."

"Me either," said Brent. "I'm going inside to reconsider my suggestions."

Heather waited until the patio door closed before she looked full on at Bob. "Are your personal financial problems clouding your judgment?"

"Who says I'm having financial problems?"

"Are you denying they exist?"

"I'm doing fine."

Steve shook his head. "Sorry, Bob. That wasn't very convincing."

Heather pressed the point. "I'm wondering how desperate you are."

Bob drew himself up to his full height. "Mr. McBlythe has never questioned my loyalty or integrity."

"I'm not my father, and perhaps he should."

Steve broke in. "Hold on, Heather. I don't think Bob would throw away his career. He's smarter than that."

"Exactly," said Bob. "I don't know who's been stealing company secrets, but it wasn't me."

"Then who is it? It's obvious you know something about it."

"It's been water-cooler talk for months. Take your pick. There are plenty of suspects."

Steve issued a challenge. "This is your chance to convince us the thief isn't you. I suggest you make the most of it."

Heather softened Steve's words. "We don't expect you to accuse anyone. Tell us who could have done it and why. We'll put the pieces together."

Bob let out a huff followed by, "All right. Don't let Janice fool you. She's a barracuda who enjoys crushing men like they were bugs."

"She's on our list," said Steve. "Who else?"

Bob's eyes shifted from left to right and back again. "Habib. Anyone can see how desperate he is to advance and eventually own a major company. He's socking away every penny he can and has a goal to make it happen sooner than later. What he can't take is a hit to his reputation by getting demoted. He's been different since we heard Mr. McBlythe is retiring and the companies will merge."

Steve asked, "What about Louis Crane? It seems to me the head of IT would be a likely suspect for selling inside information."

Bob let out a throaty chuckle. "He tops my list. Do you think a hacker like Louis doesn't know this home has a Starlink connection?"

"What are you saying?" asked Heather.

Bob lifted his chin. "Louis can hack into almost anything. He used to brag about it. It doesn't take much imagination to consider him hacking into your father's business. In fact, it might behoove you to put your IT girl to work. Check to see if someone recently hacked your laptop."

"That's not possible. I took up everyone's laptop and phone."

Bob's lips twitched in a sly smile. "You underestimate how sneaky hackers are."

"Ah," said Steve. "We didn't do a thorough search of every-one's luggage."

Heather's anger grew by the second. A computer geek had outwitted her. She gave Bob her best stare. "I suggest you and Brent try harder to finish your assignment."

The closing of the patio door gave her a chance to speak to Steve in private. As was his custom, he changed the subject. Another of his maddening habits. "Isn't it time for beach volleyball?"

Heather glanced at her watch. "It is. I'll tell Matt to round up everyone and send them to the beach."

"Not Janice and Clyde," said Steve.

"Why not?"

"You'll understand when they show up later."

Heather tilted her head. "What have you done?"

"I scored us some spies."

"Janice?"

"Uh-huh. Her and Clyde."

"Did you solve Clyde's problem?"

A cheesy grin came to Steve's mouth. "Janice said she's overdue for an island romance. She seemed to like what she saw under Clyde's blanket of hair."

Heather's hand covered her mouth to keep the laugh from escaping. She asked, "Is it all gone?"

"From what Matt led me to believe, they didn't stop shaving until Clyde was slick as a billiard ball from head to heels."

Heather couldn't help but smile, if only for a few seconds. Then another thought rose to the surface. "How did you talk Janice into being a spy for us?"

"I told her I'd eliminated her as a suspect."

"Did you mean it?"

Steve gave a partial answer with a shake of his head. "You know cops don't have to tell the whole truth."

Heather took a step toward him and leaned in to whisper. "In case you forgot, you're no longer a police homicide detective."

"Nonsense. We're operating on island rules. I appointed me and you as official detectives. I even gave us full power to detain and question suspects." He took a breath. "Speaking of questioning a suspect, I told Janice we'd question her about the others from Boston. You can start thinking of things you want to ask her. Between the exercise and how distracted she is by Clyde, we should get straight answers."

"When do we question her?"

"Tonight. But first, we need to call your father."

"Why?"

"He should be able to give us more details on when, where, and how someone attacked Reggie Scott."

Heather watched as Matt and Bella led the volleyball players down the hill. Her thoughts, however, were fixed on the crime scene in Boston. "The initial police report says it was a street mugging that went too far."

"Janice knows we're investigating a homicide. She suspects everyone from Boston."

"When did she tell you that?"

"A little while ago, while Clyde was in the shower shaving."

"That was a revelatory time you spent with Janice, Clyde, and Matt."

"In more ways than one."

"Nice double entendre," said Heather. "What's next, after we call my father?"

Steve rubbed his palm across his face. "Let's set a trap for Louis Crane and Louise King."

"Why Louise?"

"I may be wrong about them not turning in all their devices, but I'll wager one or both of them have something else with a screen."

Heather didn't say it, but she believed Steve was right. "When will we talk to them?" asked Heather. "Let's not make it too long. I have sensitive information in my files that could be worth millions of dollars."

"Then let's do it tonight, after supper. We can bluff our way through it. We'll keep Louis and Louise here after everyone goes to bed."

"Until then, I'll make sure Matt keeps Louis occupied."

25

Heather led Steve to her bedroom and closed the door behind them. She pulled the satellite phone from the top drawer of her dresser and punched in her father's private number. Steve stood with both hands on top of his white cane.

The first words came from her father. "Are you making progress?"

She didn't directly answer the question. "Steve's with me. He believes everything is going as planned. All but one of your executives are physical and emotional wrecks. We're accomplishing our first goal of breaking them down."

A chuckle sounded through the phone's speaker. "Tell me more."

"Habib has been in two fist fights and lost both. No damage to either participant. He's scheduled to compete in a more controlled battle tomorrow that involves pillows."

The chuckle morphed into a full-blown laugh. "Excellent. He's a fantastic CFO, but he could benefit from eating a large slice of humble pie. What about Bob Brown?"

Steve answered. "He's over-extended financially."

"That's what I told the police. They'll be waiting at the

airport to take him in for questioning. They already questioned his paramour. She's dropped him like a bad habit."

Heather took her turn. "Louis Crane may be in the proverbial doghouse. We have unconfirmed suspicions that he didn't turn in all his electronic devices. It's a short step from getting into computer files to selling the information they contain."

"It would surprise me if he took that second step," said her father. "Still, it makes me wonder what other mischief he could be up to. That only leaves the head of my legal department. Please tell me Janice is still walking on the straight and narrow path."

It was Heather's turn to laugh. "You wouldn't believe me if I told you what she did today."

Steve interrupted. "It's nothing illegal. In fact, she helped Heather's hot-shot attorney solve a personal problem. To top it off, she's gotten herself involved in an island romance with him."

The phone went silent for several seconds. "That sounds more out of character than the other three combined. Should I join you on the island?"

"Not yet," said Steve. "We plan to drop a surprise or two on your people and see what floats to the surface."

"What I'd give to be there to see how they respond."

Steve asked, "Isn't Dorcas keeping you informed?"

"Not as well as I'd like. I'm wondering if I made a mistake allowing her to tag along."

"She mostly stays in the background," said Heather. "Competent and loyal is how I'd describe her."

"She's excellent at keeping me informed of things going on in the office. I'm a little disappointed that she hasn't done a better job on the island."

"She's struggling more than anyone else with the heat and humidity. Her fair complexion keeps her out of the sun. There's only so much she can see and hear if she's not playing sand volleyball, swimming, fishing, or joining in with other activities."

Her father huffed. "It's my fault."

"No harm," said Steve. "We hardly realize she's here."

It was Heather's turn. "Can you give us an update on the police investigation?"

"It was a single blow to the back of the head with something made of wood."

"Like a baseball bat?" asked Steve.

"Smaller in diameter."

Heather let out a huff. "The initial reports said it was a robbery and mugging with multiple injuries."

"That was what the press reported," said her father. "In reality, it was a single blow."

Steve opined, "I'm surprised they didn't report Reggie Scott being abducted by aliens and all his bones removed before they returned him from the mother ship."

"That was in the follow-up story."

It was pure sarcasm, but fit the mood.

"Anything else of interest from the police?" asked Heather.

"It either wasn't a mugging or the perpetrator was inept. His watch was missing, but his wallet was still on him."

"What kind of watch?" asked Steve.

"A fake Rolex."

"Where did Reggie carry his wallet?"

"Inside pocket of his sports coat."

"And the position of the body?"

"Lying flat on his face with arms out."

Steve had one more question. "Who found him?"

"A college intern for a nearby company. It unnerved her so much she and her husband are moving back to Nebraska." He paused. "Before you ask, the police detective I spoke with says there's no link between the woman who found him and Reggie. She was simply the first person to come along."

Steve summed up the various bits of information. "The wallet in the coat pocket tells me this wasn't a robbery, but the missing watch suggests the perp wanted the cops to think it was."

"What about the location?" asked Mr. McBlythe.

"I thought it had to be someone who works in your building. Now, I'm not so sure. Employees from other companies must also park there."

"A few," said her father. "I had our security director check, and our people account for ninety percent of the occupancy."

Steve rubbed his chin. "That puts the odds back in favor of one of your employees committing the murder." He gulped a quick breath. "Of the people from Boston who are on the island, how many of them park in that garage?"

"All of them."

"I was afraid you'd say that."

They agreed her father wouldn't fly to the island unless an emergency arose. Heather hoped they weren't tempting fate by using the word emergency.

The afternoon dragged on, as did the volleyball games. Matt knew to give the players enough time to go to their cabanas, take quick showers, and return to the main house for dinner. She and Steve came up with a plan to keep Clyde and Janice away from the group most of the day... just in case the twice-a-day showers and spray-downs with antiperspirant didn't work.

The setting sun glowed like a fluorescent orange ball as it slipped into the ocean, somewhere beyond the mouth of the bay. Heather instructed the group to move the dining room table and chairs to the patio. It was a perfect evening to have their communal meal outdoors.

Two chairs remained open as most of the volleyball players stared at the table or into the distance. Fatigue etched their faces. "Who's missing?" asked Heather.

Steve, who sat next to her, had a partial explanation. "Pearl told me she'll be busy in the kitchen, so that accounts for one empty chair."

Louise King spoke in a condescending tone. "My teammate, Louis Crane, isn't here. It's no big loss."

Heather gave Matt a hard stare. He responded with, "Sorry.

He took a shower before me, and I thought he left to come here."

Bob Brown made his opinion known. "Was I the only one who noticed him slinking away from the bungalow?"

The group erupted in a barrage of slurs, all directed at Boston's IT director. Steve leaned into her. "I was wondering how long it would take him to make a mistake."

Heather matched Steve's whisper. "It's an addiction. He can't stand to be offline."

Steve spoke over the crowd. "Bob, could you tell where Louis was going?"

"Beats me."

"Was he reading?"

"Yeah. He likes to go outside to a spot on the lawn to read. He said eReaders didn't count as electronic devices."

Steve's voice carried so all could hear. "Matt, please retrieve our lost boy before Captain Hook kidnaps him and takes him to Never-Never Land."

"My pleasure."

Pearl delivered salads. The group fell on the first course like they hadn't seen food in a week. Matt and a sheepish-looking Louis arrived before the last fork rested beside the now-empty bowls.

"Sorry," said Louis. "I fell asleep reading."

Pearl made an appearance. "To avoid a rush, only half of you will come to the kitchen at a time. People on the left side come first. Bring your plate with you and take all the grilled vegetables and rice pilaf you want. The second group can come once the first group returns. I'll also need two people to carry platters of fish to the table."

Heather stood. "Before anyone goes to the kitchen, we have a group decision to make. We told you that you'd have to catch your own fish while here on the island. That was before Clyde arrived. He and Janice speared enough fish to feed everyone. If you'd like Clyde and Janice to keep providing fish, I'm willing to excuse them from afternoon challenges." She lowered her voice. "I'll also take this opportunity to say I'm not pleased with your progress on the mental challenges. You've shown scant originality and teamwork thus far."

Steve interjected, "Let's put that behind us for tonight. Are you willing for Clyde and Janice to be in charge of providing meat for the table?"

"Heck yeah," shouted Bob.

That's all it took to spawn a riot of voices, all proclaiming Clyde and Janice the designated providers of fish.

Bella looked at Bob. "Grab one platter of fish and I'll get the other." Her words started a stampede.

Heather stood. "Keep your seat, Steve. I'll fill your plate."

Words were in short supply as the ravenous crowd returned with loaded plates and dove into the delicious island meal.

Steve summed up his opinion of the evening's offering by asking her, "What's the chances of us hiring Pearl and taking her home with us?"

Bella, who sat beside Steve, heard the question. "Not good. The islands are in her blood. Even Heather's father doesn't have enough money to tempt Pearl away."

One by one, people settled their forks and knives on their plates. Brent Coolidge took a long look at Clyde. "What made you want to shave your head and beard?"

Janice answered before he could. "That's not all that's shaved."

Clyde moved a hand under the table. "I should have done it years ago. This island heat and humidity convinced me to take some drastic steps."

Janice couldn't hold her peace. "Perhaps you should try the look, Brent." Her right hand slipped under the table. Clyde let out a quick yelp before turning to Janice and wiggling his eyebrows.

Louis Crane was the first to stand. "I don't know about the rest of you, but I'm bushed."

Heather held up her hand. "Since you were late for supper without permission, you get to help with tonight's dishes and cleaning the kitchen."

"It's not my team's turn. We did them at lunch."

Steve pushed his chair back. "Don't worry, Louis. I'll help you. Besides, Heather and I need to speak to you after we finish."

"I'll help too," said Bella. "It's been a slower day for me."

The crew from Boston moved the table and chairs inside. Heather dismissed them with a reminder that daybreak yoga awaited them at first light.

The kitchen crew from Texas, under Dorcas's leadership, took much longer to complete their chores. Heather made it a point to monitor Louis Crane's minimal effort. It didn't surprise her that he resented having to scrub a small mountain of pans.

Once released by Dorcas, the group filed past on their way to bungalows with comfortable beds. Heather summoned Louise King and asked her to take a seat. Louis tried to hide behind Brent Coolidge. Heather waited until her father's head of IT was several steps away from the patio. "Going somewhere, Louis?"

"Huh? Oh, sorry. I forgot you wanted to talk to me."

Heather ignored the bald-faced lie. Steve was already sitting in a deck chair. She took her seat in a matching one and waited for Louis to arrive. She purposefully didn't provide a chair for him. Undeterred, he located a nearby chair and moved it to form a sloppy square and plopped down. "What can I do for you?"

"Several things," said Heather. "First, you can explain why you were late for supper."

Louis patted his stomach. "I must have eaten something that didn't agree with me."

"You made a speedy recovery. I believe you had thirds of the grilled fish."

Steve asked, "I thought you said you fell asleep while reading?"

"Oh... both."

Steve was having none of it. "I hope you remember this is a no-excuse island. You'll need to make up for causing everyone to wait on supper." He turned his head. "What do you think, Heather? One trip or two up the hill tomorrow after lunch?"

She kept a straight face. "How late was he?"

"Only a few minutes," said Louis with a plea for mercy in his voice.

"Are you sure?" asked Steve.

"Well, it could have been a little longer. I didn't pay attention to the time."

Heather kept her gaze fixed on him. "Why do you think you and Louise aren't making much progress on the problem I gave you?"

"I work at a different pace." Louis leaned back in his chair. "Don't take this wrong, but I had the problem solved in thirty minutes."

Louise cut her head to face him. "No, you didn't. The only way to cut that much time off is to have access to the question beforehand."

Steve's eyebrows raised over the rim of his sunglasses. "Do you think it's possible Louis hacked into Heather's files?"

Heather shook her head. "He couldn't. I didn't make up the questions until after I collected everyone's phones and laptops."

"Perhaps you missed something." Steve moved his head to make it appear he was looking at Louis. "You're the expert. How could a computer be disguised as something totally innocuous?"

"I've never thought of that."

"Of course not," said Heather, "but Steve and I want to know how it could be done."

Shoulders rose and dropped. "I dunno."

A sheepish look came over Louise's face. "He's lying and I have a confession to make. I kept my second cell phone."

"Not me," said Louis. "I only brought one."

Steve's voice held a hint of accusation. "It would have to be something electronic with a screen."

Heather waited for a reaction from Louis. His Adam's apple traveled up and down."

Steve continued. "Louise, we want permission to search your belongings. If you have only the one electronic device, there will be no consequences."

Louise dipped her head. "Of course. I'm so sorry. The second phone is all I have."

Heather shifted her gaze to Louis. His shoulders slumped as the response came out in a rush. "No need to ask again. You caught me fair and square. My reader doubles as a laptop. I carry it everywhere, so I always have a backup." His next sentence ran into his confession. "I promised your father I'd never hack into anyone's business files, and I've kept that promise, even though I could and he'd make a lot more money."

Steve shook his head. "That's hard to believe."

"It's true. Give the reader to Louise and she'll tell you soon enough. The only thing she'll find is that I'm a competitive gamer. That's why I needed Internet access."

Heather wasn't convinced. "You're playing a dangerous game. I already know someone's been in my files and I believe it's you."

The self-confessed gamer's head hung. "Busted again. I broke into your files to look at the question you had for me and Louise. I promised I'd never break into your father's files, but not yours."

"Did you look at anything else?" asked Heather.

"All I was interested in was getting time to rest. That meant finding the question for our challenge."

Heather added. "You're not as smart as you think you are. I didn't know you'd looked on my computer until you told me."

Louis jerked his head up. "Do you mean she didn't look to see if I hacked into your files?"

"Not yet. I'll have her check tomorrow."

"You lied."

Steve's lips danced around a smile. "I like to think of it as taking a shortcut to the truth. Isn't that what you do?"

Louis raised his hands in a gesture of surrender. "You two are really good."

Steve said, "Now that we've established that you play fast and loose with lies, let's see how you do with telling the truth. Tell us everything you know about your co-workers from Boston and their relationship with Reggie Scott."

26

Heather, Bella, and Matt placed their yoga mats in front of two rows of bleary-eyed participants. Everyone arrived on time even though they looked the worse for wear. The exceptions were Clyde and Janice. The pleasant smell of soap and deodorant wafted from him, while Janice had found time to apply makeup. It remained to be seen if two trips up and down the hill would reactivate Clyde's problem, or if the shearing plus baking soda paste would continue to work its magic.

Bella led the day's yoga session and proved herself limber as a warm string of licorice. Matt's excessive muscles prohibited a full range of motion, but he was a good example to novices that stretching could benefit all. Forty-five minutes later, Heather instructed the gathering to put on their shoes and socks. "After last night's feast, I decided we'd have an early lunch instead of a light breakfast. Are there any objections?"

Janice spoke before anyone else could. "I understand we're all going twice up the hill this morning. I ate so much last night that I don't want or need any breakfast."

"Same here," said Bob Brown from the other end of the first row.

Nods and words of agreement rose from the ranks. Heather

summarized. "There seems to be a consensus that we should switch to two meals a day, with the heavy meal at night."

Louise King shouted, "With two meals a day, I'll leave the island ten pounds lighter. That's something I've needed to do for the last year."

Several nodded in agreement.

"Then it's settled. One meal at lunch and a feast at night."

While Heather was still sitting in the lotus position, Matt slipped on socks and shoes and announced, "The trail up the hill awaits us. Who can keep up with me today?"

"I can," said Heather.

"You'll have to catch me."

"That's not fair. I don't have my shoes on yet."

Matt laughed as he ran toward the trail. "Island rules. Do what you have to do to win."

The hyper-competitive executives hurried to put on socks and shoes. It came as no surprise that Bob and Dorcas didn't race to be first.

Heather stepped to where Bob sat. "You seem to be lagging behind this morning."

"I'm remembering Aesop's fable of the tortoise and the hare. Slow and cunning beats fast and impetuous. It's going to be a full day of physical and mental challenges. I'll pace myself."

"I agree," said Dorcas. "By eliminating breakfast, you gave us extra time to finish the two trips."

Dorcas didn't move fast, but she was deliberate and once she tied her shoes, she moved out at a steady pace. Heather watched while Bob took more time than was necessary, then waited until everyone was out of sight. "What's on your mind, Bob?"

"Not much gets past you, does it?"

It was the type of question that didn't warrant a response, so she waited for him to say something that did.

"I hope you don't mind, but I need your advice."

"You know what they say about advice. If it's free, it lacks value."

The two started walking at a modest pace. "I'll take my chances." He ran a hand down his face, as if searching for the perfect words. Then, he picked up the pace, his agitation obvious. "I've made a royal mess of my life and I don't know what to do."

It was time for Bob to experience a hefty dose of reality, and Heather doused him with a proverbial bucket of ice water. "Are you talking about your mistress or your financial problems?"

Bob stopped in his tracks. "You already know."

Heather couldn't help but issue a small grin at the shocked look on his face. "You don't need to worry about one of your problems."

"Huh?"

"Your paramour is no more. She's taken up with an investment banker."

"How do you know?" His words trailed off before he snapped his fingers. "Of course. You have a satellite phone and Internet connection. You're in contact with your father, and he knows all the latest that's going on in Boston."

A nod confirmed his words. Worry lines still etched his face. "I'm glad she's gone, but the damage is done."

"You don't know that."

"How could my wife ever forgive me? I've betrayed her, and our two girls, and ruined us financially."

Heather didn't want to make him think he'd get off without consequences, but she also didn't want to pile additional guilt on him. Besides, she was on the island to solve two crimes, not to dispense marriage counseling. She focused on her field of expertise. "From what I've been told, you can repair your finances."

"Not if my wife divorces me."

"You're borrowing trouble. What's the first step you need to take to get your financial house in order?"

"Sell that stupid yacht. That thing is nothing but a money pit."

"Are you serious about selling it?"

"I'd list it right now if I could."

"Good. Let's turn around and go back to the house. Do you know a broker you can call to list it?"

"Sure. It was new when I bought it, and it's only been out of port a few times since I got the keys. The salesman said I practically stole it." He shook his head. "I thought I couldn't live without it, and now I'd kill to get rid of it."

Heather wondered about his choice of words, but kept talking. "If you're really serious, you can call the broker on my satellite phone. I'll also give you computer access if you need to sign a listing contract."

"Can I call my daughters, too? They told me they didn't want to hear from me until I dumped Mandy and the yacht."

"What about your wife?"

"That's a conversation that will have to wait until I get back to Boston. I'm hoping my daughters will soften up their mom so she'll listen to me."

"You're a strategic thinker," said Heather. "No wonder you're so good at acquisitions."

"Being around Brent Coolidge has challenged me to take prudent risks again. It serves me right for being so distracted by a pretty face."

Heather wondered how many other risks Bob had taken before he pulled out of the nosedive caused by his mid-life crisis. Selling company secrets might have been one such thing. She then wondered how Steve would read the sudden turn to repentance? One way to find out.

They arrived at the house and found Steve in a recliner facing the bank of windows. Heather explained the reason for them abandoning the two hill climbs. Steve listened with hands clasped together.

Instead of agreeing with Heather's plan, he spoke in a nonnonsense tone. "You haven't earned a phone call yet."

Bob stiffened. "What do you mean?"

"You're a guy who knows how to negotiate deals, right?"

"Sure. That's what acquisitions are about."

"You want to make three phone calls to get your life back on track, right?"

"I want them more than anything. One to sell the yacht, and a phone call to each daughter."

"Then you have to earn them. We want information and we're willing to trade."

"Heather said nothing about a trade."

Steve countered with, "Heather and I are partners. She should have discussed the terms with me also, but because we're playing with island rules, it's not too late for me to put stipulations on the deal."

"That's convenient."

"Like I said, you'll get the phone calls, but only after you earn them."

"You're taking advantage of me."

"You're the one who screwed up your life. I'm doing the same thing you do in your job—using leverage to negotiate a deal." Steve gave a toothy grin. "I'm a decent negotiator, but you're one of the best. I'd say that makes the playing field even."

Heather interrupted. "We know what you want, but you haven't heard what Steve wants in return. You should hear him out."

Bob moved a chair to within a few feet of Steve's. Heather settled in one and formed a triangle.

"What do I need to do to earn the phone calls?"

"First," said Steve, "We want you to tell us how someone could steal secrets from Mr. McBlythe."

The question didn't seem to take Bob by surprise. It was almost like he had an answer already loaded and ready to fire. "It's someone on the inside. The timing was too perfect. They knew exactly when to buy or sell to receive maximum profits."

"We already know that," said Steve. "Tell us something we don't know."

"It wasn't me."

"You'll have a hard time convincing the police of that. They're waiting for you with handcuffs when you get back to Boston."

Heather knew this was one of Steve's strategies. He used an exaggeration with enough truth in it to rattle Bob, at least for a few seconds. His mouth flew open, but he slammed it shut. "I don't care if they bring a SWAT team to arrest me. I may have shot a torpedo into my life, but I never stole a thing from the company."

"Who did?" asked Steve.

"I don't know."

"Take your best guess and tell me why."

He sighed. "It will only be a guess."

"We understand," said Heather. "There's no punishment for guessing."

"It's another island rule," said Steve.

Bob took his time. "I've given this considerable thought, and you should have the police department's computer experts take a hard look at Louis Crane. There's no telling how much sensitive information he can access."

Steve leaned forward. "Let's stay on that train of thought a while longer. How could anyone steal the secrets other than through hacking?"

Bob matched Steve's posture and lowered his voice. "A computer breach is the most likely, but there's another way." A dramatic pause followed until he whispered. "In most ways, Mr. McBlythe embraces modern technology, with one exception. He likes to read paper reports and makes copious notes and comments on them in longhand."

Steve asked, "Where are these kept?"

"Locked in file cabinets."

"In his office?"

"Only if he's actively working on them."

Steve nodded. "Let me make sure I understand the process. Each department head submits electronic reports."

"Correct."

"Who makes hard copies of these?"

"Dorcas. She gives them to him so he can make notes."

"Do the department heads have access to the notes?"

Bob shook his head. "Not exactly. Louis can hack into the original emails, but not Mr. McBlythe's notes. However, Heather's father discusses his concerns at our department head meetings. That's why I believe Louis Crane is the one selling inside information. He's the only person with access to all the reports by each department head and what Mr. McBlythe discusses at meetings."

"What else do you know about Louis?" asked Heather.

"He works strange hours. Always late for work, but you can usually find him in his office late at night. He listens to heavy metal through earbuds."

"What does he drive to work?" asked Steve.

"An electric bicycle. He chains it to a pole in the garage where everyone else parks."

"Anything else? Have you ever seen him get angry?"

"Only once, and he denied being upset. Someone took his laptop as a joke and kept it for an hour. The next day, that employee went to the garage and found his driver's side window smashed."

Steve unfolded his hands. "You've earned a phone call. Want to earn another?"

"Sure."

Heather broke in. "You can call the yacht broker after we're finished. To call one of your daughters, you and Brent Coolidge need to finish your assignment of a comprehensive strategy for future acquisitions. If you complete it today, you can make the call after supper."

"What about my second daughter?"

Steve answered for her. "That will require fresh information, and we'll determine if it merits another phone call."

Bob stood. "I'm glad I don't have to negotiate with you two every day."

Heather went to her room and brought back the satellite phone. "Go on the patio and make the call."

Steve held up a hand. "If you need an attorney to look over any documents related to the sale of the yacht, there's three to choose from."

"What will that cost me?"

"No charge," said Heather. "Steve's a hopeless romantic. He's rooting for your marriage."

Heather took her seat as Bob went to the deck and placed his call. She looked at Steve. "Your thoughts?"

"It's as I expected. They're pointing at each other. We need to come up with a plan to smoke out the thief."

"What about the killer?"

"Did I say thief? I meant the killer."

Heather knew Steve didn't make mistakes like that. Was he testing her? To find out, she'd test him. "You already know who stole Father's secrets."

He rubbed his hands together. "Knowing and proving are two different animals." He chuckled. "At least I believe I know. It seems my crystal ball is a bit cloudy these days."

"You won't tell me, will you?"

"Not yet. Let's see what happens today at the battle between Habib and Malcolm Swift. I'll want a report on how everyone reacts."

"You don't believe they'll reconcile before the match?"

"Malcolm will offer, but it takes two in any agreement. Let's make sure Habib doesn't cheat."

27

A gap of almost an hour separated Matt from Dorcas, the last person to complete the second hill climb. This left most everyone plenty of time to recover from the morning's routine. Heather leaned into Steve and whispered. "They're getting in shape. A couple more days and they'll be looking forward to climbing the hill."

"If we don't hurry and solve the case, we'll have to change things so they'll use different muscles. I'll get with Bella and Matt and see what they can come up with."

Heather looked at the bay before bringing her gaze back to the yard below the deck. "Everyone's back. Dorcas is taking on water like she's a camel."

Steve wore a chartreuse shirt emblazoned with pink sailboats and burgundy-colored shorts. "Are Habib and Malcolm ready to do battle?"

"They're in position with their sticks on the lawn."

"Form everyone but you and me in a circle. We'll stand by the rail so you can look down on the match and tell me what you see."

Heather followed Steve's instructions. "The sticks look to be the same size. Pillows cover both ends. Habib secured his pillows with twine, while Malcolm used duct tape. It looks like it would hurt more and maybe give Habib a fighting chance."

"Have them switch weapons," said Steve.

"That will make it a double switch."

Steve nodded. "Something tells me this fight won't last long."

Heather raised her voice so all would hear. "The only reason we're having this contest is because these two couldn't work out their problems without resorting to violence. Let this be a lesson for the rest of you. We're here to develop teamwork. I'm disappointed that you two couldn't reconcile, but if you insist on violence—"

Malcolm interrupted her. "I'm willing to walk away and not go through with this."

Habib grabbed his pugil stick. "My honor demands I do this." He looked at Malcolm. "Take up your weapon and defend yourself. There's no turning back now."

"You don't stand a chance," said Malcolm.

Janice shouted, "Would you two please get on with it? You're cutting into the time Clyde and I have to fish for your supper."

Bob Brown picked an extra quiet moment to say, "She needs to get Clyde in the water before his deodorant wears off."

Clyde came back with, "Perhaps you'd like to go a round or two with the pugil sticks after Habib and Malcolm are finished?"

Bob held up both hands. "No, thanks."

Heather announced. "Are you both ready?"

A hush fell on the scene as Malcolm took up his stick and assumed a stance that showed this wouldn't be an even match.

Heather shouted a last instruction. "You two trade sticks. Matt, be prepared to stop the contest when I tell you to." She took in a breath.

The two contestants switched weapons.

"Begin!" shouted Heather.

Habib mimicked the two-handed grip Malcolm had on his stick as the two made a circle on the grass, feeling each other out. Habib made a lunge with the pillow-padded end of his stick.

Malcolm flicked it away like it was a bothersome fly and countered with the opposite end of his stick. The blow wasn't hard enough to take Habib down but did land with a thud on his exposed arm.

Instead of retreating, Habib came at Malcolm with surprising speed. His second thrust hit nothing but air as Malcolm jerked his head out of harm's way at the last second. The force of Habib's jab carried him past Malcolm, who caught the inept fighter behind the knee and flipped him skyward. He landed with a thud while Malcolm again assumed a defensive posture.

"Had enough?" asked Malcolm.

Habib scrambled to his feet. Rage filled his eyes as he ran toward Malcolm and repeatedly swung the pugil stick like it was a baseball bat. Malcolm had no trouble blocking the blows with the duct-taped ends of his stick.

On the second swing, Heather noticed the twine came loose from Habib's stick. On the third swing, the pillow flew and bounced off Matt. Something glinted in the bright sun.

"Stop!" shouted Heather.

There was no stopping Habib. He took another wild swing and the sound of something tearing shot forth as Malcolm blocked another blow, took three steps back, and inspected the end of his stick.

Habib was charging again as a narrow-eyed look came over Malcolm's countenance. He blocked the next swing then drove the end of his stick into his opponent's stomach. Habib leaned forward, which exposed his face. Malcolm took full advantage of the moment and brought what was now a shredded pillow over a stout stick into Habib's jaw.

Matt plowed into Malcolm, driving him into Brent Coolidge, who caught him before both went to the ground.

Heather jumped over the rail and went directly to where Habib lay. Her focus was not on her father's chief financial officer but the pugil stick. Strapped to the end of it was the blade of a chef's knife.

Gasps rose from the crowd. Malcolm announced, "He tried to kill me."

Habib made it to his knees, dazed by the blows he'd absorbed. Heather had the lethal weapon in her hand. "Did you make this pugil stick?"

He tried to focus. "What?"

"Is this the pugil stick you built?"

He held his stomach and took in his first full breath. "What's that tied to the end of it?"

"A knife."

"Then it's not mine."

Clyde spoke from where he stood beside Janice. "You're going to need a good lawyer to get out of this, Habib."

28

Heather took the stick with the knife attached back to the porch where Steve stood at the rail. She hoped a plan would come to her. Something had to be done to Habib, but there wasn't a jail cell handy.

She directed Steve away from the rail. "Do I need to explain what happened?"

He shook his head. "I caught enough to know. The problem now is what to do with Habib. He can't stay in the bungalow. Aren't there a couple more bedrooms in the main house?"

"Only one."

"Have Matt go with Habib and gather all his belongings. Put him in the open bedroom and tell him to stay there."

"What about the others?"

"Let's give them something else to think about. Swimming laps across the bay should do the trick."

"Do you think we should contact the police and have them take Habib to St. Thomas?"

Steve didn't need to think about it. "We're getting closer to the truth. Let's stay the course and see what else happens."

"Does that mean you think someone tried to make it appear Habib tried to kill Malcolm?"

"That's one theory. Tell all the executives they're not allowed to go anywhere on the island alone. We already have them partnered with their counterpart."

"Except Habib and Malcolm."

"Malcolm can tag along with any of the other two-person teams."

"Janice and Clyde won't like it if he chooses them."

"I have a half-baked idea of something special for Clyde and Janice to do."

Heather put extra emphasis on her next words. "You will not keep this plan from me. You've had enough secrets and things are getting out of hand."

Steve flicked away her concern. "Everything's progressing better than you think."

"Your idea of progress and mine are as different as night and day."

Steve pointed to the crowd. "You may not hear them, but the natives are getting restless. Put Habib in solitary confinement and have everyone else burn off energy. When you're finished, come find me and I'll tell you my plan."

"I hope it's better than the one with pugil sticks."

"That one was better than you realize."

Heather moved to the rail and spoke in a tone that didn't invite comment. "Matt, take Habib to his bungalow. Gather everything he brought and return here."

She shifted her gaze. "Habib. You'll stay in the main house until further notice. You'll not leave the bedroom we're assigning you to."

"That's not fair," shouted Habib. "I've done nothing wrong. Someone else put the knife on the stick."

Steve made it to Heather's side. "You have two choices. You can either stay in a bedroom here on the island, or Heather will call the police in St. Thomas and you'll go to jail today."

Matt moved toward Habib. "Let's go. You'll sleep in luxury and won't have to listen to anyone snoring."

"This isn't right. I demand to see an attorney."

Heather said, "You're looking at one." She pointed. "There's two more over there. What's your advice, counselors?"

"Keep your mouth shut," said Janice.

Clyde added, "You'll have a private bedroom and bathroom. Make the most of it while you can."

"I agree," said Heather. "You've now seen and heard from three attorneys. Go with Matt and get your possessions."

Heather looked at her watch. "Everyone else will go to your bungalow, and put on bathing suits and the quick-dry shirts we gave you. Meet Bella on the beach. You'll swim until it's time for lunch. Be sure you put on sunscreen."

Habib found a silver cloud in his otherwise dark day. "At least I won't have to swim."

Clyde added a thought as the group dispersed. "Don't get too close to the pier. Janice and I need to spear more fish for tonight's supper and tomorrow's lunch."

The group scattered. Bella climbed the steps and approached Heather and Steve. "How long do you want me to play lifeguard?"

"About an hour," said Steve.

Heather added, "I want you about forty yards from the pier and Matt, the same distance from the reef on the far side. All we're trying to do is expend the adrenaline and take their minds off what happened this morning."

That was all the explanation Bella needed. She pulled the door open and Heather led Steve inside. He went to the recliner he'd staked out and sat without saying another word.

Bella soon reappeared with a shine of sunblock on her face, wearing a straw hat, and carrying flippers. "Just in case," she said, while walking past.

Heather didn't speak until Matt delivered Habib. She rose and said, "I'll take him to his room. Go to the beach. Bella knows what to do and when to come back for lunch."

Matt cut his eyes toward Habib. "Are you sure you don't want me to stay?"

"I've seen him fight. There's nothing to worry about."

Heather then directed her words to Habib. "I'll show you to your room. You'll receive meals there unless we tell you otherwise."

Habib surrendered to his fate, but got off one impotent protest as he walked toward the hallway leading to the bedrooms. "I'm a proud man, not a thief or a man of violence."

Heather pointed to the open door that would mark the boundary of Habib's captivity. She entered and rolled his suitcase into the room. It still had an airline luggage tag laced through the handle. She stepped back and he passed her carrying a backpack, a gym bag, and a plastic sack containing what she assumed was dirty clothes or extra shoes. As soon as he was inside, he kicked the door shut.

Steve was waiting for her by the sliding patio door. Instead of inquiring about Habib, he asked, "Did you take a head count of everyone swimming or fishing?"

"I assume everyone is in the water except Habib and Pearl. She's in the kitchen."

"What about Dorcas?"

Heather picked up binoculars and opened the patio door. "She should be easy to spot. She can swim, but doesn't want to. I told her she could avoid the sun, so I bet she's lying down in the women's bungalow."

Steve gestured with his cane and said, "Let's go on the patio. I'll sit in the shade while you look for Dorcas."

Heather scanned the beach, paying attention to the spots under the few palm trees that offered shade. "Like I said, she has to be in the bungalow."

"Good," said Steve. "She won't be able to hear us."

"No one can with the door closed."

"Pull up a chair and I'll tell you my plan."

Heather did as he instructed and sat where she could see the bungalows and the beach with a simple twist of her head. "I'm ready."

Steve folded his collapsible cane and placed it on the planks next to his chair. "I want Habib to think we believe he didn't strap the knife to the pugil stick or make it so the pillow would fall off so easily."

"You're doing the same thing with Habib that you did with Janice," said Heather. "You convinced her that we thought she had nothing to do with the thefts or murder. Please tell me you didn't change your mind and take her off our list of suspects."

Steve's chin came down and then rose back to its original position. "Everyone from Boston is a suspect. Let's talk about Habib."

Heather gave him a sideways glance. "The tone of your voice tells me you're up to something sneaky."

She neither expected nor received a response to her verbal jab. Instead, he kept talking. "Habib believes the police will charge him with attempted murder. It's possible that someone took the pugil stick during the night and turned it into a deadly weapon. They knew Habib and Malcolm spent yesterday making padded sticks they would use to strike each other. It's my understanding it took very little for the pillow to fall off and expose the knife."

"I looked at the twine holding the pillow on. Someone cut it."

"That's what I suspected. Let's talk to Habib and tell him we need his help to find the person who's trying to frame him."

"How is he going to help us?"

"By staying in his room for the next day or two. I'm hoping whoever set him up will make a mistake."

"And if they don't?"

"There's several days before we leave. We'll think of something."

Heather sighed. "Our week hasn't turned out anything like we planned. What's one more adjustment?"

The patio door slid open, interrupting the meeting. Pearl stood in the doorway. "I heard that fancy phone ringing in your room, Miss Heather."

"That could only be Father." Heather placed a hand on Steve's shoulder as she passed him. "I'll bring the phone out here, and we can both talk to him."

29

T he tile floor was cool on Heather's bare feet as she walked
    to her bedroom. She thanked Pearl for notifying her that
the satellite phone had come to life while she and Steve were
outside. She reached her room and looked at the phone's screen.
Sure enough, her father's name and number appeared.

Once back on the patio with the door shut, Heather
returned the call and enabled the speaker. Her father wasted no
words on pleasantries. "I'm calling off your investigation. Get my
employees back to Boston as soon as possible."

Heather bristled at the command. She and her father had
butted heads all their lives. They'd mostly reconciled in the last
few years, which only came about by realizing their tempera-
ments were so similar they functioned best by owning separate
companies. There were still days, like today, that their reconcilia-
tion hung by a thread.

Steve must have sensed that father and daughter were two
shifting tectonic plates. A major earthquake was imminent if he
didn't stabilize the conversation. He spoke as Heather was
inhaling a full breath to deliver a salvo of stinging words. "Good
morning, Mr. McBlythe. It's clear you've spoken to Dorcas.
There's more to the story than she told you."

"She told me enough to make me realize there was an attempt to kill Heather's CFO, and Habib Patel is under some sort of house arrest. Is that true or not?"

"Not entirely," said Steve in a calm voice. "I'm responsible for the contest and knew the skill level of both contestants. Believe me when I say this couldn't have been more of a mismatch. The contest resulted in giving us much needed physical evidence that will help us reveal the person or persons responsible for the crimes in Boston."

"From what Dorcas told me, Habib is responsible."

"That's what Heather and I want people to think."

Heather had heard enough. "Father, you're an amazing businessman, but you don't know a thing about solving crimes. That goes double for murders."

Allister shot back. "That may be, but I understand risk. It doesn't take a genius to see you're playing fast and loose with the lives of my most valuable employees."

"Didn't you hear what Steve said? We orchestrated the event."

"Of course I heard, and that's the problem. Despite your careful plan, someone on the island tried to kill your CFO. I can't believe you're so cavalier with people's safety."

Steve inserted himself into the fray. "Let's take a deep breath before we continue. Sparring with each other won't bring us to a resolution."

Heather puffed out her cheeks and released the trapped air.

Steve made sure his exhale was loud and long. He added a second deep breath for good measure.

"I'll mediate between you two," said Steve. "Mr. McBlythe, what do you propose?"

"I want you to call the police in St. Thomas and have them arrest Habib as soon as possible. I also want Heather to charter a boat and have everyone off the island by nightfall."

Steve held up a hand to halt Heather's immediate reply. "Heather. What do you propose?"

"That Father abides by our original agreement, and we continue our investigation in whatever way we determine is best." She added a postscript. "Without his interference."

"That's progress," said Steve. "We now have a starting point. Heather, are you willing to compromise on the time we'll stay on the island?"

Steve prompted her with a firm nod. She grudgingly said, "I guess we could cut it short a day."

Steve then asked, "Mr. McBlythe, are you willing to hold off on involving the police?"

"No."

Heather shot back. "Then I'll retract my offer to end our investigation early. In fact, I'll call the police and tell them there's nothing illegal going on here and you're an overprotective billionaire who received a false report from a misguided and possibly delusional employee whom you sent to spy on us. Who do you think they'll believe? Two former cops who helped them solve a murder last year, or a man sitting in an office a thousand miles away?"

"That's not fair."

"It's called leverage, and I have it. I'll put my offer back on the table if you'll negotiate in good faith."

Several long seconds passed. "I still want the police involved."

Steve nodded, so she said, "The police can come, but not until our investigation is complete."

"I want input into that decision."

"No way."

Steve interrupted. "Heather spoke too soon. She needs details so she can make a more informed decision."

"A well-informed decision is what I want to make, too. I'm coming to the island."

"When?"

"Today."

Heather shook her head. "You couldn't make it today, even if you tried."

"Then tomorrow."

"Give us one extra day," said Heather. "You can fly to St. Thomas or St. Croix tomorrow and arrive by either boat or helicopter the next morning."

"Agreed."

Steve grinned. "Well done. That's genuine progress. What have we missed?"

Silence again settled in before Mr. McBlythe said, "I still want to end the investigation early."

Heather shook her head, but held her words. Steve filled the void. "When do you want your employees to leave?"

"Thursday evening at the latest."

Heather countered with, "Our investigation didn't start until last Saturday, and my people didn't arrive until Sunday."

Steve burst in. "Heather wants Saturday and Allister wants Thursday. They'll leave on Friday. That concludes negotiations."

The end came so fast that it left Heather and her father with nothing to say. Steve told him they were looking forward to his arrival and handed the phone back to Heather. Her father had already disconnected the call.

She spoke with a grumble in her voice. "You gave up the extra day too soon. I could have gotten him to agree to take everyone from Boston home on Saturday."

Steve quirked a smile. "I didn't tell him what time they would leave on Friday. I interpret that to mean before midnight."

It was an insignificant victory over her father, but a victory all the same. Heather leaned forward. "It's times like this that make me glad you're my business partner."

"That's good, because we need to find a killer before they strike again. Let's discuss what we know so far, but first I need some water. I'm detoxing."

Heather couldn't help but chuckle. "You never detox."

"I'm getting a jump on what I'll eat and drink when we get

back to civilization. You didn't tell me this makeshift fat-farm wouldn't have dessert on the menu." He raised an index finger. "Before we review the suspects, let's get Habib out here and tell him we don't think he tried to kill Malcolm."

"I'll get him and bring your water."

30

Three knocks on the door failed to yield a response from Habib. Heather tried to turn the doorknob, but it wouldn't yield. She banged louder. "Habib, it's Heather. Steve and I would like to speak to you."

"Leave me alone."

She didn't blame him for being upset, but the testy conversation with her father had left her in a sour mood. "Don't be childish. We have good news for you. We'll wait for you on the patio, but only for the next twenty minutes. It won't be long before the rest of the executives return from swimming and we'll be ready for lunch."

"I don't care. You've turned them all against me."

Heather didn't expect to encounter a petulant CFO and wasn't sure how to handle the situation. She pounded louder this time. "I refuse to shout at this door. Come out now or stay locked in there until the boat comes to pick us up. I don't care."

"You said the police would come for me."

"Steve and I will explain when you come outside. I'll have a glass of cold water waiting for you." She spun on the heel of her bare foot and stomped toward the kitchen. The click of the lock on Habib's door sounded behind her.

Habib came to a stop as she was filling two regular glasses and a larger one for Steve with ice and water. She handed him two of them. "One for you and the big one for Steve."

He took them and tilted his head. "I don't understand. One minute you tell me I'm under some sort of house arrest and the next you insist I come out of my room."

"Take Steve his water and we'll explain."

Heather slid the patio door shut behind her as Steve sat in the shade. "Ah. There you are, Habib. How's the room?"

"I'm not used to having my freedom restricted. Otherwise, it's a very nice room. I brought your water."

"Excellent. Pull up a chair and let's talk. I can tell by the sound of ice in your glass that you have something to drink. Isn't it nice on the patio? I love the sound of the breeze as it rustles the palm fronds. I can also hear the voices of the people in the bay. They're having some sort of swimming contest."

"I'm thankful that didn't include me."

Steve let out a chuckle. "You're finding things to be thankful for. Well done."

Habib flashed a quizzical look at Heather before returning his gaze to Steve. "Am I in trouble or not?"

"Yes, and no. We want everyone to believe you are, but we know someone tampered with one of the pugil sticks to make it look like you tried to inflict serious harm on Malcolm."

Heather asked, "Who would do something like that?"

Habib shrugged. "No idea."

Steve took over again. "There's no doubt someone tried to pin the blame on you."

"But why?"

"That's what Heather and I are trying to find out. Do you think they intended you and not Malcolm to be harmed or possibly killed?"

"What makes you think that?"

"The double switch of the pugil sticks. If I hadn't told you and Malcolm to change sticks at the last minute, he would have had the weapon with the knife strapped to it. You experienced how skilled he was in its use. He could have killed you before he realized there was a knife attached."

A shudder coursed through Habib. "That's not a pleasant thought."

"Not at all," said Heather. "Did you know Malcolm before he arrived on the island?"

"I looked him up on your company's website, but I'd never met him."

Steve asked, "What about any of Heather's other department heads?"

"Only what I gleaned on the computer."

"That's what I thought," said Steve before he added, "Here's what we want to do in case you were the intended victim. It's a simple assignment. We want you to stay in your room a while longer."

Heather quickly added, "It's for your protection."

"Just in case," said Steve. "By the way, do you have any fresh ideas about who could have altered the pugil stick?"

Habib answered with a shake of his head, which prompted Heather to tell Steve about the non-verbal response.

"Sorry," said Habib. "I'm not used to communicating with a blind person."

Steve flipped away the apology. "No offense meant and none taken."

Habib dipped his chin and cast his gaze to Heather. "Might I ask a favor?"

"Sure. You're doing us a favor by staying in your room."

"Might I have some books to read? I noticed several on the shelves in the living room."

"Of course. Take all you want to your room."

"Before you go," said Steve. "Heather tells me you displayed rage at the contest with Malcolm. Is that true?"

"Yes."

"And you've had two other fights since your arrival. Have you always had trouble controlling your temper?"

"It is my biggest weakness and has caused me untold shame. I thought it was under control, but so many things this week caused me to act irrationally."

"What things?"

"It started with the intolerable flights and boat ride. Next came the heat and humidity of the island, the fatigue caused by exercise, having to learn to swim, the pressure of having to fight for my job, family pressure, and defending my dissertation. All these squeezed my mind like a vice."

Steve nodded. "You've earned a break. Go to your room and lock the door. Don't think of it as punishment, but as a sabbatical from all your problems."

Habib stood. "I'll tell myself I'm locking the world out instead of locking myself in."

"It's only for a couple of days," said Heather.

"Two days of peace and rest. It sounds like heaven when I say it out loud."

Habib rose, but Heather remained seated. He asked, "Aren't you going to escort me to my room?"

"Why should I? You're on vacation, not under arrest."

Thirty seconds later, Steve asked, "Did he return to his room?"

"He's still in the living room picking out books."

"Let me know when he's gone, and we'll review the suspects."

31

S teve took a long drink from his glass of water before lowering it to the patio. Heather had spent a few minutes organizing her thoughts while monitoring Habib's movements in the living room. She turned to Steve. "He took a stack of books and a couple of magazines back to his room."

"The first thing we need to do is provide a room for your father. He's supposed to be here in two days, but it wouldn't surprise me if he shows up tomorrow."

"What makes you think he'll arrive early?"

"Because it's something you'd do. He didn't enjoy not getting his way on everything. He'll also realize that you outfoxed him on when his employees will leave the island."

"Me? You're the one who shouted 'Friday!' and closed the discussion."

Steve chuckled. "Yeah. That was a nice touch. He'll blame you all the same. Expect him to be here tomorrow afternoon."

Heather released a huff. "You're probably right about him doing something I won't be able to stop. I hope he doesn't come with the police."

Steve reached down and picked up his glass of water again.

"We're short a bedroom in the main house. Matt will need to go to the men's bungalow tomorrow morning."

Heather's words came out sounding sharp. "If Father comes tomorrow, he can share a room with someone in the bungalow. It will serve him right for violating the terms of the agreement."

Steve shook his head. "You're thinking with your emotions. We have a sales job to do, and it doesn't include poking the bear who happens to be your father. There's nothing we can do if he insists his employees leave the island, by boat or helicopter. Like it or not, we have to make him believe we're close to solving at least two crimes, and possibly all three."

"You're counting the knife attached to the pugil stick as the third."

"Correct."

Heather knew Steve spoke words of wisdom about her father, but she didn't like it. Her next words came out like they were being dragged by a rope. "All right. Matt goes to the bungalow tomorrow, and Father takes his room."

Steve reminded her of something that had slipped her mind. "Don't forget that your father has the connections that allowed us to use this island. That makes him responsible for what takes place here. I'm sure that inconvenient fact hasn't escaped his mind."

Heather held up both hands in surrender. "You made your point. Let's move on. Who do you want to talk about first?"

He answered her question but not directly. "Before we start, I've heard no one talk about Clyde or his problem. Is it safe to say the remedies worked?"

"Much better than expected. Louis Crane saw how much cooler the loss of hair made Clyde and showed up at yoga this morning without a visible follicle. It made him look like he hadn't gone through puberty."

"I had him pictured as being a computer geek with wild hair and a scraggly beard."

"That's the way I described him to you. Louis told me he doesn't much care what he looks like and needed to do something about heat rash. Clyde set the example of how to make the stay here more comfortable. Now there's three slick Willies on the island."

Steve didn't cover his grin. "Clyde might set a fashion trend."

"The best thing that's come out of our time on the island is nobody shuns Clyde anymore, especially Janice."

Steve got down to business. "Let's agree that we're talking about three crimes." He held up his thumb. "First, stolen company secrets. I believe there's sufficient evidence and testimony to verify at least one person stole and sold information from your father's company."

"I agree," said Heather. "I find it interesting that there's been no recent reports."

"Good point," said Steve. "We'll discuss that later." He unfurled his index finger. "The second crime is the assault and resulting murder of Reggie Scott in the parking garage. You and I verified that was the original crime scene."

"*We* didn't determine it was the original crime scene. You did. That gift of associative chromesthesia gives me the shakes every time you use it."

"Me, too. Imagine what it's like living in a dark world and suddenly you can see red or some variation of it."

A few seconds passed before Steve held up the next finger. "Third. Someone tampered with the pugil stick and turned it into a lethal weapon."

"It was likely intended for Habib to be the victim, not Malcolm," said Heather.

"That's a reasonable assumption. We need to come up with a plan to discover who did it. Let's also brainstorm reasons someone would want to set up Habib."

Steve turned toward the beach. "Everyone is getting out of the water. It won't be long before they take showers and come to lunch. We won't have time to complete our review of suspects until this afternoon. What's on their schedule?"

Heather shifted gears mentally. "Showers, lunch, another three-hour session of two-person problem solving. Then, beach volleyball, followed by showers and dinner."

Steve drained his glass of water before lowering it back to the deck. "What we don't finish in the next few minutes, we'll take up while they're wearing themselves out playing volleyball."

A random thought escaped Steve. "We talked a little about Clyde. Are you sure there's no problem with odor now?"

"He's careful to shower at least three times a day, but so far I've smelled nothing but soap and antiperspirant concoctions. The only problem he and Janice have is getting enough sleep. I'm blaming it on the late night walks on the beach."

"Have you noticed anyone else wandering around after supper?"

"Only the two lovebirds."

Heather could tell by his one-syllable use of *huh* that something had crossed his mind. He confirmed it when he asked, "Where did you store the pugil sticks last night?"

"On the patio. They were off to the side with the fishing gear."

The importance of the question hit Heather. "Janice had access to the sticks and an excuse to be out in the middle of the night. She could have left her bungalow any time during the night and people would have thought she was meeting Clyde."

"Do you know what time they went back to the bungalow?"

"I went to bed at eleven. They were sitting under the stars when I last saw them."

"Sitting?" asked Steve with a chuckle.

"More like leaning back on their elbows, but I only glanced."

Heather wanted to use the time wisely, so she said, "Since we're already talking about Janice, what are your thoughts about her?"

"She's near the bottom of my suspect list."

"What about this new information that she could have tampered with the pugil sticks?"

Steve gave a quick response. "So could anyone else. The disadvantage to mentally and physically wearing people out is they're likely to go to bed early and sleep soundly. It would be easy for anyone to rise in the middle of the night and rework the stick."

"True, but Janice was already awake."

"Don't misunderstand me," said Steve. "She's still on my list of suspects. All I'm saying is I can't find a motive for her committing any of the three crimes. She's well paid, the top person in her department, and was content with everything but her love life. That was lacking until Clyde arrived and..." His words trailed off.

"What is it?"

Steve rubbed his chin. "Have you heard anything about Janice and Reggie Scott having a relationship? Wasn't he single?"

"Yes, but I'm not sure anyone on the island would know if they were spending time together in their off hours."

Steve came back with, "Janice knows how to keep secrets." He took a quick breath. "I bet Dorcas would know."

"You're probably right, but she's not been very forthcoming since we pressured her for information. Her loyalty to my father is back stronger than ever."

"Would your father know if they were involved?"

"He can't stand to talk about office romances."

Steve jerked his head up. "It may be out of character for him to ask, but Dorcas will tell your father anything he asks her."

"Does that mean you're moving Janice up on your list of suspects?"

"If Janice and Reggie were romantically involved, and he dumped her, that could give her a powerful motive. I can imagine a shrewd woman like her trying to implicate others, especially Habib."

Steve issued a word of caution. "Even if Janice and Reggie were involved, that's not proof enough for the police to charge her."

Steve had hit on a major problem. Janice was nobody's fool, and if she attacked Reggie, she'd plan it out and cover her tracks. Getting an admission of guilt from such a seasoned attorney would be as likely as snow falling on the island that afternoon.

Heather's gaze shifted as the water-soaked executives trudged up the hill. Most headed for the bungalows. The exceptions were Janice and Clyde, who came to the patio bearing snorkeling equipment and heavy stringers of fish. They were mostly dry, and Janice explained the reason. "It didn't take long for us to spear all we needed for today. We took a short walk, found a shady spot, and took a nap."

Clyde's smile made Heather wonder if Janice had given a full report on their activities. He cleared his throat and said, "We need to clean these fish."

The door slid shut behind them and Heather whispered her thoughts. "I hope she doesn't break Clyde's heart."

"And you accused me of being a romantic," said Steve.

Bella arrived, climbed the patio steps, and pulled off her wet shirt, revealing a perfectly sculpted body covered by a none-too-modest two-piece bathing suit. She would have been more discreet in front of her father. Steve's blindness had a way of reducing her modesty. Likewise, Heather had grown so used to Steve's loss of vision that she thought nothing of wearing sleep-wear in front of him.

Steve must have recognized the sound of her footsteps because he launched into his first question. "Who's the strongest swimmer?"

Bella wrung the water out of her quick-dry shirt. "Louise King, and it wasn't close. She went to college on a swimming scholarship and swims almost daily."

Heather said, "Swimming and computers are her passions."

Steve asked, "Are the others holding up physically?"

"The water and sun took a lot out of them. Louis Crane developed leg cramps. Matt put him in the shade, gave him a liter of cold water, and fed him a banana. I thought Bob Brown was struggling, but he was pacing himself."

Steve shifted in his chair. "Does Matt think we're pushing them too hard?"

"Not if we keep them out of the midday sun. He believes most will acclimate to the heat, humidity, and schedule by tomorrow." Bella wadded her shirt into a ball. "I need to get the salt water off me and out of my clothes. Is there anything else?"

"One more thing," said Steve. "Have you heard anyone talk about the case?"

"Whispers," said Bella.

"Oh?"

"About half believe Habib is responsible for what happened today and they're glad he's locked in his room. Others aren't convinced, and some don't seem to care. They're just trying to make it through the week."

"Thanks, Bella," said Heather. "Keep looking and listening. You're helping more than you think you are."

"The only thing that could make this island better is if Adam was here. Otherwise, who can complain about getting great exercise, wonderful food, and watching you two solve crimes?"

It was Steve's turn to speak. "We'll try to live up to your expectations."

Lunch was a quiet event. Next came hours of brain-stretching problems to solve, followed by beach volleyball for the executives. During the contests, Heather and Steve spent two hours reviewing the four primary suspects: Habib Patel, Bob Brown, Janice Peltier, and Louis Crane. They concluded that the best course of action was to ask Heather's father to question Dorcas and see if she knew more than she had been willing to tell them. Steve believed Allister would arrive the next day. She wasn't so sure.

By the end of the day, Heather began to question Bella's confidence in her and Steve. She went to bed and tried to assign motives to each suspect. Her pillow seemed to pull her downward.

Heather believed she awoke to the sound of beating helicopter rotors outside the home. She went outside and saw her father striding across the yard, his face stern, as yoga mats flew into the air. Two policemen in uniform followed close behind Mr. Allister McBlythe IV,

She shook her head like a dog would after chasing a stick into a pond. She looked at her watch and realized her father's arrival was only a dream. Or was it a look into the future? Either way, her confidence in solving the cases flowed out on the tide.

Perhaps Steve had come up with a plan. She rose and crept barefoot into the living room. He hadn't moved from the recliner. Sonorous breaths were deep and regular. If he'd had a revelation on how to proceed, it would need to wait until daylight peeked over the island's tall hill.

32

It was out of the ordinary for Heather not to rise from a night's sleep when her alarm first sounded. It was also highly unusual for her alarm to be followed by a man's voice calling for help. She threw back the covers, sprang from the bed, and made for the living room. Luckily, she'd worn pajamas that were modest compared to the lingerie she normally wore.

Steve lowered the recliner's footrest and sat up straight as he groped to find his sunglasses. Matt stood by the sliding glass door with Louis Crane's arm draped over his broad shoulders. Her personal trainer offered a word of explanation. "I found him by the patio steps. There's blood on the back of his head."

"What happened?" asked Louis. The slurring of his speech reminded Heather of dealing with drunks when she wore the badge of a Boston police officer.

"Bring him to the couch," said Heather.

Pearl appeared from the kitchen. She had a dishtowel draped over her shoulder and offered it. Heather said, "Bring an icepack." The chef beat a quick retreat to the kitchen.

"Let's look at his head," said Heather. Matt stopped and helped Louis sit on the couch. She maneuvered to inspect his head. "The cut looks small and shallow. There's a nice lump rising, which is a good sign. I'm glad you shaved your head. I can see everything without having to move your hair out of the way.

She stood in front of him and held up her hand with fingers spread. "How many fingers am I holding up?"

"All five on your right hand."

"Very good. Follow my finger with your eyes. Don't move your head." Heather watched as his eyes moved in unison with her finger. "Your pupils look even and you're able to follow my finger. How do you feel?"

"Better than I did a few minutes ago. Did a coconut fall on me?"

Heather shifted her gaze to Matt, who said, "I didn't see one, but it was still dark."

Bella came into the living room dressed for yoga. "What's going on?"

Steve answered, "That's what Heather's trying to find out. You and Matt go outside and look for something that could have struck Louis."

Pearl appeared with crushed ice inside a plastic bag and a folded dishtowel. Heather took them from her, wrapped the bag of ice in the towel, and handed it to Louis. "Can you hold this on the lump?"

He grimaced when the icepack pressed on the back of his head, but he left it in place. Heather then asked, "Do you feel dizzy?"

"Not anymore."

"Is your vision blurred?"

"No. Everything's clear."

"Close one eye, and then the other, and tell me if one is clearer than the other."

He did as instructed, then said, "Nope. All clear in both eyes."

"Good. Can you tell us what happened?"

"Beats me. One minute I'm taking the first step up to the

patio and the next I'm lying in the yard with a shooting pain in my head."

Steve took over. "Did you hear, see, or smell anything?"

"Not that I recall. I went out early to put the yoga mats in the yard."

Heather checked his eyes again. "No yoga for you today. You'll need to take it easy."

"Bummer. I was getting into the stretching and meditation. It's pretty nice to take your mind out of gear and chill."

Steve wasn't giving up on trying to gather information. "With injuries of this type, it's not unusual for people to remember things after the pain subsides. If you recall anything else about what happened, tell Heather or me about it. Don't worry if it makes little sense or you think it's not important. We want to hear anything and everything."

Bella and Matt opened the patio door. Bella motioned for Heather to come outside. She nudged Steve on the way and whispered. "Come outside."

Heather shut the door behind them. Matt did the talking. "No coconuts."

Bella took over. "The only thing we found was the priest. It was on top of one of the spearguns."

Matt added his contribution to the story of the search. "Bella told me not to touch it. She said it looks like it might have blood on it."

Bella quickly added, "It's probably fish blood, but I didn't want to risk contaminating the evidence."

"Good girl," said Steve. "Heather will bag and tag it. That bat could be a crucial piece of evidence. Let's get back inside."

Once the door slid shut behind them, Steve asked, "Is everyone who knows Louis received a bump on the head where they can hear me?"

"All but Pearl," said Heather. "She's in the kitchen."

"Get her. We don't have much time before the others show up."

Heather scurried to the kitchen and soon returned with the chef. Pearl announced, "Coffee's ready if anyone wants a cup before Yoga."

Steve ignored the offer. "Listen, everyone. Louis slipped going up the stairs and fell backward."

"I did?"

Heather knew this was the story Steve wanted to spread, so she played along. "Louis first thought a coconut fell on him, but Bella and Matt found nothing when they searched. The only plausible explanation is he slipped and hit his head."

Bella chimed in. "That's right. We both searched the yard. No coconuts."

Pearl might have wondered why she had to hear the announcement, but simply shrugged and went back to the kitchen. Heather followed her and came back with a plastic trash bag. She walked to the door and placed her hand on the handle. Bella followed her and whispered, "I'll get it. People are arriving from the bungalows, and you're not exactly dressed to bag evidence or do yoga."

A huff of exasperation came from Heather as she looked down at her sleepwear. "Start yoga without me after you retrieve the bat. I need to talk to Steve and drink a cup of coffee. Not necessarily in that order."

The day started out of sequence and continued that way. Heather grabbed a cup of coffee on the way to the bedroom and started on it before she put on her exercise clothes and brushed her teeth. She then went to the living room where Steve had an assignment that prevented her from taking part in yoga for the time being.

"Are there chairs on the beach?" he asked.

"There's two Adirondack chairs under a palm tree near the water and the pier."

"That's perfect. Take me there and leave me. I was waiting for someone to make a mistake. I believe they did."

Heather waited until they were halfway down the hill before

she said, "You're on the verge of a breakthrough. When are you planning on telling me?"

"I need several hours of uninterrupted thinking to make sure all the pieces fit together."

A tingle went up Heather's spine. "How sure are you?"

"Ninety-nine percent, give or take. We may need help from your father to seal the deal. I'm glad he's coming."

"I dreamed he came by helicopter with two burly policemen."

"Detectives or uniformed?"

"They were both Matt's size and wore dress uniforms."

Steve shook his head. "Cancel that portion of the dream. Send detectives if you have to, but I don't think we'll need them."

Heather settled him in the chair as waves lapped to shore a short distance away. "Do you need anything else?"

Steve didn't respond. He'd already placed himself in a world that shut out sound. It occurred to her on the trip up the hill that two members of the Boston staff wouldn't be present for the day's activities and challenges. Habib was pretending to be under house arrest while Louis would spend the morning with an ice pack on the back of his head. She'd need to check on him periodically to make sure he hadn't suffered a concussion. What would her father think? Perhaps he wouldn't arrive until tomorrow.

Heather let out a laugh and spoke out loud to herself. "Fat chance of that. He's likely halfway to St. Croix already."

She made it to the front yard and tried to still her mind. Yoga might help, so she assumed all the positions on Bella's command, but her mind wouldn't cooperate. Thoughts of suspects and possibilities of matching people with crimes spun her thoughts as if they were on the last cycle of a washing machine.

The session seemed to go on forever. The facts simply wouldn't go into an order that made any sense. She finally gave up and decided if yoga wouldn't help her think clearly, perhaps a couple of hard runs up the mountain would do the trick. She led the pack and tacked on a third hill climb for good measure. Some joined her for the extra trip, including Janice and Clyde.

The two stopped at the house after their third hill climb to gather snorkeling gear and spearguns. They ran down the hill, slipped off their shoes and socks, and plunged into the water. Once again, Heather hoped Janice hadn't done something stupid back in Boston. She'd never seen Clyde so happy.

Heather followed the couple's lead and cooled off by taking a quick dip in the bay. She stopped where Steve sat. "Are you ready to go back to the house?"

He shook his head. "Not yet. I'm enjoying listening to the lovebirds swim. Janice announced her first catch of the day. I didn't know if she was talking about Clyde or a fish."

"I'm guessing both," said Heather.

Steve shifted in the chair. "I'll get Bella to bring me up the hill. You'd better prepare to receive your father. Whatever you do, don't get into a fight with him. I'm more convinced than ever that we need him to solve these crimes."

"I might have to bite my tongue. We both know how to push each other's buttons."

"Then wear shorts with deep pockets and keep your hands in them. No button-pushing today."

"That's never worked in the past, but I'll try to behave myself." She considered leaving him alone with his thoughts but only made it one step. "I'm sensing you've solved the crimes."

Steve gave his head a slow nod. "Evidence is in short supply."

"What about motive?"

"That's what we need your father's help with. There may not be enough hard evidence." He reached and patted the arm of the chair next to his. "Have a seat. If we were playing poker, this is when I'd show you my cards."

"I was wondering how long I'd have to wait."

"If your father arrives today, and he agrees to our plan, we should wrap these cases up tonight."

This was the moment Heather had been waiting for. One by one, Steve reviewed the crimes, the suspects, and possible motives. The session took the better part of an hour.

Heather did her part by challenging him on every conclusion he'd reached. It was the attorney coming out of her, and Steve said he appreciated it. Better to face tough questions by a trusted colleague than be wrong and accuse the wrong person.

They were down to the motive for the assault at daybreak when Steve raised his chin. With dark glasses on, he seemed to look out to sea. "Unless I'm hearing things, your father is approaching from the direction of St. Thomas. Do you see a helicopter?"

Heather shaded her eyes with her hand. Steve was right again. "Let's hope he's in a mood to listen to us."

Steve's feet found his sandals and slipped them on. "It's a simple plan, and your father's a reasonable man. If I miss anything, you can add to it. I hope your acting skills are in excellent form."

33

The thump-thump of the helicopter's rotors sounded as Heather looked over her shoulder. "Oh, for heaven's sake," she shouted. "I didn't tell anyone to pick up the yoga mats before I attacked the hill this morning. The yard is where the helicopter will land."

She let go of Steve. "Stay here. I need to wave off the landing."

"Go on. I'll find my way."

Heather sprinted up the hill, waving her arms, making frantic X's. The pilot either didn't see her, paid no attention, or was under instructions from her father to land. Regardless, mats fluttered and folded. The pilot must have had extensive military training as he came in fast before lifting the nose and settling the skids on the giant H painted in white on the grass.

Mats flew in every direction, some going skyward, and one stuck in the top of the palm tree that shaded the patio. The back door to the helicopter opened and out popped her father with an overnight bag. He reached behind him and extracted two large wooden boxes and sat them on the ground. Once out from under the path of the beating blades, he crossed the yard and climbed the steps to the patio.

Rotors increased in velocity as soon as the lone passenger was clear. As quickly as it had arrived, the chopper lifted off the ground. It turned to face the bay and pointed toward the water as it rose.

Heather fumed when she scanned the landscape. Mats lay scattered as if a waterspout had paid a quick visit. She jogged up the patio's steps and approached her father, who was pulling a comb through his gray hair. "Was that necessary?"

He answered her question with one of his own. "Don't you know that helicopter pads are to be free of obstructions at all times?"

"You could have told the pilot to circle. This isn't a war zone."

"Are you sure? The reports I've received tell me there've been multiple instances of violence since you arrived."

"Nothing that we haven't handled."

Heather looked away and noticed the patio door stood open. Inside were the executives from both offices. There had been no attempt from her or her father to muffle their words. Some seemed to enjoy the display of raw emotions, their smirks giving evidence to the fact that she and her father were mere mortals.

The tap of Steve's cane sounded from behind her. "Hello, Mr. McBlythe. How were your flights?"

"Satisfactory. I wish I could say the same about the investigation."

Heather attempted to change the mood. She noticed her father's personal assistant standing in the doorway. "Dorcas, would you mind taking Father's bag and showing him to his room?"

"My pleasure," she replied as she addressed her boss. "I cleaned your room, bathroom, and made sure there are fresh sheets on your bed."

"Thank you."

Steve spoke next. "Once you get settled, we'll have lunch."

"Everyone?" asked Allister.

"All but Habib Patel," said Heather. "He takes meals in his room."

Allister responded with a grunt that could mean anything.

Heather wanted Dorcas to perform one more task. "Would you mind introducing Father to my employees? I'm sure he knows them by name, but he hasn't met them in person."

Dorcas gave her head a rather regal nod. "Of course."

Heather and Steve waited outside while her father took time to speak to each of his employees and those from Texas.

Steve leaned into her. "So far, so good."

"I have my fingers crossed."

"Let's take things slow and allow the island to work its magic."

"What do you propose?"

"Your father likes to be in control. The last time I spoke with him, he said he wanted to spend time with everyone from both offices."

She suspected Steve hadn't told her everything. "When did you speak with him?"

"This morning while you were running up and down the big hill."

"Why didn't you tell me?"

"I wanted you to have a natural reaction to things." He chuckled. "You didn't realize it, but everyone but you stacked their mats on the porch before they ran up the big hill."

"Did you put them back in the yard?"

"It was mostly Bella. I wanted your father to make a dramatic arrival. One more thing to distract the killer."

Heather shook her head and stared at him. "Your secrets are going to be the death of me. Now I have to get a yoga mat out of the top of a palm tree."

Steve shrugged. "That's easy. Make getting it down the first challenge of the afternoon. Whoever comes up with the best solution has their option of playing beach volleyball or resting in the shade."

Since the palm tree didn't provide enough shade for the long table, they took the noon meal inside. Heather surrendered her seat at the head of the table to her father. Steve anchored the other end with Bella at his right hand. Conversation ceased as the group dug into lunch.

Steve expressed Heather's sentiments when he said, "I was wondering if I'd tire of eating so much fresh fish. The answer is a definite no. I'm so thankful for the skill of Clyde and Janice in providing the fish and Pearl amazing us with the variety of dishes she cooks."

Allister put his fork down and swallowed. "I've never tasted better. This gives me hope that something good will come out of this retreat."

Janice spoke up. "I'm not sure I could stand it if things were any better."

Clyde's shaved head dipped. Heather never thought she'd see the bulldog attorney blush, but his face took on the color of pink rose petals.

"Knock it off, you two," said Bob Brown.

Heather challenged him. "I may be wrong, but are you missing someone back in Boston?"

"More than you know. It's amazing how much this trip has straightened out my thinking."

Allister looked at his acquisition specialist. "I'd like to hear more about that in private." He cast his gaze to the employees from both offices. "In fact, I'd like to meet with each of you privately this afternoon."

Steve spoke from the far end of the table. "Great idea. Heather can arrange a schedule. How long would you like each interview to last?"

Heather spoke up. "Since we're on island time, why don't I post a list of names, but leave it up to Father to decide how long each interview will last?"

Her father leaned back, took in a deep breath, and released it. "I've been rushing to and from appointments all my life.

Perhaps it's time to slow down. The idea of being on island time appeals to me." He faced Heather. "When everyone's finished with lunch, I'll start with Habib in his room. It seems he has the most to answer for."

Heather made a point of looking to see how those assembled around the table reacted to her father's words. Janice looked at Clyde with raised eyebrows. Bob Brown either took the news in stride or had other things on his mind. Louis Crane shifted his gaze from left to right, before taking another bite of blackened fish.

As for Heather's employees, her CFO gave a slight nod. Was he signaling he believed he had the inside track on keeping his job? Perhaps.

Louise King cast a quick glance toward her counterpart in information technology, Louis Crane. No change in facial expression occurred.

Heather concluded they were a tough group to read. Not surprising for a gathering of top professionals.

The meal concluded with a round of applause given to Pearl. The rotating schedule meant washing dishes and cleaning the kitchen went to Heather's employees. It came as a mild surprise that Janice and Clyde volunteered to help. She explained by saying, "It took so little time to get fish this morning that we feel guilty for not doing more to help."

Louise King chimed in with a proverb. "My mother always told me that many hands make for light work. Count me in for helping clean the kitchen."

Bob Brown asked, "Would it be all right if I went fishing instead of playing volleyball this afternoon?"

Heather answered, "That depends. If you and Brent win the first brain challenge of the afternoon, you can do whatever you want during the time you normally play volleyball."

"Anything we want?" asked Brent.

Steve spoke up. "You need to stay in sight."

Allister joined in. "I'm the one responsible for that island rule. After the incident with the knife, I decided it's best to monitor your whereabouts. It's not meant to spy, but to protect you from potential harm."

"That's fine with me," said Brent. "Even if Bob and I win the competition, I'd like to play beach volleyball. What's the challenge?"

Heather rose from her chair. "Everyone come out on the patio and I'll tell you."

Chairs slid backward on the tile floor as the gathering rose and walked to the patio door. Once outside, Heather gave the assignment. "Wind from the helicopter sent the yoga mats flying. Those of you who aren't cleaning the kitchen will gather the mats and return them to the deck. Once completed, you'll divide into your two-person teams and solve today's first brain challenge." She pointed to the top of the palm tree. "You're to develop a plan to retrieve the mat lodged in the fronds of this tree. You cannot cause damage to the mat, the tree, or any other natural vegetation."

Heather added, "You must submit your plan before attempting to retrieve the mat."

The group filed back inside and cleared the table. Steve waited in the recliner he'd claimed as his own. It was either the sound of her footfalls or the smell of Bella's lavender-scented soap that caused him to hold up a hand to signal the young woman to stop.

She knelt by his side. "What can I do for you, boss?"

It wasn't unusual for Bella to give him this title when he included her in one of their investigations.

He crooked a finger and motioned for her to lean close. Heather couldn't make out a word. He kept talking while Bella jerked back and said, "Really? That's..." Tears choked off any additional words.

After planting a kiss on Steve's cheek, Bella made for her room.

Heather took Bella's place beside Steve. She tried to sound

serious. "That's one secret too many, Mr. Smiley. What did you tell Bella?"

He wagged an index finger from side to side. "No, you don't. It's an island secret."

Heather lowered her voice. "I can read Bella. Those were tears of joy. What have you done?"

He grinned. "I'm reclaiming my title as the top romantic on the island. Adam's flying in from Puerto Rico tomorrow morning. He's meeting her at the airport on St. Thomas."

The shock of the announcement soon wore off. Heather didn't know whether to hug him or lambaste him for keeping one more thing from her. For once, she practiced restraint. "What time is Bella leaving?"

"I'm not sure when the police helicopter will be here to pick them up. Sometime tomorrow morning. I thought Bella would get a kick out of helping transport a prisoner."

Steve kept talking. "By the way, I need to talk to you about tonight."

"Oh?"

"Yeah, let's go back to the beach and I'll fill you in on other details. I've been thinking so hard it occurred to me that I forgot to tell you who committed the crimes. I hope you can forgive me —again. Old habits are hard to break."

Heather clenched her teeth to keep her anger from spilling out in words she would later regret. She put Steve's hand on her forearm and led him to the chairs on the beach. Without saying a word, she left him there and walked away. She'd need to have another long talk with Steve, but not until she brought her emotions under control. She stepped to the pier, and continued on until she stood on the last plank. While looking out to sea, she took in a huge breath and screamed as loud and long as she could.

After easing herself down and dangling her feet over water so clear it seemed unreal, she stared at the fish and wondered why she was so angry. Steve always told her everything she really needed to know, but not on her timeline. He'd done the same thing to every partner he'd ever worked with when he was a homicide detective. It was a part of Steve she didn't particularly like, but she couldn't deny his results.

Her thoughts went to her employees. She did virtually the same thing to them on this trip by not divulging the real reason for them being on the island. Steve had said that the best way to keep a secret is to tell no one. They both had practiced that simple truth.

She rose and walked on the weathered wood back to shore. Heather eased down in the chair beside him. He asked, "Are you all right?"

"I am, but I won't be if you don't start talking."

Steve's stomach jiggled. It was a prelude to laughter spilling out. "You and your father are so much alike. He insisted I tell him everything, just like you are."

"That's what partners are supposed to do."

Ignoring her dig, Steve dragged a hand down his cheek. "It's going to be tricky, but I believe we have an excellent opportunity to get a confession tonight."

Time lost its meaning as Steve explained all as the waves washed to shore.

34

Heather patted Steve's hand at the conclusion of his explanation. She rose from her chair before speaking. "Confessions are hard to extract from shrewd people. I hope you're right about how everyone will react." She looked toward the house on the hill. "I need to check on the teams working on the challenge."

"Who do you think will win?"

Heather considered the participants before stating, "Clyde and Janice. They're both brilliant. Legal training helps people come up with unique solutions to tough problems."

"You may be right, but I don't believe they'll win this time."

"Why not?"

"They're too distracted. I didn't turn into a decent cop until Maggie and I were married for five years." He scratched his head. "Or was it six?"

While she'd used cold logic to form an answer, Steve looked at the bigger picture, which included deep emotions. That ability set him apart from anyone she'd ever known; he could see more facets of people even though he was blind.

When she arrived at the house, the teams were all inside. Bob and Brent must have finished early as they were both napping. Louise sat at the table reading a book while Louis, the second IT expert, sat on the couch with feet thrust forward, snoring. Janice and Clyde were nowhere in sight.

Malcolm Swift, Heather's CFO, stood and stretched. "I came up with a plan for getting the mat down, but it's not very good."

Instead of responding to Malcolm's comment, she asked, "Do you know where Clyde and Janice are?"

"They said they were going for a walk. Their solution to the problem is on the table."

The conversation roused those sleeping. Heather gathered the proposals and went onto the patio to read them. All were short, including Clyde and Janice's two sentences. *Shoot it with a speargun. Make sure the line is long enough and drag it down.*

It was a workable solution, but one that would damage the mat. Not good enough, and Steve was right again. One down and three to go.

She read Malcolm's. He proposed finding downed branches, lashing them end to end until they were long enough to reach the top of the tree and dislodge the mat. This might work, but would require a multi-part, unwieldy pole. Her company money-man was right. It wasn't a good solution.

The third solution came from the two computer geeks and didn't deserve a second look. *Either wait for a tropical storm or we'll buy you a new one.*

Hope for a decent solution was running low when Heather read Bob and Brent's proposal to save the mat. *Cast a fishing weight over the mat, snag the edge, and slowly slide it off the frond.*

She went inside and declared the two procurement specialists the winners. They would both receive their previously stated desires. Bob could fish while Brent played beach volleyball. None of the losers seemed disappointed, and all cheered as Bob put his solution to the test. The mat fluttered down and saved Bob steps by landing on the deck. If only all problems were so easy to fix.

An hour remained before beach volleyball. Steve still sat in the shade near the water, clearly visible in a royal purple shirt.

She didn't have the heart to tell him the penguins sliding down large chunks of ice didn't match the tropical theme of his other shirts.

A passing thought went through her mind. Should she assign the teams another brain-teaser? The question fled faster than it had arrived. The executives from both offices deserved a break. She announced, "You're free to do whatever you want until it's time for volleyball."

The executives thanked her. Those that had spoken with her father retreated to their bungalows. When she reentered the main house, her father was waiting. "That was nice of you." He pointed toward the deck. "Let's go outside."

"It's warmer than what you're used to."

"Good. I spend far too much time indoors."

The ever-present breeze provided the perfect amount of cooling. Her father closed his eyes and allowed his normally rigid posture to droop. He spoke in a soft tone. "Your mother didn't like the tropics."

The statement took her aback. "How could anyone not enjoy this?"

"She didn't allow herself to. I was just as bad until I became interested in investing in cruise lines. It helped that you told me the only way to investigate the different companies was to get on their ships. The voyages gave me enough time to grieve and to open my eyes to something besides spreadsheets and prospectus reports."

The conversation wasn't what Heather expected. Was her father trying to tell her something? Her natural inclination was to make her questions direct and to the point. This time, something told her to hold off.

Her father talked about several of the cruises he'd taken and which companies he'd purchased stock in. As usual, he'd made timely investments and the returns exceeded his expectations.

She limited her questions and waited for him to broach whatever was on his mind. After a few seconds, he lifted his chin and sat up straight. "I've been rambling."

"That's fine. The islands have that effect on people."

He inhaled a full breath and said, "I've made a decision that might someday affect you."

A sense of panic swept over her. Her words tumbled out before her brain engaged. "You're too young to retire and I'm not prepared to run both companies."

His head tilted to one side, and his mouth opened for a few seconds. A laugh spilled out, followed by several more. It took a while, but he brought the mirth under control and asked, "What in the world made you think I was retiring?"

Heather didn't have a decent answer, so she dredged up a plausible excuse. "I've lived with the cover story of you retiring and our offices merging for weeks. That's been the undercurrent on the island and I guess the story settled in my brain." She looked around. "This place has a way of affecting your thinking."

He took her hand in his. "I know exactly what you mean. That's why I'm choosing this place and time to tell you I'm considering…" He gulped another breath. "I don't know how to say this without sounding juvenile."

It was Heather's turn to tilt her head and allow her jaw to drop. She composed herself and asked, "Are you saying you're hunting for a lady friend."

He issued a toothy grin. "In a word, yes."

It was Heather's turn to laugh. "What a relief! Do you have anyone particular in mind?"

He gave her a coy smile.

Heather held up a hand. "Don't answer that question. It's none of my business and I can't clutter my mind until we get this case solved."

"Speaking of the case—Steve hinted at who's behind all the crimes. I think I've figured it out."

Steve's trip up the hill had gone unnoticed until his cane

tapped the lowest step on the deck. He asked, "Did I hear my name?"

"Father wants to know how to find eligible women to date. I was telling him you weren't the best person to ask."

Steve placed his hand on the handle of the sliding glass door. "That's amazing. You followed a lie with a statement of absolute truth." He removed his hand from the handle. "Allister, I have a favor to ask."

"Ask away."

"Heather and I will explain all tonight and we'll complete the assignment you asked us to help you with. Can you wait until after supper for us to reveal everything?"

"Do you know who stole the secrets?"

"We do."

"And who's responsible for the death of one of my employees?"

"Yes, sir. We also know who tried to shift the blame to others on your staff."

Her father huffed a sigh that seemed to release a heavy burden. "The advantage of age is it teaches one patience."

35

A sense of trepidation fell on Heather as she took her seat next to her father at the dinner table. She mentally reviewed Steve's plan for the evening. It should produce the desired results, but had they missed something? If so, she couldn't imagine what.

Doubts circled her head like seabirds, landing for only a moment before taking flight again. Had they sufficiently distracted the participants? She believed they had, but these were some of the brightest people she'd ever met. Had the killer seen through the smoke?

She refocused and looked around the table. The banter preceding the meal was strong. Tiki torches cast shadows on the faces, giving the scene a spectral glow. As a show of mercy, Habib was allowed to join the feast but remained quiet. Dorcas sat directly across the table from Heather while Steve and Bella sat at the far end. It was showtime.

Heather placed her napkin on her plate and stood. She took her knife and tapped a call to order on her wineglass. "Attention, everyone. Once again, Pearl has worked her magic. Be sure to let her know how much we appreciate her skill and dedication." She paused for a breath. "In case you didn't notice, Bella added wine glasses to each place setting. I'd like to thank my father for bringing two cases from his private stock to help us celebrate."

"What are we celebrating?" asked Janice.

Steve shouted out an answer. "Surviving Christmas Cay."

Laughter rose and fell, and Heather continued. "This will also be a farewell dinner of sorts. Bella's husband will arrive in St. Thomas tomorrow morning. A helicopter will take her back to civilization."

What wasn't said was she'd leave in a police helicopter with a handcuffed passenger.

Bella cast her gaze at each one around the table. "No offense to any of you, but Adam and I have only been married six months. Starting a new career has made me an absentee wife for much of that time."

Janice spoke in a loud, husky voice. "I don't blame you a bit for leaving."

Heather took over again. "We're very thankful for all she's done."

"Amen," said Steve. "Let's eat."

Heather replied with, "Let's drink."

Her father joined the chorus. "Let's make merry."

The feast began. Wine served the purpose of lowering inhibitions and loosening tongues. This was also part of the plan Steve had outlined to her earlier that day. Heather tried to relax, but had a hard time enjoying herself, knowing the confrontation that would come. She took a large drink of superb wine to brace herself, but made sure not to drink any more. The possibility of the plan failing seemed slim, but she'd been involved in enough investigations to realize things could go wrong. She would need all her wits about her tonight.

36

D inner under the stars ended with an apology from Pearl. "The gelato machine stopped working. No dessert. I'm so sorry."

Clyde expressed his thoughts about what Pearl considered a major issue. "After a meal of that quality and quantity, who needs dessert?"

Janice came back with, "I ate so much I'll need at least one extra trip up the hill tomorrow morning."

Heather stood and announced, "Leave your plates where they are for now. Steve has something important to tell you." She looked down the long table. "Everyone is here."

Steve remained seated, preferring to set a more relaxed mood. "Thanks for your attention. Heather, Allister, and I have a confession to make to you all. We brought you executives to Christmas Cay under false pretenses."

A hush fell over the table as wrinkled brows and questioning gazes responded in ways he couldn't see.

"Not only did we deceive you, but it was all part of a plan that I'm primarily responsible for."

Heather interrupted. "Don't you dare try to take the blame. This was a group effort."

Allister took his turn. "It's an open secret that someone from our office in Boston stole and sold company secrets. I called on the two best private detectives I know to help solve the problem. Over time, a plan emerged to find the guilty party. I'm the one who initiated the investigation."

Steve assumed the lead. "What began as a case involving theft took an ominous turn when someone assaulted and gravely injured Reggie Scott. The press took little notice of the event, but Heather and I kept an open mind." He took in a deep breath. "Reggie died while the management team from Boston was in transit to this island."

Heather looked around the table for a reaction. Stoic faces took in the information but didn't react. It came as no surprise that Steve failed to mention the quick trip to and from the crime scene in Boston. His being able to perceive the color red in the parking garage, and its implications, was not for anyone else to know.

Janice raised her hand and spoke as she did. "What was the reason for the awful, red-eye flight to Miami and a second one to St. Croix? I thought Dorcas had something against us to schedule such torturous flights."

"I'll take credit for that," said Allister. "Part of Steve and Heather's overall plan to catch the thief was to distract you by wearing you down physically and mentally."

Heather added, "Sleep deprivation and fatigue are two of the oldest tricks in the book to get people to reveal things they normally wouldn't. Military interrogators and police officers have used the technique for centuries."

Heads turned to look at Steve as he grinned and asked, "Was it effective?"

Bob Brown had an answer. "It worked too well. I could barely walk off the dock when we arrived."

Allister chuckled. "You might also recall that I doubled your workload in the days leading up to your departure."

"Who can forget?" said Louis. "I lost an important online computer game because I fell asleep at the keyboard."

Clyde's eyes traversed back and forth. When they came to a stop, he fixed his gaze on Heather. "Do you know who stole company secrets?"

She pointed at her partner at the far end of the table. "I'll let Steve tell you."

Steve spoke without further prompting. "Let's save that for the end. What's more important is who killed Reggie Scott and why."

"Before we get into those details..." said Allister. "Let's make sure everyone has a full glass of wine. I've made a significant decision that gives me cause to celebrate and I prefer not to drink alone."

Bella, Matt, and Pearl poured wine to within an inch of the rims. Heather raised her glass and offered a toast. "To my father. May all his decisions be as joyful as this one."

Questioning looks abounded as everyone saluted the patriarch and his momentous decision... whatever it might be.

Heather lowered her glass. "I'm sure you're all wondering what would cause such a toast. You'll learn the nature of Father's decision before you leave the table tonight. But first, turn your attention to Steve and listen closely."

Steve stood and projected his voice so there was no mistaking his words. "Allister and Dorcas helped Heather and me immensely. They told us about office procedures, security measures in place, division of labor, and a host of other things that gave us a clear understanding of how the business in Boston functions. We also learned details of the information that was stolen and sold."

Steve's pause for a breath was long enough to heighten the impact of his next words. "We concluded the thief, or thieves, had to be company employees."

Heather chimed in, but only after allowing Steve's words to hang in the air for several seconds. "Even though we didn't want to believe someone inside the company was responsible, the people with the most access to sensitive information were the department heads."

Steve quickly added, "Good investigators must first clear their minds of any preconceived notions of the guilt or innocence of any person and focus only on the facts gathered. Allister has done a stellar job of protecting his company from theft from outside sources. In addition, very few people inside the company have access to information outside their area of expertise. The exceptions are department heads who gather for regularly scheduled meetings to discuss buying or selling companies, stocks, real estate, or other investments."

Heads swiveled as Heather called out the specific departments. "This meant that the heads of legal, acquisitions, information technology, and the chief financial officer attended these meetings."

Habib was the first to speak. "That proves nothing. I am not a thief."

Clyde made his presence known. "Listen more carefully to their words. They've yet to accuse anyone."

Heather gave her attorney a nod of approval. "That's good advice."

Steve spoke next. "Once we had a list of suspects, we implemented our plan to separate the department heads from civilization, wear down their defenses, and uncover the thief. What we hadn't expected was the assault on Reggie Scott. I'll admit this threw us for a loop. Neither Heather nor I like coincidences, so we adjusted our thinking to include the possibility we were looking for a thief and a killer."

Steve reached for his glass and took a sip of what Heather knew to be grape juice.

Pearl shot from her seat. "Oh my gosh! I forgot the charcuterie boards. I'll be right back."

37

P earl's interruption wasn't planned, but served to heighten the anticipation in the room as everyone waited for her return. Heather signaled Bella who whispered something to Steve.

He responded by standing and picking up where he left off. "Let's talk about each of the department heads individually. The plan to wear you down worked better than we expected. We discovered strengths and weaknesses in each of the four, not to mention a significant amount of personal information. Let's start with you, Bob. What reason did you give us to think you would steal and sell company secrets?"

"I'd rather not say."

Allister stiffened. "Did you do it?"

"No. Something like that never crossed my mind."

"I believe you," said Allister in a much softer tone.

Bob seemed to find his backbone and said, "They say there's no fool like an old one. I certainly qualify. To make a long story shorter, I came to this island deep in debt and on the verge of divorce. I had plenty of motive for stealing from the company. If you want to know the sordid details of how a middle-aged executive nearing retirement might be tempted to throw away his career and family, I'll share it with you in private."

Allister spoke next. "I'm happy to report that Bob has taken steps to right his financial ship and his personal life."

"Exactly," said Bob. "I sold that stupid boat, and can't wait to apologize to my wife and girls."

Heather lifted her glass. "To Bob and his family."

Everyone followed Heather's lead and toasted Bob.

Steve moved on. "Next, we have Louis Crane. He caught our attention when we discovered he hid an electronic device from us and hacked into the island's Internet connection. It wasn't a great leap for us to think he had access to the company's business files and was selling information."

Louis cleared his throat. "The problem with IT is it can be addictive. I've been hooked since I was four years old. Before coming to this island, I'd never missed a day of being on a computer or some other electronic device. Heather and Steve caught me and took away my highly modified eReader. I can't blame them for suspecting me of selling secrets."

"Did you?" asked Allister.

Louis shook his head. "People don't understand the difference between a gamer and a thief. Winning a super-difficult game against skilled players is a rush like no other. So is hacking into a system that's supposed to be secure. Believe it or not, money doesn't mean that much to me. If I wanted to, I could take it out of almost any account in the world and not leave a trace. What I'd receive from selling company secrets would be small change. To me, it's all about winning a game, not money."

"Thanks, Louis," said Steve. "Let's move on to Habib. As chief financial officer, he had the most detailed information concerning profitability for all investments and potential sales."

Habib stiffened. "Am I to understand I fell under suspicion for doing my job too well?"

Steve shot back, "Not any more than the other three. What

made us suspect you more than the others was your temper and pride. You kept these hidden in Boston, but the physical challenges on the island exposed some rather unsavory attributes. You're under a mountain of personal pressure and it only took a little more to push you over the edge."

"Running up and down hills and being forced to learn to swim has nothing to do with my job," he replied stiffly.

"Stop trying to justify your actions," said Allister. "I sent you here to take part in team building exercises. That's covered in the *Other Duties as Assigned* clause in your contract. You responded with petulance and violence. Don't forget your pugil stick had modifications that could have seriously injured Malcolm Swift."

Steve took a breath and lowered the pitch of his voice. "You're missing the point, Habib. You made it easy for us to believe you posed a danger to the group. We couldn't dismiss the possibility that you'd harmed Reggie Scott."

"I've given this much consideration," said Habib. "Someone has worked very hard to cast suspicion on me."

A smile crossed Steve's face. "On that point, Heather and I agree. What I want you to see is how much you cooperated with the person who tampered with the pugil stick."

Janice spoke next. "You're running out of suspects. I've followed Clyde's advice and listened closely. You've accused no one, and I'm the only department head left. What do you have on me?"

"Nothing specific, but I have a few questions for you. How well did you know Reggie Scott?"

Janice took her time before answering. "To the best of my knowledge, I spoke to him on two occasions. The first time was at a Christmas party. The second was in the hall outside Mr. McBlythe's suite of offices. I was on my way to a meeting."

"That second meeting intrigues me," said Steve. "If it was such a casual passing, why do you remember it?"

"It took place not long after the Christmas party. I remembered how entertaining he was. He dressed as an elf and
performed magic and card tricks."

"Did you ever see him socially?"

Janice hesitated and looked at Clyde.

38

Several people leaned forward, waiting for the attorney to answer Steve's question. It was anticlimactic when she spoke a firm, "No." She followed it with, "I grew up poor and didn't like it. I swore an oath that nothing would keep me from becoming a success. A couple of failed relationships in college showed me I needed to focus exclusively on my career. That's what I've done... at least until I came to this island."

Janice took a breath and rested her hand on Clyde's shoulder. "I want my man to act like a real man, not a cartoon character wearing a green costume and fake ears."

Clyde's smile threatened to permanently stretch his mouth.

Janice leaned over and planted a kiss on Clyde's lips.

While most giggled at the love-struck duo, Steve cleared his throat, drawing everyone's attention back to him. "We were mistaken about any of the department heads being the thief."

Bob Brown raised his hand. "The suspense is killing me. Who sold company secrets?"

"Isn't it obvious?" asked Steve. "Dorcas, tell us how Reggie Scott used to come to your office."

Dorcas began with halting words. "I recall little about him other than he'd hand-deliver reports every so often."

"Would he stay long?"

"He'd try to make small talk. I'd be cordial, but I'm not being paid to chit-chat."

Steve kept pressing. "Did you think it odd that he hand delivered reports when all the other departments communicated via email?"

"Not really."

"It's my understanding that your office is part of a suite of offices. Is that correct?"

"Yes. Visitors pass through my office to go to a conference room or Mr. McBlythe's office."

"Is your office kept locked?"

"Not during office hours."

"What about your file cabinets?"

"I make sure they're locked every night before I leave."

Steve gave a firm nod. "Thank you for your patience in answering these questions. Just a few more and I'll move on to something else. Do you sometimes go into Mr. McBlythe's office?"

"Of course. I'm his personal assistant."

"And do you sometimes speak with Mr. McBlythe with his door closed?"

Dorcas bristled. "If you're implying—"

Steve held up a hand with palm facing outward. "I'm not implying anything other than Reggie Scott was stealing and selling company secrets."

Janice responded with a wide-eyed stare. "Of course. It all makes sense now. He was very good at sleight-of-hand. If Dorcas was in the conference room or Mr. McBlythe's office, he could be in and out of a file cabinet in no time."

Habib added, "I bet he familiarized himself with the files over multiple visits. All he had to do was catch Dorcas away from her desk."

Allister added, "Once Steve discovered the thief, I called some people I know in Boston P.D. They tracked down Reggie's bank records. He was good at stealing, but didn't know how to hide money."

The tiki torches flickered as a breeze swept over the deck, sending a chill down Heather's spine. One crime down, two to go.

Murmurs floated on the wind as the group spoke among themselves. Steve allowed the conversations to continue until Clyde spoke over the crowd. "We still don't know who killed Reggie Scott."

"Patience," said Steve. "After all, we're on island time." In a complete change of direction, he addressed Mr. McBlythe. "Allister, we could use a break. Can you wait until we return to give your announcement?"

Heather answered for him. "Of course he can."

39

Once reassembled, Heather watched as her father slowly rose from his chair. He picked up his glass of wine and said, "I'm so pleased with Steve and Heather. I have no words to express myself, so instead, let's salute them for a job well done."

He set the example, and everyone followed. Once empty glasses dotted the table, he continued. "Now for my announcement." His chin rose, and he cleared his throat. "Life surprises us, and I'd like to tell you about something that surprised me. As everyone knows, I lost my wife some time ago. She was a fine woman, and I reconciled myself to a life of contentment with my memories. I now find that living only with memories isn't for me. Life is precious and I want to experience all of it."

He turned and looked at Heather. "This may make me sound like I belong in a lonely-hearts club, but I'm ready to dip my toes into the shallow end of the pool of romance."

Clyde couldn't contain himself. "Come on in. The water's amazing."

Laughs sounded from both sides of the table. Heather then prompted her father by saying, "Tell everyone how you came to this decision."

"Looking in retrospect, it's been building for months."

Heather looked across the table. Dorcas stared with unblinking intensity.

"It started on a voyage. I met a woman of incredible grace and bearing. She possessed the type of beauty that doesn't fade with age. For some unknown reason, she seemed attracted to me. Like a short-lived teenage romance, the cruise ended all too soon, and we parted as something more than friends."

Clyde spoke again. "Go after her before she slips away."

"I plan on it, but I'm not sure where the relationship will lead. If nothing else, we agreed to travel frequently. She's already filled our calendars with several places to go for pleasure, and a little work, if necessary. She has excellent administrative skills, which could be very useful when I'm away from the office. I don't mind telling you, that I plan to be gone most of the time."

Concern shone on Dorcas's face.

Allister squared his shoulders. "Clyde, thank you for your words of support. Watching you and Janice has bolstered my resolve to proceed."

He shifted his gaze to Dorcas. "Don't expect me to be in the office for the foreseeable future."

He addressed each of the department heads by name. "In my absence, I'm appointing Habib Patel as my executive assistant. He'll add that to his current duties as CFO and make the day-to-day decisions for the smooth running of things. I expect him to keep me informed of any problems that require my attention."

"What about me?" demanded Dorcas.

"You'll report to Habib."

Dorcas stood with fists clenched. "Who is this woman?"

"If you must know, she's a widowed duchess from a rather small European country."

Steve chimed in and spoke with certainty. "You always make good deals. This is a two-for-one. I guess you could call her a very personal assistant as well as a royal."

Rage filled Dorcas's eyes as the flicker of the torches cast menacing shadows on her face. Heather motioned to Matt.

"Is this how you repay my years of devotion to you? How could you, after all I've done?"

Allister quirked his head. "Are you suggesting you deserve a bonus of some sort?"

"Of course not. What I've done is something more valuable. Something no one else would do."

With chin lifted, Allister asked, "You're not making sense. What have you done for me?"

"I discovered the thief and made him pay. I protected you! Now you're throwing me aside like I was a complete nobody." She grabbed the nearest shiny object and lunged at her employer.

Allister parried the flash of silver with a raised arm. Matt pulled her away as deep sobs replaced her screams of anger.

Heather was at her father's side in a flash, examining his arm for blood. He fixed his gaze on Dorcas's hand. "I've never heard of anyone being seriously injured by a spoon."

Matt and Bella dragged Dorcas away from the table and into the house, her cries of anger and despair fading.

Stunned expressions covered the faces of the executives.

Steve apologized. "Sorry about the excitement. It was the only way I could think of to get a confession."

He kept talking. "We can now finish our evening in peace. Pearl is in the kitchen making coffee and, by the way, the gelato machine works fine. We'll have cookies, gelato, and answers shortly."

40

Unanswered questions hung in the air like balloons at a child's birthday party. The expression on the executives' faces showed confusion regarding the unexpected events that landed Dorcas in the island's version of jail. She'd reacted so fast and violently, it defied comprehension.

Hushed talk turned to absolute silence when Heather called everyone to order by tapping on her wineglass. "Pearl will serve coffee, but we'll delay dessert until after we've explained a few things. My father wants to go first."

Steve took the chair previously occupied by Dorcas on Allister's left, with Heather sitting to her father's right.

Allister stood. "I apologize for putting you through such a trying ordeal. You've been physically and mentally abused, brought here under false pretenses, and fed misinformation. I'm complicit in all these. There are also two additional things that I took upon myself to do. I'm responsible for bringing two cases of wine. I'm sure you noticed your glasses never ran dry, plus you received double portions. The purpose of that was to break down inhibitions."

Before Allister could continue, Heather interrupted. "Do you remember when we spoke of breaking you down so we could

238

expose the truth? We told you mental and physical exhaustion are techniques used by interrogators. Plying people with alcohol is another time-tested way of getting people to divulge things they normally wouldn't. In the name of health and fitness, I deprived everyone of alcohol this week. That was my mistake. It could have been a very useful tool in helping us solve this case sooner."

Her father took over again. "I'm also guilty of telling another partial lie. I did meet a gracious lady on a cruise, and we enjoyed each other's company. However, the relationship and the cruise ended at the same time. I embellished the story for dramatic effect."

Steve stood. "Island rules allow exaggeration, deception, and embellishment."

Janice asked, "When did you first suspect Dorcas?"

Steve gave an incomplete answer. "Not soon enough. The first mistake we made was not linking the thefts to the assault on Reggie Scott. Looking at things in hindsight, I should have put more emphasis on what everyone, including the police, called a coincidence."

He took in a full breath. "This case was like following wooden signs with arrows painted on them to show the way. The problem was, many of the signs sent us in the wrong direction. To begin, the first sign told us we were dealing with two unre-lated crimes, so we focused only on the thefts. Our sole purpose in coming to the island was to discover the person responsible for stealing information and selling it."

Clyde asked, "Who painted the signs that led you in the wrong direction?"

"Ah," said Steve. "That's a great question. Everyone from the Boston office said something to make us suspect at least one of the other department heads. Again, that was our fault. We pres-sured you to speculate."

Heather hadn't planned on speaking much, but she chimed in anyway. "I have to hand it to Dorcas. She waited until we turned up the heat on her before she implicated everyone from Boston."

Steve continued. "After hearing from each of you, we went back to basics."

"What Steve means is, *he* went back to basics. For him, that involves countless hours of serious thinking. I was busy climbing hills, playing volleyball, and trying to keep people from harming each other, or themselves."

Steve nodded in agreement. "Everyone who traveled from Boston to Christmas Cay had equal means and opportunity to commit both crimes. Of the suspects, Bob stood out first. He was in financial and personal trouble."

Bob spoke up. "I'm happy to say that stupid yacht now belongs to someone else. Thanks to Heather and Mr. McBlythe, my bank account is in the black and things are looking up on the home front, too."

"Excellent," said Allister.

Steve took up where he left off. "I concluded that even though I could invent reasons for each of the people from Boston to steal and sell company secrets, each one proved themselves trustworthy when it came to company money." He paused. "That included Dorcas. By process of elimination, we were left with Reggie Scott as the thief. Don't get me wrong; there were clues we should have caught."

"Like what?" asked Janice.

"He wore a fake Rolex watch, and he lived above his means. The watch showed an unmet desire to be rich."

Heather added, "Reggie had no reason to come to Dorcas's office, but he did."

Steve added one more. "His wallet was left in his coat pocket. Only a novice thief would miss that. We had to look for a different motive for the murder."

Heather took a glance at the faces of those gathered around the table. The term *fully engrossed* came to mind. They were each leaning forward, eyes wide open, hanging on Steve's every word.

"Keep going, Steve," said Heather.

"He also practiced magic and sleight-of-hand tricks."

Janice shouted as a second revelation came to her. "That's why you asked me if we had a romantic thing going on. You were trying to find out if I was in on the thefts with him."

"You made me curious when you said how much you desired a meaningful relationship."

Heather spoke in a matter-of-fact voice. "You weren't alone. Steve had to rule out everyone from Boston."

Bob raised his hand. "Let me get this straight. Are you saying that Dorcas killed Reggie, but it wasn't for money?"

"Correct," said Steve.

"Was she in love with him?"

"No."

"And she didn't do it for money?"

"Nope. When I said it wasn't for love, I meant it wasn't for romantic love. There's more than one type."

Heather spoke up. "Listen carefully, everyone. If you don't catch this, you'll stay confused about why Dorcas killed him."

Steve filled his lungs before speaking. "Dorcas is a name that's gone out of fashion, but it fits her perfectly. She possesses an old soul and looks at life through an antique lens. She thinks in terms of unconditional loyalty. That can include many things, but in this case, it involves her employer. She views Allister's company as an extension of him."

Bob interrupted. "Are you talking about hero worship?"

"Not exactly, but you're on the right track. Go back several centuries and consider how a servant regarded the lord of an estate. You can go back even farther and see more striking examples where people in many cultures counted themselves as slaves, serfs, or indentured servants. It's hard for us to wrap our minds around it today, but not that long ago, societies practiced slavery. It went by many names, but don't get bogged down with the label. Absolute loyalty to a person and their property was the norm."

Habib raised a hand. "Coming from my culture, I have better insight into this truth than the rest of you."

Heather gave a nod. "Thank you, Habib."

Steve wasn't through. "I want to emphasize that Dorcas's loyalty wasn't the result of any sort of romantic interest in Mr. McBlythe. She didn't react when she heard of Allister's renewed interest in a woman. It was only after he revealed she'd lose her position as his personal assistant that she came unglued. In that moment, I believe the wine helped."

Heather summarized. "In a matter of speaking, she was being demoted from the lord's private secretary and steward over the manor to that of a scullery maid. And that was after she'd caught and killed a thief who stole the family silver. An act, which, in her mind, should have earned her a permanent position beside her master."

"Nice analogy," said Steve.

Janice asked, "Was there any physical evidence that linked Dorcas to Reggie's murder?"

"None," said Heather. "Closed circuit cameras caught all the suspects going into the garage and leaving on the day of the assault. Remember, the original investigation labeled the attack as a mugging. Reggie didn't die until much later. All we know about the weapon used is that it's made of wood."

"Was it like the bat I used to kill the fish?" said Habib. "If so, that made you suspect me even more."

Heather nodded. "It did make us wonder. You had no qualms about using it."

Clyde gave his legal opinion. "If she hadn't confessed, Dorcas would have gotten away with it. A good lawyer would have torn your theory about motive to pieces."

"I knew that," said Heather. "That's why Steve and my father baited her the way they did. They were counting on her emotions overtaking her."

Steve took over again. "Dorcas made other mistakes. The first was she pressured Allister to allow her to come to this island. Had she kept her head down in Boston, I don't think we would have caught her."

Allister added, "Looking back, it was out of character for her to go anywhere. She never took vacations."

Steve immediately added, "The reason she came was to cast suspicion on each of the department heads. I'll give her credit, she waited until we pressured her before incriminating you. Looking back, the accusations didn't sound off-the-cuff. She gave a lot of thought to that part of her plan. Next, she overplayed her hand. As time passed on the island, Habib became her choice as the person to take the rap for both crimes. Her final mistake was putting a kitchen knife on the pugil stick."

"Will they charge her for that crime?" asked Habib.

Heather answered, "Again, there's no evidence that Dorcas did it. We intentionally didn't ask her about it."

"Why not?"

"I'll take this one," said Clyde. "The answer is judicial expediency. Even if the cops file charges, the D.A. won't prosecute. Their aim in a situation like this is to extradite the accused as soon as possible."

Heather nodded in agreement. "Dorcas has more than enough to answer for back in Boston."

Steve rubbed his hands together. "That should cover most of your questions."

"Not quite," said Janice. "What happens next? Will the boat come to pick us up tomorrow?"

Heather hadn't considered this. She wasn't sure if Steve had either. Her father came to their rescue. "There are several days left before you're scheduled to leave. Bella will fly out tomorrow morning on the police helicopter with Dorcas. My employees don't have to return to work until Monday morning. It's your choice whether you stay on the island or fly back to Boston with me tomorrow. If you stay, it's first class tickets for the return flight."

Bob raised his hand. "Count me as one who'll go back with you."

Heather spoke up. "It's optional for my employees, too. If you stay, it will be as someone on vacation. No mandatory sunrise yoga, hill climbing, swimming competitions, or beach volleyball. Also, no made-up brain-teaser exercises."

Clyde seemed to speak for the majority. "I'm getting in the best shape I've ever been in. My vote is for staying and continuing with exercising and fishing."

Janice followed Clyde's lead, which surprised no one.

Louis Crane asked, "Can we have our laptops back?"

Heather chuckled. "Of course."

"Then, I'm staying."

"By the way," said Steve. "In case you missed it, there's no merger of companies... except for whatever happens between the lead attorneys."

"Darn right," said Clyde as he smiled at Janice.

Pearl arrived with bowls of gelato and mounds of cookies. The meeting came to a noisy end as the department heads from both offices found room for dessert and conversation.

Heather made her way to stand between her father and Steve.

"It appears everyone but Bob is staying," said Allister. "Does that include you, Heather?"

"I've done everything but relax since I left Texas. If I'm going to finish strong in completing the development, I'll need to rest. There's a massive job waiting for me that includes building lakeside homes for me, Steve, Bella and Adam, and Bella's parents. I want to be in by Christmas."

"That's ambitious, but I'm sure you can do it."

Steve said, "Perhaps my new companion will move in with me for Christmas."

Allister took a step back. "I... er... hadn't heard about..."

Steve rescued him. "I'm looking for a combination service and guard dog. You could say I'm in the research stage. He, or she, needs to be big, gentle with children, but extremely protective. Any ideas?"

"Leave it to me," said Allister. "Expect a Christmas bow on something special. It's the least I can do to repay you."

Heather added, "Make sure the beast doesn't eat cats."

Steve had the last word. "I'm hoping Max doesn't develop a taste for dog."

From The Author

Thank you for reading *A Killer In Christmas Cay*. I hope you enjoyed your escape to the Caribbean as you turned the pages to find out whodunit! If you loved it, please consider leaving a review at your favorite retailer, Bookbub or Goodreads. Your reviews help other readers discover their next great mystery!

To stay abreast of Smiley and McBlythe's latest adventure, and all my book news, join my Mystery Insiders community. As a thank you, I'll send you a *reader exclusive* Smiley and McBlythe mystery novella!

You can also follow me on Amazon, Bookbub and Goodreads to receive notification of my latest release.

Happy reading!
Bruce

Scan the image to sign up or go to brucehammack.com/the-smiley-and-mcblythe-mysteries-reader-gift/

The Fen Maguire Mysteries

**He invested years in making his county safe.
He's not about to give up now.**

Newman County was clean and safe when Fen Maguire left office as sheriff nine months ago. But the dead drug dealer floating down the river says things may be changing.

When he discovers a stash of drugs and a coded notebook, Fen launches his own investigation into the murder. Can he uncover the layers of corruption in his beloved county? Or will this be one time justice doesn't prevail?

Scan below to get your copy of *Murder On The Brazos* today!

brucehammack.com/books/murder-on-the-brazos/

About The Author

Bruce Hammack, a native Texan, began his professional writing career in the tenth grade when the local Lions Club sponsored a writing contest for students in civics class. To the amazement of students and teachers alike, he won the prize of a twenty-five-dollar savings bond.

After retiring from a career in criminal justice, Bruce picked up the proverbial pen again. He now draws on his extensive background with law enforcement (and criminals) to write contemporary, clean read detective and crime mysteries.

Bruce has lived in a total of eighteen cities around the country and the world, but now calls the Texas hill country home with his wife of thirty-plus years. When not writing, he enjoys reading a classic mystery, watching whodunits, and travel.

Follow Bruce on Bookbub and Goodreads for the latest new release info and recommendations. Learn more at brucehammack.com.